He was the King of Arcadia Prep,
until she came for his throne…

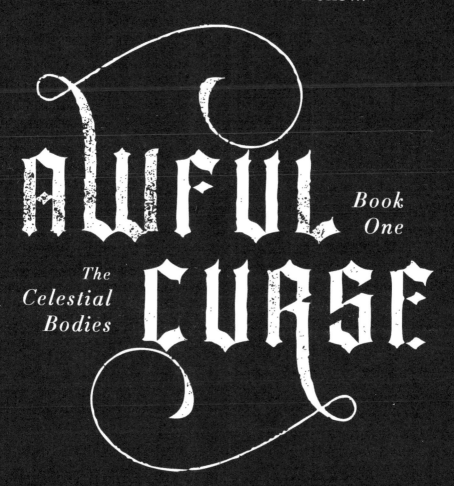

AWFUL

*Book
One*

*The
Celestial
Bodies*

CURSE

Elena Monroe

The Celestial Bodies Series book I

Copyright © 2020 by Elena Monroe

Cover Design: Maria with Steamy Reads
Editor: Sarajoy Bonebright
Proofreader: Liz Argote
Interior Design: Stephanie Anderson, Alt 19 Creative
Photographer: Michelle Lancaster
Cover Model: Lochie Carey

ISBN 9798615826115

First edition

Dedication

Mac

Your love of Astrology sparked something in me to dive into the cosmos. Awful Curse isn't awful at all, but a journey that has stained me forever. I will forever be addicted to my horoscope, moons, and stars as a tool to guide me. Thank you for all the chats that made this book happen.

Liz

For keeping my myth game strong, being my day one and supporting every crazy idea I have. Seriously, I don't write without your approval first.

Amber

How could I not mention you? You read everything I send (not edited in any sense of the word) and still love these characters as much as I do. BIGGEST hype woman—ever.

CHARACTERS

ARIANNA : Sagittarius

BOLTON : Aries

NYX : Scorpio

AUSTIN : Pisces

LEO : Leo

BEAU : Libra

OMARI AND CHEYANNE : Gemini

LUNA : Cancer

DR. MILO ALBA : Virgo

KATE : Taurus

JASPER : Capricorn

CAELLUM : Aquarius

"In all

CHAOS

there is a cosmos, in all

DISORDER

a secret order."

—CARL JUNG (Astrologer)

Henry Jon

Spring 1694
Seattle

We were long *past the darkness of the trials, but we soon found out we would never be done fighting the evil among us. The days were longer, giving us more light to work in our* favor. An ache in my bones told me something was coming and I needed to be prepared.

Every night I prayed, and every morning I woke in the same bliss, I could have cried a grateful tear.

When the mysterious settlers came across our village from the woods, I knew God was frowning upon us and preparing me in my sleep. This was the battle I was waiting for. Those deranged girls with their dead flowers and book of evils went quietly into the night, too quietly. These were the demons crawling up from Hell as penance for sending their sisters home by fire.

Revenge.

Retribution.

We disrespected the balance.

1

I waited, counting my blessing and watching them settle on the edge of our village with ease. They mocked me when they evinced in my direction at the market or walking past the church bells. It came as no surprise when their leader caught the fair eye of my Rosalia.

She was beguiled quickly by the evil I knew him to be. My child of the one true God was dancing with the Devil.

The children were never seen at worship. They didn't carry the Bible, and they let the mischief in their irises make questioning who made them simple. They went about town sharing their stories, their beliefs shaming our dedication to God with their myths. The false gods they worshipped were nothing but a bad nightmare to scare the children into faith. They were using it to convert my people, my town, and spitting on my religion.

They wouldn't escape my watchful eye.

THANK YOU so much for all the ♥

AWFUL CURSE

cosmic!

Arianna

You know that storm of butterflies that induces a slight sweat and your anxiety kicks into gear, readying to drive you into fight or flight? That was me every six months.

I never adjusted to being permanently new. I never felt rooted to anyone or anything. I was always willing to say goodbye at every moment, through all of my firsts, making them suddenly lasts.

The new kid ... again. Great.

I stood in the middle of the room I was assigned to at the Arcadia Preparatory School for the forgotten, left behind, and otherwise independent.

I didn't begin to ponder which one I was. I wasn't ready for that kind of truth.

Painfully real observations are my specialty when it comes to the rest of the world. I had a sharp tongue, constantly breaking its cage of teeth to tactlessly hurt people in the wrong way. I was still learning to wield this kind of power in my words.

My dad was brand A military grade quiet, which only made my tongue even more antsy to do the talking for someone else too. It was only him and I after mama passed when I was ten. Naturally I

1

absorbed her silence too, turning it into blabbering. Synchronously, that was the exact time we lost our grip on our sanity. We took her for granted, every minute, up until we lost her. Suddenly, we were fighting to learn how to do anything for ourselves.

I stumbled my way through puberty, barely making it to womanhood with no real female gracing my presence—not a permanent one anyways. Just my highly decorated military dad, who was a ranger and who spent more time overseas than actually in the country he swore to protect. He left me constantly to bounce around from different extended family and friends.

I assessed the old, ancient even, iron gates of Arcadia Prep, while our car was stopped, waiting for them to open. My dad had to press a button on a com for the iron to break down the middle and let us in.

I was hoping it'd stay closed.

The driveway was more like a dirt road being stalked by thick woods on either side, lined with old streetlamps and nothing giving away that this was, in fact, a school.

Everything after we passed through the iron gates seemed eerie. This didn't seem like a normal boarding school—at least not a happy one. There was a thick fog as the temperature shifted from the blazing highs of summer to the slight chill of autumn.

Seattle wasn't Texas; that much was obvious. The only gloomy parts of Texas were in the outskirts, away from the cities, where the land was flat and resembled *The Texas Chainsaw Massacre*'s aesthetic. I was in Austin with my aunt last, which was far from horrific. The city was the power source for starving artists and hip cafes.

Arcadia Prep wasn't home—not even close.

The main building was all stone and brick, historically old and not impressing me. History was my least favorite subject. The building sat much further away from the rest of the campus, with pathways reaching out in every direction to other larger buildings. I grabbed my bag and tossed a stick of gum into my mouth, as I unwillingly got out of the car with a nudge from my dad, hitting my knee.

A woman in an all-black, floor-length dress, with a long face that hollowed at her eyes and cheeks, "greeted" us, which didn't help me see this change in a positive light. It was all still creepy as fuck.

"Welcome to Arcadia Prep, the school for the wise and intelligent leaders of tomorrow. You must be Arianna?"

I laughed at her saying my name. She tried to say it with an upscale twist like I was some elite leader of tomorrow. "No, it's pronounced the shitty way. Just plain Arianna."

She crossed her arms unamused. My dad scolded me silently, while he introduced himself and dragged my bags behind him. I refused to make this transition any easier for anyone involved.

The woman who was guiding our Arcadia Prep tour wasn't even close to friendly. Her voice was a shrill tone that made goosebumps along my spine.

She actually used skeleton keys to unlock the door we finally stopped at which sent the goosebumps further down my arms. I had watched my fair share of scary movies, wondering too hard how those people felt, in the middle of sheer horror.

Now, I knew.

She was tall but that was no reason to literally look down at people. I was painfully aware I didn't belong here with my purple hair, Doc Martens, and jean jacket that was from the 80's. I let people associate me with being a *Stranger Things* super fan, instead of telling people it was my dead mom's.

I made that mistake at school number three this year with what I learned later was the mean girl. Suffice to say, it didn't work out in my favor when I landed in the principal's office after she thought of using my dead mom to torture me.

Our creepy guide huffed, waiting for my father, who was trailing too far behind us, carrying my duffle that really looked like a body bag and wheeling two suitcases I refused to wheel in myself. I had looked at the brochure the whole way here, like it would magically illuminate a way out of bad behavior. My attitude could grow into a monster which got me kicked out of my last three schools and made a good case for having me banned in the tri-state area from public school. Guess that's how I ended up at Arcadia Prep—at boarding school.

Did I mention that it was my senior year, on top of being new? Double whammy.

The room was suffocatingly small and even the walls were wood paneling. The one small window dividing the twin-sized beds in the room barely illuminated the completely dark side belonging to my roommate.

Yes, a roommate my senior year of high school. What could go wrong putting two hormonal girls, who are strangers, together in one room for a year?

I desperately missed my bedroom that was all to myself at my last stay-cation. That's what I called long vacations with no real destination. I was the residency guest at various homes.

My aunt drew the line when the cops brought me home and my then boyfriend's mom lodged a formal complaint with our school and law enforcement, after he got hurt during our last adventure.

That was my strike three with disobedience.

To be clear, we snuck into the dam after hours, and security didn't feel like giving us a warning—not with my reputation and not when I was with the son of the mayor. I couldn't even hold it against him. I dragged him there, craving an adventure of my own. He was completely innocent if we didn't count the heavy make out session and his fingers slipping between me and my underwear.

The tall, slender woman with hooded eyes, and the kind of nonchalant air that could knock you over, handed me a piece of plastic doubling as an electronic keycard and debit card to pay for my meals. I tucked it in my back pocket absently. I was not focusing on staying but escaping. They could keep the doors locked all they wanted, as long as I wasn't locked behind them.

My dad's heavy hands landed on my shoulder as she ghosted her way out of the room. She moved like she hovered above the ground, and I couldn't even tell how, because her legs were covered by the length of her dress.

"Okay, kiddo, this is it. You're gonna be on your own, but the school knows the deal. I'll call when I can, so keep your phone on you."

I couldn't force my eyes up further than our shoes between us. Ironically, we were both wearing boots. Mine were rooted in rebellion and his in order.

I hate goodbyes with so much passion it crippled my heart. After saying goodbye to my last boyfriend, I vowed to cage my heart. I shoved the organ in a box, filed it deep below my lungs and threw away any idea of a key. I had to start protecting myself. This new home didn't seem to yield any promises of permanence either, not when it was my senior year and I had dreams to be in California, not Seattle.

"Dad … " was all my dry voice choked out.

He pulled me into his broad, solid chest and held me to him as my eyes welled up and I held my breath. He finally pulled away after what seemed like longer than a typical hug, and he couldn't resist tousling up my hair like I was still his little broken girl who lost her mom too young and couldn't manage to find stability.

"No boys. Seriously. Aunt Dee really let that slide."

I pulled the delicate skin under my eye with my pointer finger, wiping the tears away before they were spotted and smeared with makeup that wasn't waterproof.

"I'm almost eighteen, old man. I can date. You're the only person who thinks that way."

He saluted me in the doorway as he typically did every time he left for some secret mission and location. As he created distance between him and me, I heard him shout loud enough for it to echo. "I mean it, no boys! I'll hunt them down person-ally, and you know my aim is aces."

I couldn't help but chuckle as I still wiped away stray tears. I thought I'd be used to goodbyes by now. I had plenty of practice, but they never got easier.

The mattress was wrapped in plastic, and it made an obnoxious noise as I sat down and wilted. My beat up Doc Martens were no longer white but stained with every kind of dirt from at least six different states. I was a walking road map, and I grew to like my shoes collecting pieces of where I had been.

I didn't even bother to unpack this time. I simply laid my suit-cases down and threw my duffel on the dresser meant to be mine. I closed the door to the room, barren and all, before I went to investigate my surroundings.

My dad joked that I was surveying the land, mentally marking threats, and doing exactly what he does on a much more precarious scale. He loved finding small things connecting us since I was my mama's shadow. It made him feel important so I never harped on it. Small victories.

CHAPTER 2

Arianna

I transferred in a few months into my senior year, which meant everyone started classes and most likely fell into their groups already. I would be the odd one out, finding certain classrooms and trying not to eat lunch alone outside, until someone took pity on me.

I roamed around with nowhere to be, since it was the weekend and knew no one in this God-forsaken town. The campus was large and reeked of old money. The buildings looked like churches with the moldings and stone appearance.

They mocked us–out living us all.

The Seattle overcast created a strong sense of doom that didn't help brighten my mood one bit. I looked up at the light gray sky, cursing my existence and questioning the chain of events leading me here out loud.

"If you keep doing that, people are gonna think you're crazy. Don't want you stealing my role around here."

The slender, brooding, raven-haired boy sat up against his elbow from the laying in the lush grass. His eyes were strikingly green with flecks of dark emerald. I squinted, trying to pinpoint any signs of imperfection but his skin was smooth and glazed with a brush of bronze. His pile of necklaces weighted his neck like chains, and my eyes scanned down the length of his barely buttoned red shirt that had a black palm trees pattern on it. The ends flew open threatening to detach the only button holding his shirt around his body.

"The only ones here who are this quiet are the nerds ... or you're the new girl the school's been buzzing about."

His words crashed down around me, breaking the thick layer of fog he induced around functioning.

"The latter-new-always new," I responded.

His gaze fell down to my beat up shoes. A snort shook his body, as he said, "At least something about you is new."

My peculiar set of eyes, a hue of violet rimming the ocean blue, darted down to meet his. "Can't say your brand of fashion is my favorite either."

He took inventory of me, looking at my expression, as the sass slipped out of my mouth, for any insecurities. He wasn't going to find a hint of apprehension.

I struggled to find the shame in the words I said—that was the problem with my silver tongue.

He stood up pushing a hand out between our bodies and offering his name: "Austin-resident crazy. Empath. Running back."

I looked at his hand, debating if I was going to go down this road again-for the fourteenth time-of having to say goodbye again in a quick nine months when we all chose separate colleges. An ache as heavy as all my other goodbyes made me painfully aware, and I locked my heart away before I looked down again.

"Look, I'm only here for nine more months 'til college. There's no point of getting to know me." My hands were up, and I even backed away to drive it home—a clear warning to stay away from me. I was heartache waiting to happen at the ring of a relocation phone call.

He stepped forward anyways, pushing his hand out even further. I noticed the rings, all big and bulky like they were heirlooms, not just jewelry. "Nine months is a long time. You want to be miserable? Come on."

Who shook hands anymore? Who was this guy, and why wouldn't he give up?

I sighed, letting my shoulders bounce, before I pushed my hand to meet his.

"I'm Arianna. You should feel accomplished." I stopped talking as soon as his palm touched mine to yelp out an "Ow!" instead, when the shock sizzled against my palm.

He looked up at me devilishly. "Well, isn't that a sign? Besides, I'm supposed to be showing you around campus, and Mr. Alba would lose it if I actually blew you off."

He waved me along with a graceful hand gesture and I followed. Of course I followed, he was perfect, and we literally had sparks just fly between us. Even with my heart safely locked away, I couldn't ignore some kind of divine intervention.

I stopped suddenly, logically. "Why were you in the grass then?"

He laughed, turning around in his funky button down, barely held together still and ripped jeans. "I blew you off but now I'm into it. Curiosity piqued."

My eyebrows jumped up into an arched position, looking at him in mock shock. He had the infection of an independent tongue too; all his honesty was a breath of fresh air.

I didn't ask where we were going. The futile journey around campus fed my hunger for an adventure. He pointed out various buildings unenthusiastically. His vibrancy faded quickly, and he was just as gloomy as the sky. Now, I understood the crazy he dubbed himself.

I was on board with his self-diagnosis and positive Web MD would confirm. He didn't perk up until he pointed out the faculty building—a whole building, just for the teachers. I really didn't belong here. In the public school system, teachers were barely paid a decent wage, never mind having a building to themselves.

He turned around, walking backwards. "Off limits. Keycard won't work." His voice was soaked in curiosity and misguided behavior I found irresistible in men. The willingness to break a rule for a good time wasn't only something I admired but a trait I valued in myself. My own version of fearless, much more reckless.

Who would want to break into the faculty building? Nothing about that seemed fun, even though his childish grin spurred me on exactly how intended.

He clutched my arm, dragging me past the building as he announced our journey to the dining hall. Something about the faculty building drew my eyes back for one long, last look taking in the details of the old structure. The whole campus was out of an old gothic novel, complete with gargoyles at the entrance paired with an iron gate. A prison had come to mind as we drove through the gate earlier.

He opened both doors to the dining hall dramatically, letting them open widely for us to walk through. Someone should have given him a bullhorn or mic to just shout my presence to the flooded room.

Thankfully, no one was looking my direction, and if they were, then I was willing to add it up to the vibrant guy next to me, not actually me. He turned towards me, clasping his hands together in a praying motion, even though this campus gave more of a witch vibe than a come-to-Jesus one.

"So this is the dining hall. Overwhelmed yet?"

I squinted my eyes and smiled sweetly, giving him the perfect pair of salty and sweet in one look. "I've been the new kid fourteen times. I'm a pro now."

He snickered, not a full laugh, as he stood in the same place next to the doors that closed behind us, overlooking the room, scanning it expertly.

"So what's the deal here? Everyone is stuck up? Rich?"

He waved a finger back and forth into a "no" in front of my face. "Here at Arcadia Prep we are inclusive, offer four scholarships a year, and wear uniforms to create unity."

I snipped, "I read the brochure, asshole."

His face immediately melted into a full laugh, slapping his own leg in amusement. "Arcadia Prep is every other cesspool of stereotypes, drama, hookups, and break ups."

I scanned the dining hall with the long tables pushed together drilling in the inclusiveness the school was clearly built on. There was one table sitting horizontally on a pedestal of four steps that looked like an old stage. A group lounging all over the steps, like they reigned over the rest of the students, caught all of my attention. I wasn't doubting the truth in my assessment when my eyes glued themselves to the girl dead center of the group.

Austin's shoulder crashed into my focused body, and I felt my balance immediately absorb the hit, catching myself before I fell over.

"That didn't take you long. Kate, senior, and she's Queen Bitch in these parts."

I looked at him, trying not to be disgusted. It wasn't my first time being met head on with the Miss Popular type. I didn't have the same flare for dramatics. I held my own when it came to snide remarks, dirty looks, and pretty much pissing those kinds of girls off with just my mere presence.

"Not my first rodeo. Who are the rest? Some kind of cult? Her slaves? Followers?"

His carefree face turned dark, serious even, as his head snapped to me. I stared back at him, unsure of what I said that turned our conversation sideways. I wanted to bump into him in the same playful way but we didn't have that rapport yet. His serious expression honestly put me on edge, so much on edge I fell silent, waiting for him to speak.

The silence didn't last long before he dove in, telling me exactly who each person was on the stairs: "The one next to Kate is Luna. She's class president and going to make the perfect mom. Jasper is the one stealing all the attention without trying. Beau and Leo are our resident gay couple—probably the only one this school has ever seen. The twins? Cheyanne and Omari. It's pretty clear which one you don't wanna be on the bad side of. Nyx is our man of mystery. I'm surprised we even know his name. I can't keep up with the rumors explaining why he's so off limits."

My eyes slid over the group, putting names to faces, when I realized he left out the guy sitting on the top step with his forearms resting on his legs. He was wearing red suspenders that looked like restraints. His intense and impatient glare wasn't directed at anyone particular, but in fact, everyone. He looked like he despised everyone equally.

Mental eye roll. A bad boy mad at the world at his feet. I am drawing a line and thanking myself later for caging my wild organ.

Otherwise, I'd be screwed.

If my heart was free to swoon, it would've.

His dirty blonde hair with darker roots was the best mix of good and bad I had seen. Apart from the scowl warding people off, his eyes did the opposite. They drew me in, dark with depth I wanted to understand.

Damn it, even caged, my heart still swooned for his muscular body and attitude to match how highly he thought of himself.

I was going to ignore he existed.

Pretend I hated him.

Austin started walking and my gaze followed, wondering where he fit into the hierarchy of high school. "What about you?"

Before I knew it, we had made our way through the dining hall and were only a few feet away from the group that you clearly needed an invite from to even speak to. That much was obvious when no one even attempted to sit near them, even at the tables close by. I never wanted to fit in that way—the kind of way that makes you compromise some part of you. I was content making people uncomfortable. It was easy being brave when everywhere was temporary.

"Queen Bitch? My girlfriend." His voice was flat as he ambled over to her, leaned down, and proved it by having their lips meet with ease.

I felt my jaw suddenly go lax with shock, when the guy sitting above everyone quickly got up and fled the scene. He breezed by me angrily, like the presence of two more people set him off. He didn't say a word as he left dust in his wake. I found myself twisting around to watch him storm off, stuck on his crimson suspenders and the necklace around his neck hanging perfectly in the V of his shirt, showing off a pair of ram horns hanging from the thin chain.

How fitting. Aggressive, angry, powerful, and drawing me in—all at the same time.

I was so focused on him bolting from my presence I didn't notice every set of eyes on me. I turned back around, letting the noise creep in, a skill I was born with, the ability to drown out anything around me and focus. This time wasn't on purpose and certainly not the best time.

"New Girl! Hey!"

The snapping of the Queen Bitch's perfectly manicured fingers cut through the haze left over, making my head snap in her direction.

"It's Arianna. Not 'New Girl'." I stressed the *not*, and she dropped her hand to her lap and smiled back at me placid, neither offended or excited. She was a tiger, lying in wait to pounce, completely unseen but lethal.

"Okay, New Girl. We aren't the enemy. Bolton, the guy who darted past you ... ? Debatable."

Austin made eye contact with each person left sprawled along the stairs purposely when introducing me officially. I never knew someone to put so much value on eye contact, except parents when they drove home the same unsolicited advice for the tenth time. Eye contact did not mean you were soaking in whatever they wanted you to. Words were messy. Meaning was a hurricane made of feelings, motivation, and maybe some of your astrological sign feeding off the position of everything else.

"So what's his problem?" I asked in pure curiosity but a small part of me took it personally. How could I not?

Another guy, Nyx, the one Austin told me was a total mystery spoke, and the group fell silent from their small chatter. "She doesn't look that special to me, Austin. Purple hair, really? I'm out. I got better shit to do."

He stopped in front of me, letting his fingers clamp around a runaway strand of my purple hair, giving it a swift tug as his eyes bore into me. Austin scoffed, with his arm around his perfect girlfriend, who had no reason to be a bitch. She was perfect on the outside.

That was the second guy to bolt from the room since I walked in. Was I missing something? And what did he mean special? Was I supposed to be? I raised an eyebrow, not sure how I fit into this environment yet. Solitude was so much easier. I didn't know why I was entertaining Austin and his insulting group of friends anyways.

Actually, I did know why. Even with a caged heart, I was still trying to fill the spaces left vacant by the love that was hard to feel between continents and a parent whose love was something I had to dredge up past memories to feel.

Bolton

A few days had gone by since the new girl had settled in Arcadia Prep, like she had been here the whole time and wasn't, in fact, new. She blended in with the group with no real proof she belonged.

I wasn't wasting my time on another flawless face. I was trying to find the last person our circle was missing, not a girlfriend or best pal.

The rest of the circle forgot that when they integrated her in without my approval. I let them pretend she was special—the one we had waited for, for fourteen years. They knew better than to cross me and get too attached.

Austin said he felt the impact of a shock as soon as their hands touched. I wanted lightning and the world to split open undeniably. I wanted unequivocal proof she was the one, so I watched her every move—not in the bathroom or her bedroom. I had boundaries. I'm not that much of an asshole.

She was painfully normal. She was naturally curious, though, which made observing her a dangerous game.

My new favorite game.

Every time she went by the faculty building, her gaze scrutinized the doors, willing its secrets loose. Secrets I protected fiercely for the group's safety, tucked into the basement, behind limited access. No one could know why the unlikely bunch of us were friends, why we snuck into the building every Wednesday, or what Mr. Alba's involvement was.

We weren't *just friends*.

We were Fate and Destiny wrapped up into unavoidable responsibility. None of us were able to move on until Fate and Destiny were satisfied with us, enough to spit us into the real world.

Arcadia was too small to not have classes together. The senior class was maybe pushing one hundred at this point. Everyone knew everyone's business.

We all had one class together, Ancient History, taught by none other than Mr. Alba himself. He referred to this class as babysitting us, even though there weren't enough students to get lost in a crowd.

Ancient History was more than the history of the United States, but about gods and goddesses, magic, and everything we didn't have to play down. We could talk freely and arrogantly as we wanted, because we knew our own history better than the books.

Alba made it clear that was our problem: *arrogance*. He was convinced if we just gave in to our humanity, we wouldn't be in this prison.

We knew we were above humans, and we flaunted it just as much as our over-privileged asses or off-putting personalities. Each of us was slightly different.

I preferred a scowl above talking, listening, or any real effort for anyone else. Kate, our Queen Bitch, preferred pointed jabs, while Nyx preferred not talking at all. I would have loved to not talk but nothing would get done if my lips were sewn together. I was the only one making decisions.

Heavy is the crown who wears it, right?

I refused to learn her name or let anyone else deviate from the path of only labeling her as "New Girl." I watched her clumsiness guide her into History, nearly tripping over her own feet as she juggled too many books.

This was the only part of her not adjusted.

Arcadia Prep was a college-level preparatory school, and everyone was already the smartest person in the room. She obviously came from public.

Nyx twisted in his seat in front of me, giving me a smirk and a raised eyebrow. We were both judging every part of her messy appearance.

Her uniform didn't look ironed, and her wrinkled white shirt was only half tucked into her skirt. One knee high sock landed at a different place on her shin, and her distastefully purple hair landed disheveled at her jaw line. It begged for attention, and without even trying, she had it.

Everyone's. Except mine.

She sat down next to me to with a loud huff displaced, shaking Alba's disposition at the front of the class. Out of all the scholarship kids that came through here, she was by far living up to pity.

I glared at her, wondering why she sat next to me when I tried so hard to seem un-relatable and unpleasant. "Seat is taken. Move it, New Girl."

Nyx started laughing into his closed fist, making it hard to deliver the statement without grinning too.

She glanced around the room at the empty seats and back at me before she quipped, "Finders keepers." The shrug drove her lack of caring home.

I couldn't blame her adolescent answer when I was acting the same way. The seat was only taken by my annoyance of her being in this class too.

Alba's presence between us demanded attention but I didn't bother looking up for the scolding. "Do we have a problem, Bolton? Hate to send my best student to detention."

Nyx stepped in, speaking before I had the chance, "Come on. She's disrupting the fucking class."

I looked up as soon as I heard the word, and I knew he was purposely taking this lick. That's what people did for their sovereign; they kissed the ring, any way they could, if it proved loyalty. Nyx was the most loyal person I had ever come across. His loyalty was fierce and dangerous for others.

"Detention, Nyx. Windows after classes. Same for you, Arianna. Your student handguide has the uniform standards. Please brush up." He shook his head in disappointment before standing at the front of the class again. "Page fifty. Greek Mythology."

Arianna leaned in towards me. "Would they all jump in front of a bullet if it meant protecting you? Or sometimes, do you fight your own battles?"

I slammed my book shut, ready to leave class and pay for it later. This might be why he called this class his babysitting duties.

"Let's start at the beginning for our new student. We'll summarize what we've gone over. Bolton, most common myths?"

He was battling for dominance. Here he was king, even though he had no followers. I had to fold under him. He was our teacher and that alone labeled him an authority figure.

"New Girl better do some reading in her spare time. The myth of Hades and Persephone; the myth of Aphrodite and Adonis; the myth of Pandora's box; the myth of Eros and Psyche; and the myth of Perseus and Medusa."

The challenge in his voice was heavy and stern. "Why is mythology relevant today?"

I was telling her all of the secrets without her knowing. She wasn't even bothering to write any of this down. She was blissfully unaware of this being the only time I would open up to her.

"It's all around us. Most people don't notice. Companies, products, motivations … all plucked from mythology and shoving it down their throats."

Her fist was pushed into her cheek, holding her up like this conversation was boring her to death.

She spoke again almost to herself, murmuring, "Nike is named after the Greek goddess of victory, and Starbucks is a siren, also mythology."

Alba asked her to repeat herself louder, clearly impressed and now certainly in agreement with Austin's theory that she was, in fact, the one.

I wasn't convinced. She still wasn't special, and I still wasn't blown over by some sign.

I felt nothing—certainly not complete.

CHAPTER 4

Bolton

Nyx had detention with New Girl.

She was working her way through the group, stealing private time with each one of them.

I didn't bother to text him and see how it went. I didn't really care. I didn't care what anyone had to say about her. It was my decision that mattered.

I would see him tonight for our weekly meeting with Alba. Really, it was a festivity of complaints that I was against completing our circle. Nothing productive ever came from the wasted hour of my time.

A series of complaints I had heard so many times before.

Asinine.

Did they think I wanted to be immortally stuck in my senior year? No. It's what I called my own personal hell.

Never mind the circle being stuck at Arcadia was throwing the world out of whack. All our gods were dead. There were no gods serving up retribution or pulling the strings anymore.

Trump was fucking president; people were worshiping the Kardashians; and social media was determining fucking worth. Being here was the last thing I wanted.

We needed to balance the world by being a part of it—not by repeating senior year for a 100th time.

I dipped into the faculty building unseen exactly at seven o'clock. I was always early as our unofficial and unelected leader; it made scolding everyone who was late easier. I liked being first, in control, and god-like above everyone else. I had been like this since I could remember, even on the playground as a younger, less vile me, I would dominate the monkey bars and charge a hefty fee for the sweet treats their loving moms put in their lunchboxes as payment.

Both my parents thought it was endearing. I was raised in an environment of ruthlessness, to be unafraid and to not follow but lead.

The faculty building was never used after four; none of our teachers were dedicated enough to put in extra hours. They already just chalked up the student body, minus four scholarship students yearly, as over-privileged and over-stimulated by our circumstances.

Alba wasn't like the rest of the staff, he was just like us, waiting on us all to arrive and stuck in a loop. He took a special interest in us and led the charge in our search. Years of the same shit can make someone a dangerous type of motivated.

He even started the scholarship program to move the search along quicker by integrating new students every year—four to be exact. We had four chances every year.

I pressed my student ID to the secure pad and waited for the little light to go green before I squeezed the handle to open the door. We were the only students with access.

I looked at my phone, which I always had on "Do Not Disturb," overlooking the group chat and focusing on the time. I had plenty of it to look at her file the way I originally planned to.

Watching her basic ass behavior wasn't enough. I needed ammo in the war against her infiltration.

Getting a file out of a locked filing cabinet was easy. I had been picking locks since grade school, once I realized all the best things are the ones you can't have.

I took what I wanted, no apologies.

Especially if I was forced to repeat senior year until *the one* showed up—the only one not drawn to Arcadia or us.

Adventure kept her away, roaming, and hard to pinpoint. Despite popular belief, magic could only do so much. We weren't even at our full strength as a broken circle.

This was our fourteenth time stuck as seniors, never aging or moving on. It was Pandora's punishment for being separated outside the clouds of Olympus. The gods loved a good sadomasochist torture session.

The lock almost begged to unhinge, falling apart instantly, as I jammed my key into its mechanism. I pulled the file cabinet open with a yank and a creek like the drawer hadn't been opened in years. I propped my phone up on its socket letting the flashlight beam down on the files as I fingered through them to find her first name.

I still didn't know her last name and her first didn't really matter either—she was New Girl. I finally found her file. It was all new and protected between as files as old as someone repeating senior year as many times as we had.

My resentment for this place behind the gate grew each year I was stuck here. There were only a few holidays when the boundary was lifted and we could sneak out into the real world: Halloween, Harvest Kickoff, and Summer Solstice.

The hours and days between were a long drawn inhale, and I wasn't breathing until I could exhale outside these grounds.

I opened the file, only finding one piece of paper with her demographics, like a medical office: height, eye color, address, emergency contact, and nothing else. The lone, thin piece of paper had a Post-it attached.

Nice try. It's not that black and white.

I recognized the handwriting instantly.

Alba.

He knew everything, with good reason; he was actually two-hundred years old, stuck in the body of a forty-year-old teacher.

I closed the file as hard as I could and kicked the filing cabinet against the wall in the office I broke into.

Mad didn't describe how I felt when I didn't get my way.

It was a poison rushing through my veins, turning every ounce of me into a villain. I was no hero.

That was an easy label when I could do and say what I wanted. That kind of comfort irritated people so much that it landed me in their hate category. I had played the villain for so long I didn't even know what heroes were anymore.

Fuck heroes.

Fuck their golden rules.

Fuck their self-sacrificing, courage, and humility.

I was selfish and unafraid, and everyone knew it just as much as I did. I wasn't ashamed. I was the essence of Aries, trapped in a teenager, doomed to this repetitive punishment—all because of the one who got lost.

Again.

I barely lifted my feet as I padded out of the office, letting them drag against the vintage hardwood as I made my way to the basement. I still had time to kill but at least I could do it in a place of comfort. Nothing was more off putting than this faculty building. All the ancient furniture, paintings of people I never concerned myself with, and the lingering scent of sharpened pencils ... it made me choke on the saliva my mouth was producing.

The basement wasn't your mom's basement. Our basement was finished, dark, housing so many candles we could have created a forest fire, and looked like it belonged to a cult—the non-religious type, something darker.

I thumbed through books of our history, waiting for anyone, even Alba, to arrive for our consistent meeting. New Girl would be the topic of focus; the new scholarship student always was.

Alba was the first to arrive, giving me a once over, like my body would convey the secrets of my most recent trouble.

"You're here early, Bolton."

I didn't bother looking up from my comfortable hunched over position at a desk with my feet planted into the ground and a book in my hand. Nothing ever demanded my full attention, so everyone got a small portion instead.

"Yep. You know me."

"Thought you'd be at practice; don't you guys have a big game against Fillmore Prep?"

"I don't know. I just show up, smile, and wave."

I could feel the annoyance seethe from his body, trying to reach me. I was the only one he couldn't control. We played nice for everyone else, to the point of everyone thinking I was his favorite. In private, we were at each other's throats, comfortably.

"Maybe if you took being stuck here as a blessing in disguise, you could enjoy yourself more … like the others."

"You think I wanna enjoy this shit? I don't belong here, Alba. I'm not 18; I'm not a high schooler; and I'm not gonna fucking pretend like we are."

He gave me the worst case of side eye he could, while he started lighting his candles in preparation for the others to arrive.

"She could be the twelfth, but you're determined to be miserable."

"She's not. There's no way. She's got goddamn purple hair."

He didn't laugh or agree, instead he looked to the door and announced the others before they even reached the basement door. I didn't move one inch as they entered the room as one big group, like they met up before coming here. It didn't bother me, I declined 99% of invites anywhere just for the simple reason: I disliked other people. I was my best company.

Nyx was my best friend, actually the perfect best friend. He was quiet, loyal, and brooding, just as much as I was. Misery loved her damn company.

He sauntered over to me, looking more serious than ever. He still wore his workout clothes from football practice. "We have to talk."

I looked at him with my eyebrows tense and then dropped them down to my eyelids, searching for a hint as to what about. Nyx was stone cold, and he never revealed any hints.

I got up slowly and walked out of sight of the group. It was a maze down here, tunnels leading off campus, to nothing, to other buildings. I had them mapped in my head perfectly. I slithered down a hallway, waiting for Nyx to spill his new as I leaned against the door frame, expertly blocking the tunnel entrance. Depending on what kind of news this was, we may need more privacy.

This group had abilities. Like Austin, he could sense power. The rest of them mastered manipulation, enhanced hearing, strength, empathy visions, shadow play, and things I deemed special, simply because I was born without them, like nurturing, timing, and understanding.

Unlike the rest of them, my only ability was to continue to be an asshole, and my voice boomed with enough authority to demand that people listen.

Nyx pushed his fingers through his long hair, looking (Dare I say it?) stressed out. "We have a problem."

Now, I was interested in his detention with New Girl. I waved an impatient hand for him to continue.

"She's not just some girl. Austin felt it ... and so did I, man."

I rolled my eyes unapologetically. Sure. She was the infamous one. The sarcasm alone felt uncomfortable even silently in my head.

"Felt what?" I snapped in his direction.

"The zap, the shock ... whatever it is. When you touch her ... something in us remembers her, Bolton. You're the only one that remembers shit from before here."

"You know I don't remember anything useful. Shit. Now I have to actually touch her just to prove to you guys she's just some shiny new toy."

He leaned against the wall, free of the burden he just unloaded. His eyes closed, and I watched him swallow hard. "She's cute, bro."

I rolled my eyes, folding my arms against my chest and leaving him to crush on New Girl alone. I wanted this meeting to be over as quickly as possible. Sitting in a room, whining about our circumstances, wasn't my priority. My priority was acting my age in the privacy of my room.

Cheyanne had AirPods in, almost always, and was swaying her hips to nothing but silence, before Omari gave her a stern look. They were twins, connected in a way we wouldn't ever understand. In one glance, you could feel a whole conversation surge between them without any real words being said.

She plucked the AirPods from her ear, finally joining the group sitting in the circle. "Jasper is having a party tonight at the abandoned building."

The estate was the abandoned building on the edge of campus, not used anymore. Naturally, it was used for whatever trouble you could conjure up.

Jasper was notorious for his parties that sprung out of boredom. If I ever showed up, it was out of desperation on my part, and it was only for a half hour. My presence kept the others in line, even in small doses. We were stuck as teenagers, but we weren't getting close to that kind of immaturity. Not on my watch.

Everyone chatted about the party, and I stayed silent, waiting for the hour to be up so I could leave, regardless of whether or not we made any headway on the topic.

I wasn't naïve; they wanted to blow off steam. That's what football was for me: A place where aggression and fighting was allowed.

The girls didn't have the same kind of relief; they were forced to fit in and keep up appearances that we guys didn't need to. Our standards could be lived down with an irritated grunt, multiple girls in our bed, and bad behavior. However, the women couldn't do the same without being labeled names that were cruel and unusual.

CHAPTER 6

Arianna

That was the worst part of Arcadia Prep: There was no escaping. We were all closed in behind a gate, guarded by middle-aged security that I could outrun but to where? The other side of campus? No thanks.

It was 7:50, and I was in my room, "behaving."

Having trouble being so far from me, I felt lonely.

My head hung off the edge of the bed as I held up my heavy textbook, trying to soak in whatever ramblings crowded the pages. My eyes floated over the same words more than once as I tossed the book to my side and groaned.

My roommate came back from wherever she was; she had a busy social life, even as a girl wearing hand-knit sweaters, while I suffered in silence.

Luna.

She reminded me of the world's best helicopter mom, stuck in a state of complete worry over everyone else.

She immediately asked me what was wrong and simultaneously handed me a Ziplock baggie of grapes, like whatever it was would be cured by her gesture. I popped one in my mouth, unmoving from letting the blood drain to my face, hopefully numbing the parts of me that were on fire with cabin fever.

"I'm bored, Luna. I'm dying here."

She smiled sweetly at my dramatics. "There's a party tonight ... Cheer up! Do you wanna come with us?"

I sat up, ravenous for more information. I pulled my Doc Martens on and grabbed my hoodie to pull on. She giggled in such an innocent way at my rushed enthusiasm.

Nothing could be bad about this girl. She didn't know what mean was. I quickly wondered how her easy-target attitude didn't land her in a less than desirable position in the high school hierarchy. Maybe the group was her way of protecting herself.

"Guess that means you want to come ... ? I just need to change my shirt."

I drew my eyes back from critiquing her demeanor and gave her the privacy I would want. I unlocked my phone, still waiting for any kind of message from my ex-boyfriend. The same boyfriend I got into trouble with and stomped on his heart, all in the same week.

He didn't try to reach out after everything happened. I didn't expect him to, but my mind kept wandering back to the precious moments we shared—all the casual "I love you's" we exchanged and how he took my virginity. I may be hard to pin down, full of sass, and operating solely on dangerous adventures but when it came to love ... Well, I was as sappy as the rest of them. I could commit to anything if it meant love.

Apparently to the *wrong people*.

I wasn't bitter or anything.

My eyes traveled back to Luna, who was still picking between two different tops she would cover up with her chunky knit sweater anyways. I noticed a tattoo on her shoulder, and all the excitement bubbled to my surface.

"Is that a tattoo? Omg! I knew you weren't all goody-goody."

Her innocently smooth face was overcome with embarrassment as she quickly turned around and stammered over her own words.

"It's... it's a birthmark, actually. It's from birth."

I stood up and crossed the small room to get a better look at the light mark on her shoulder. "That's where birthmarks do tend to be from: birth. Can I see?"

She reluctantly turned away from me, displaying it not so proudly.

I was sure she had never said no to anything, ever.

I looked at the mark more closely, and it looked like an old scar or a burn. I recognized the shape; it was on the tip of my tongue, teasing me to think harder.

Cancer—not the terminal kind, the astrological kind.

"It's like the astrological sign. You ever notice that? Weird."

Her features sank into panic, like it was a sore spot for me to have mentioned it, yet she'd never discourage someone. She turned around, throwing her shirt on, to cover up any more of my inquiring.

I moved back, grabbing a lipstick off my nightstand and perfectly coating my lips in a deep red. I held it out in a silent gesture to match her grapes from earlier.

"No, thanks. I just wear a clear gloss."

I watched her pick a teal sweater from her closet and pull it over her arms.

All that was missing was some grandkids and cats.

She playfully bumped her shoulder into mine, and we both pulled back when the shock zapped us both.

I laughed. "See? Dying. It's been happening since I got here. Even the school doesn't want me here."

Her laugh halted into a smile that resembled strong sympathy.

I guess I was only half joking, most people just took all of me as sarcasm.

"Who's party is it anyways?"

I hadn't met anyone here who had even seemed like they had ever been to a party, let alone would throw one on campus. Everyone was so rigid here—rule followers. The only exceptions were Nyx and Bolton. I was still trying to figure out how anyone fit here.

"Jasper. He's on the football team. You'll meet him at games and pre and post celebrations. Pretty much a party follows him everywhere."

"One of those, huh?"

"He's certainly something. He's gorgeous, though, so his flaws get overlooked."

I muttered to myself in discontent. I had met every type of Jasper at every new school I went to, from coast to coast. Entitled, gorgeous, and always the one to make high school harder than it needed to be—for everyone but himself. I despised the Jaspers of the world.

I followed her out of our room, out of the building and into the field behind it. She walked through the tall grass with ease, and it wasn't until that moment that I wondered where the party was. Boarding schools didn't offer much privacy. I staggered behind her, kicking the blades of grass against my boots and watching the moisture of Seattle cover the toe.

"We can walk there. It's on the other side of campus, the old abandoned building past the field. They stopped using it in the 90's because of a fire in one of the labs."

She willingly gave information without me having to ask. She was too giving, and it made me suspicious.

"Anyone off campus come to his parties?"

She slowed down her focused pace and smiled in my direction. The lamps illuminating the campus after dark put her smile perfectly on display. "Not interested in anyone at Arcadia?"

I shrugged. I wasn't interested in any aspect of this place. Maybe a boy would anchor down some wild part of me I couldn't control—the part of me that craved adventure and danger.

Detention with Nyx wasn't the worst thing I had ever suffered through, but Nyx didn't illicit the same interest I had in Bolton, the boy who breezed by me so quickly my head spun around before I could give him my mean mug. I didn't know what my interest was in him, but something about him held my curiosity hostage.

All my ex-boyfriends were wholesome and nice, basically the opposite of Bolton in every way.

So why did I care if he didn't like me? Why did I feel this hell bent need to get his approval? Why did he seem like the most dangerous adventure I'd have yet?

I heard Luna's soft voice smooth my thoughts down to a whisper when she spoke. "Not even Nyx? Every girl wants him, because they have zero chance with Bolton."

"He's the strong, silent type, right? He barely spoke during our hour sentencing."

She looked down at the sidewalk instead of at me. "He's just been through a lot … he's moody. He's on scholarship too. He only transferred in last year. No one knows much about him."

That sounded about right. Brooding was always in some abusive relationship with mystery.

It was all just too much work for me. I wasn't the type to hug it out until you hit your head into some epiphany.

I liked the kind of guy who knew exactly who they were; it wasn't silent but ruthlessly deafening.

It would take more than a strong silence to tame me.

The abandoned building was exactly out of a horror movie, and for a minute, I briefly wondered if this was a type of hazing as the new kid. This place was already creepy and sinister enough, but the threat of dying of boredom had me even accepting my own innominate death.

My body tensed with just the thought. I could be walking into a situation I wasn't prepared for, all because I was letting my boredom drive my actions.

We got close, and I saw the small string of lights and lanterns decorating the stairs and door, like some sort of messed up beacon of hope in the hell called Arcadia Prep.

I was elated to see rich, snobby kids could still have fun free of their pretenses.

Luna prepped me as she pushed the door open to what now would be known as heaven. Everything needed a balance. "Things get wild sometimes. Just take it in stride ... "

I didn't know if that was supposed to be a warning, but to me, it sounded like an invitation.

The party was still timid, like people only gathered out of boredom not rebellion. I was taken aback by the tone being so relaxed that I wasn't sure where to put my displaced energy. I was ready to walk into relief but this felt like a library instead. I turned to Luna, letting my eyebrow pop up in criticism.

"Real wild, huh?"

She slapped my forearm lightly, jokingly ... Let's be real, this girl probably wouldn't kill a spider if it meant hurting another living creature.

"Jasper and the boys aren't here yet, duh. Nothing good happens without them."

Now I was making more sense of this place, even the rich had no even playing field. These boys ruled school, and no one made a move without their permission. This was more common than individuality, trust me, I had lived in most of the United States. Seattle was no different.

Luna had a bounce in her step when she reached her friends, minus Nyx, Bolton, and Jasper. Kate's glare didn't leave my direction as her wrist twisted in a broken manner, holding the Solo cup like it clashed with her outfit and she was pissed no one told her what colors to wear.

I could barely hold my snarky laugh inside without biting the inside of my sensitive mouth.

"What's so funny, New Girl?"

I was looking for adventure, not confrontation. Her eyebrows stretched up into her forehead, and her lips tensed, waiting for me to respond.

"You. Worried the Solo cup doesn't match your outfit?"

I looked her up and down once more for effect, even though I was impressed. She wore mom jeans in a way mom's only wished. She was the school's obvious bombshell, dressing like a mom's desperate attempt to relive this part of their adolescence and embarrassed the cup clashed with the ensemble. Kate was ironically a cliché in every way.

I pivoted on my heel, making a clean getaway after my verbal hit-and-run. I wanted whatever she was drinking, because this "party" was not up to my standards.

Pretty tame high schoolers. Parents must be proud.

I wandered around until I found the keg nudged in a corner, and I wondered how many of them had done a keg stand, stayed out too late, or broken any kind of rules, besides being nice to the new girl.

Arianna

I strutted around, proud of my cup of room temperature beer. I started exploring past the party and into the rooms breaking off like veins from the heart of the party. The building was huge, and the only part truly off limits was the top floors that still held a faint stench of smoke.

I wasn't interested in damaged. Damaged was different than dangerous. I was a pro at knowing the differences.

All the rooms resembled science labs of some nature with the islands, stools, and even some beakers left behind.

Abandoned.

Sneaking a look into each room, I swayed my hips down the hallway, moving to the music leaking into the spaces.

I got to the end of the hall, curiosity completely un-sparked, until I heard different music erupting from the hallway competing with the Top 100 playing in the distance.

Alternative music swelled as I inched closer, wondering why someone would be all the way down here, by themselves, during a party.

Curiosity was piqued.

Slinking up to the doorway, I scoped out the room, but I could hear their voices over the music. I took my chances, pressing my spine against the door frame and sipping my beer like I was completely unaware of anyone but the music.

I heard someone shout as the music stopped. "This room is private!"

I lazily turned onto my shoulder, facing the contents of the room and rolling my eyes. It wasn't until my dramatic, yet childish, move that I noticed the three boys lounging in their own private party.

I snipped in Bolton's direction, sure he was the one who shouted, "Public property."

He sat up, no longer relaxed, but strained, as his forearms ground into his thighs. "Actually, you're trespassing. This building is closed and off limits."

He pushed me into the wicked parts of me as I did him. We were so far equally matched.

"And? You're too cool to smoke and drink with anyone else?"

He got up, slowly making his way to the doorway I was in, and every nerve inside of me was frying under the pressure of all his unknown.

"Did this act work at every other school you've been to? It doesn't work here. Wash the purple out and lose the attitude. It's not having the effect you want."

His shoulder checking skills ran over me expertly. I was knocked right into the door frame as the boys followed behind him, but not before smirking at his burn.

I smirked at the flames of his burn too.

He challenged me in a way no one else even tried to. Thirteen schools before Arcadia, and I finally found my match in Bolton Hayes.

The one I hadn't met, Jasper, stopped only when he was in the doorway across from me, leaving him in my personal space. "Guessing you're New Girl."

"Well, we don't get to pick our names. Birth names or otherwise."

We exchanged our birth-given names, and he seemed more personable than the others—dare I say normal.

"He's not warm and cuddly. Don't pay attention to him. Coming to the party?"

As soon as the boys entered the party bubble contained to the front half of the building, it seemed like time stopped. Every pair of eyes were now in our direction, and the scrutiny of why I was trailing behind them was burdensome.

I took the first opportunity I could, to break away and make a shortcut to the beer, which I hadn't had since the last time I was in trouble.

Every time I got in real trouble I would lay low, be the person everyone wanted me to be for a while. That meant no fun, no alcohol, no pot, and no boys. At this point, I was famished for all four.

I didn't search Luna out again after filling my cup with the room temperature beer, even though I should have. I came with her and now I was ditching her in search of what she couldn't provide with her hugs and sweaters.

I ended up on the porch outside the party looking up at the stars. My mom was really into astrology, the signs, crystals, and sometimes magic. Now that she was gone, it was like she left the stars in the sky for me.

That's how I really started getting in trouble—sneaking out to be under the stars. I'd point out the constellations she taught me, and I could hear her stories resurrected in my mind—her soft voice, the smell of her shampoo, and the purple stone that was cold against my skin when she hugged me.

My good memory was ripped from me with footsteps I wasn't paying attention to.

Jasper stood tall behind me, lighting the end of his joint and mumbling around it hanging from his lips. "You know the party is inside, right?"

My face contorted into annoyance at his obvious remark. It didn't need a reply, and I wasn't giving out ones that wasted my time. I turned towards him, pushed my ass on the banister of the porch and faced him, wordlessly.

He didn't step closer like I thought he would. He let the porch between us swallow the words before reaching each other.

He took an exasperated inhale from the joint that looked small between his fingers. He was all muscle and perfection, leaving no room for flaws. He had cut the arms off his t-shirt, unevenly displaying his toned arms, clearly from the discipline of football.

I tried not to bite my lip in front of him; I wasn't giving this gorgeous man an upper hand on me.

He moved forward slowly, not to catch me off guard, erasing the space between us with each step. His pinched fingers gestured towards me offering me what was his. I didn't take it from him, instead I leaned forward and pushed my lips up to his fingers still holding the joint. I inhaled the bud I hadn't tasted in months.

I wasn't prejudiced against whatever fun meant here ... as long as it was dangerous and got my blood circulated.

I watched Jasper's body stiffen as he watched me pull away with the inhale still in my lungs and burning my chest. My eyelashes fluttered involuntarily as I looked up at him.

He was slow to act and it confused me in every way.

The King of Arcadia Prep himself shouted Jasper's name from the doorway, and he sighed like it was enough to send this guy into a pissed off mode with just syllables alone.

I guessed steroids were another avenue of fun here.

His body twisted, facing Bolton and leaning against the banister next to me. For all intents and purposes, he looked caught.

Why did he care what Bolton thought? Who voted him the pointless king? Was he the sex police too?

Bolton stormed closer to us and demanded Jasper go inside. Jasper didn't even attempt to talk back, and I suddenly found him less attractive than I previously thought.

Jasper let his hand with the joint fall down and he gave me a look instead of any words.

Bolton's head cocked behind him, looking over his shoulder at Jasper and Nyx going inside and closing the door behind them quieting the music.

"What the fuck do you think you're doing?"

I felt like I was being scolded by my father, when his hands grabbed his own hips and his face looked so severe I wondered if looks really did kill. I waited for whatever nonsense he was gonna throw my way with his disgusted tone he perfected for me now.

I slid off the banister and stood up, "Seriously, isn't there some kind of rule you have to tell people you're a narc?"

I didn't bother sticking around for his jabs. I had seen so many versions of Bolton that I was pretty positive I had heard all the insults worth hearing.

Walking away stole his majesty's right to put me in my place, but his hand grasped around my bicep as I walked away holding me in my place. Another sharp prick came with another person's touch. Jesus…this campus either truly hated me or wanted to tell me something. Either way, I didn't speak in electricity.

I could hear his voice in my ear so clearly that I didn't need to grant him the pleasure of making eye contact. "He can't smoke in the season. Maybe while you're bulldozing through our school, you can use your head."

I jerked my arm back and turned to finally face him, as pissed off as I felt at his attempt to make me feel small.

"He's old enough to not have you baby him," my voice shook with my immature comeback.

I wanted to affect him, shake him, but nothing did. I was pretty sure he was made of the same shit demigods were and had the attitude to match.

I was ready to storm back into the party. My hand reached for the door, just as his hands grasped my hips with such strength I felt realigned in a way only chiropractors knew how.

His head bowed down into the crook of my neck, and I felt his warm voice hit my neck. "Stay away from my boys, New Girl."

This party wasn't enough rebellion or adventure to satisfy a photojournalist in the middle of a war zone. I turned around in his grasp facing him. I made sure to make eye contact while I spoke.

So much for keeping my nose clean here. Sorry, Dad.

"And what if I don't?"

I didn't have to see my reflection in his dark eyes to know there was a twinkle of victory in mine. I finally found the chink in his armor: questions he wouldn't answer.

I was celebrating long before I should have ... before he leaned down, letting his closeness pin me against the door frame in a distracting way. He was purposely making me feel off center with his body and that sultry voice that was borderline too rough and coming into my space. It was like my whole body needed the next breath to come before I became deprived of oxygen.

"Don't test me. We aren't your typical rich kids."

His body pushed off of mine, and I felt the colder air rise between us. The air was deprived of the bickering and it was giving us the cold shoulder.

The party was still going strong inside, and I found Luna again after realizing boys are a lost cause here.

Luna could read facial expressions like a more in-depth personality test. She saw the disappointment in my mouth without any delay.

"Don't worry…the game day is this weekend against our rivals Exeter Academy. There will be a whole new meaning to *trouble* soon."

I was sure she had never used the word in a sentence before now. She was trying very hard to comfort me with it anyways.

"Rivals? I can see why. No offense but I might cheer for the other team."

Kate's snicker was like a flicker and quick fade. She didn't snap and call me New Girl when she turned to me, so I took it as progress.

"Good luck with that, really. Bolton will love that."

"Who crowned him King of Arcadia Prep?"

Kate didn't laugh or even sneer when she looked at me for the first time since I arrived. Every other time was a glance in my direction, seemingly trying not to make direct eye contact.

"Himself, duh."

CHAPTER 1

Bolton

The gods had ways of torturing you with mediocrity and driving you mad by making you think things were coincidence or karma.

I'd watch people turn themselves inside out looking for the one infected part of themselves to cut off, finding religion, breaking up with their partners, or even creating a more disastrous situation for themselves, when the whole time it was my gods simply toying with miniature versions of hell.

Mediocrity was hell.

Routine was hell.

And New Girl? My own personal torture from the gods.

She spoke out of turn. She was confident in the ways girls this age shouldn't be, and she knew exactly how much she was annoying me every time that grin took over her face, like it was her favorite sport.

I pushed off my locker just annoyed with her being in the same hallway as me. We had a game to play against our rivals, and I was consumed with my own personal hell.

That was the thing about hell: it was on a loop, and there was no escaping.

I thought being stuck as a high school senior more than once was hell.

I was mistaken.

The only time I will admit to being wrong is to prove how much she didn't belong here.

The boys' locker room wasn't typical. We had the state of the art equipment and funding that would well exceed one season. Boarding school parents weren't afraid to trade in their guilt for donations.

I threw my duffle bag down with force, making Nyx and Austin look at me with so much concern that I wanted to throw up.

"You good?" Austin was a lot like Luna; they both sensed too much with the emotions other people wore. It was unsettling.

Nothing was private in their presence.

"I'm fine, Austin. Let's just focus on the game."

Nyx was changing into his under armor we wore under our pads when he picked up his head. "Did you feel anything the night of the party? Did you touch her?"

Nyx was always a baseline: calm, collected, secretive. This version of him, who was asking me questions like she was a desperate way out of being stuck, wasn't anyone I knew.

I ignored him until he got himself under control enough to ask me with his balls firmly attached again.

Austin looked towards us, also waiting for an answer. "Well? Is she the one or not?"

I slammed my locker closed behind me, facing both of them again. I tried to loosen my lips and shake off the intensity in my face.

"No, the fucking new girl isn't gonna save us. Drop it. We have a game."

I pulled the spandex under armor on and proceeded to put my pads in place when Coach entered the room for his traditional speech meant to hype us all up. To be honest, I stopped listening after we first repeated the year. He recycled his words and fed them back to us.

Nyx was our defensive line. No seriously, he pretty much was the only player paying attention out there.

Jasper was captain, only because he cared and I don't. He was willing to put in the effort if it benefitted him outside the field, and it did, tenfold.

Austin was our quarterback—out of the way and the least amount of contact if we all did our jobs right.

Beau and Leo, who were together, respectfully cheered us on, even though they preferred a good makeover show (of any kind: people or houses).

The girls came to the games, too, even though they had no real stake in who wins or loses.

On the field, I could see our rivals gearing up to make this the game of the season—all but one, Caellum, who used to go to Arcadia before he escaped and landed at Exeter Academy. He was still forced to repeat his senior year, just like us, except that he found a way around being around us.

Fucking Aquarius.

Cold.

Clever.

Stubborn.

Big on loyalty, which was ironic, because not one bone in his body was loyal.

Our hard stares locked onto each other, and I felt my fingers clench around my helmet tighter. He betrayed the circle, and the fucked up part was we didn't know how he did it.

Cheyanne was convinced he used some kind of black magic to lift the enchantment of the campus when it was weakest.

Now he was free to be himself without the chains, but he'd always fall asleep and wake up in the same senior year. Everyone forgetting the heavy feeling of deja vu that tingled inside them as they redid the year.

Caellum was the only one at Exeter Academy, having no balance in his influence. Without the collective everyone around him fed off his traits, making the entire academy mirror what he focused on most, his flaws.

Nyx pushed his helmet down and pushed the mouth guard in place, as Austin stood on the other side of me ready to go.

My gaze at Caellum wasn't wavering. I wasn't going to break first. He pressed his gloved hand to his lips and blew us a kiss before putting his helmet on. I felt the anger nearly explode in my chest as my team jogged to the field, waiting for my approval.

I didn't have to be captain for everyone to need my approval.

All I told the team was to kill them, and anyone not giving everything they had to this game needed to get off my field.

We got into position, and for some idiotic reason, my eyes shifted towards the stands. I swept over people, finding familiar faces quickly and then there was one I didn't expect to see:

New Girl.

I didn't have time to contemplate her ulterior motives for being here.

Caellum whistled, before calling out, "Come on, pretty boy. You've got some losing to do!"

I felt everything in my body tighten in preparation. My breath was steady, and I was focused in a way I never felt. We weren't losing to the one person who left us.

The game went on forever, a push and pull the whole game, with neither of us having an upper hand.

I was still confident, until I felt a hit taking me down with a hard thud. I clenched my teeth and my guard, absorbing the hit like fuel.

A few seconds later, fingers laced through my helmet. "Haven't you learned by now, Bolton? I never lose. You chose the wrong team."

I heard the buzzer, and I knew we lost. I didn't bother to get up or fight. We lost, even after leaving every ounce of our motivation on the field.

My fist rose up just to hit the turf with an angry blow, blaming the field for our loss. I let the memory seep in. In my weakened state, it was hard to keep anything out.

I didn't choose the wrong team.

Caellum only told me he was leaving, Halloween night, three years ago.

I knew, and I kept it from the group.

I knew, and I didn't stop him.

In fact, I had to convince myself not to go with him. If I went with him, I'd always be in his shadow. We'd be a broken circle with no way out of this. So I stayed and let him think I betrayed him.

I became King of Arcadia with Caellum gone. No one questioned me; no one even thought about betraying me. Plus, I had the circle.

I was still lying there defeated with my helmet ripped off and pissed-off rage still coursing through my veins when New Girl stood above me.

Great, I forgot she was here. Now she had ammunition.

She offered her hand. "You played really hard. Trust me, I'm originally from Texas. Football is basically religion there."

I got up without taking her hand. I didn't need her help or her pity. Just as the scowl crept onto my face from my poisoned blood, Caellum appeared.

His timing was impeccable at his worst. When he went to Arcadia, he was known for hearing and seeing everything.

There were no secrets with him. He'd tell you just how wicked he was if you just asked.

"Having New Girl nurse your broken, black heart? That's a new low for you."

I watched him laugh, eyes roaming over both of us critically, looking for soft spots to prod. He smirked without another word, before slapping her shoulder. I watched the exchange, knowing he felt exactly what everyone else did—the spark radiating off of her.

I slid into place almost instinctively, blocking most of her from him.

I knew his demons better than my own. He wasn't dangerous, but cruel and reckless always made the short list.

I don't know what made me protect people from his wrath, maybe the bullshit title of Arcadia King?

Even other schools caught onto the nickname, and at every game, someone twisted it in insults and jabs meant to piss me off.

Knock off pretty boy's crown.

Show them who's really king.

Slay the king.

I blame Game of Thrones for people being so comfortable with old English and throwing the word "king" around like a dagger.

Caellum's hand landed heavy on my shoulder as he leaned in keeping New Girl out of this.

"Your face still doesn't hide anything from me. Don't let me find out you're hiding how to get out of this."

I shook out of his space, pushing myself up taller and being the asshole I always was. "Guess that fucking scar Nyx gave you doesn't warn people enough to stay away. You left, so get on your damn bus and get off my campus."

He stepped forward, so did I. I wasn't shying away from him gloating his win in my face along with the circle he abandoned. He wasn't physically tough, not enough to carry his constant need to challenge everyone around him. His team did that for him. Their job was creating clear paths to the goal, keeping the contact of the sport away from him.

I didn't challenge anyone. Why would a king fight a knight?

I was so close I could see his skin glistening from the sweat of the game and his eyes almost burning an ember color. There was a red hue circling his pupils, and his fists clenched as the only parts of him capable of anger, while others were dormant.

I wasn't backing down. Every part of me was pissed off and ready to fight at all times.

Nyx shouted from the sidelines, making Caellum break his focus on me.

"Bolton, get to the damn showers already!"

He knew what he was doing when he shouted our way. He never spoke without thinking. He never actually spoke without it meaning something so much deeper.

I watched him fold his arms, standing firm, until I dropped whatever bullshit that was between us.

I made sure I pushed my shoulder into his aggressively, letting the padding of my gear take him off guard. I felt satisfied walking away and shouting, "New Girl!" without looking behind me. My lips were pursed tightly together hoping she would just listen for once, without forcing me to overdose on sarcasm.

When she jogged to catch up to my side, I finally let out an exhale.

Of course she needed to be equal. God forbid she trail behind me like everyone else.

This girl was constant trouble, torture, and now Caellum knew that too.

He wasn't going to let this go; he felt the same spark.

I wanted to banish her from my kingdom, but now I was forced to protect her.

She followed me into the tunnel leading to the locker room. I hadn't realized as I threw my helmet against the cement wall, waiting for it to crack, when she yipped in a way that girls do with loud sounds. So easily shaken. I turned around already pulling off my pads.

"This is the guys' locker room, New Girl ... Is that the reputation you want?"

She leaned against the wall, her Doc Martens pressing into the concrete. "I let Billy kiss me in eighth grade when we lived in Georgia. Gwendolyn didn't approve, so she told the whole school I slept with him. In a week, I was the youngest whore that town had seen. So been there, done that."

I held my jersey and pads in my hand, completely shirtless and comfortable. Life before this was filled with gods—literally, the most perfect race ever created.

This body I was stuck in was nothing in comparison to the beauty I had seen before. I was a sliver of the perfect I once was. I could tell she was accustomed to this form, human, when her eyes trailed down my abs, and her lips parted only slightly, like I was too much to take in before she forced her eyes down.

"Gwendolyn was a jealous bitch."

She smiled without any cleverness to go with it, and I saw something I hadn't before. I didn't know how to put it into words as I squinted in her direction, trying to place it.

Common ground?

She was as lonely as I was?

I was finally seeing her, Arianna, instead of the new girl I despised. None of that was real. The sarcasm, the clever smiles, the taste for trouble, and pissing people off on purpose was how she protected herself. Now I wanted to know why.

Why did New Girl need to protect herself?

I didn't pry. I was a lot of things, but greedy wasn't one of them. Not today. We were both wounded from our own losses.

I threw my pads in the bin at the door and walked over to my locker. I left it open, letting the door of my locker cover my gaze towards her. Her eyes took it all in as she pushed her back against the wall closest to the exit.

"Unless you're offering to shower with me, I'd get out of here."

I watched her tawny complex turn red with my words and she shifted almost uncomfortably. She gave me all the clues to figuring her out without knowing it. I kicked off my cleats and stood in front of my locker. Facing Arianna, I came to terms with replacing her nickname with her actual name. New girl didn't seem to fit anymore.

I waited to continue to strip until she safely left the room. The locker room was heavy with hot air reacting to our awkwardness at my own sarcasm.

For a brief moment, I debated if she would have stayed if I simply made a move. Instead, I chose to belittle her like I did everyone else.

CHAPTER 6

Arianna

I tried to ask Luna who the guy was at the game before we left the bathroom together. Kate was busy re-applying her gloss, even though she wasn't trying to allure any boys. She had Austin—a drop dead gorgeous and completely nice boyfriend. I saw him even hold her purse before we came into the bathroom.

Who does that?

He was too nice for Kate. Maybe he was anchored down to her humility buried way down deep, under all the pink.

Luna stayed quiet, like she hadn't heard me, and I waited like she wasn't avoiding answering me, while I tapped my fingers against the counter, impatiently waiting.

Kate let out a labored, yet annoyed sigh, before her hand dropped from primping herself. "Caellum, okay? Jesus. Nosey much?"

I had nothing to adjust in the mirror. I was comfortable in my jeans, a t-shirt, and boots. Comfortable meant not having to stress and using setting spray took care of the rest.

"And? That's all? Obviously they have beef."

She didn't even ask who or wait for clarification when she spun around and jumped up more gracefully than I walked to sit on the counter top.

"You know he's gonna kill you for prying into his business, right?"

I looked at her like I was still waiting for more, and now I was insatiable for the answers.

She actually rolled her eyes at me before she spoke, "Bad blood. It's a real Taylor Swift song. He used to go here, was Bolton's best friend, and now he's not."

Luna was finally paying attention only to snub Kate for spilling the beans. I didn't see the big deal but maybe there was more history than my vagabond life was used to.

I dropped it, not asking anymore. I let it mull over in my mind, fermenting and letting it grow on me.

We headed back into the pizzeria on campus. I knew I was in a whole new world of rich when the boarding school had a pizza place on campus and opened for after game celebrations.

No one was actually celebrating; the boys were recovering.

I slid into the corner booth big enough for all of us. I was sandwiched between Luna and Nyx. My eyes were searching for Bolton but came up empty.

"Wasting your time, sweetheart. He doesn't come here," Nyx spat out, in a too-exhausted-for-words kind of way. His Australian accent really made even insults sound sweet.

I watched him pull a nip of vodka out from his jacket pocket and pour it into his soda expertly. I was sure no one else even saw him do it. I popped an eyebrow at his actions, wondering too many things to articulate quickly.

He put the empty nip back in his pocket and stirred in the vodka. "New Girl, I can see the judgment."

I stayed silent, he was just as intense as Bolton, maybe more explosive, and less calculated.

He continued, "It's a Friday night. We lost. Do I really need to make more excuses?"

The two trays of pizza came, and I shifted focus, letting him have his secrets ... for now.

Everyone was laughing and a relaxed tone cascaded over us. That didn't last long.

Bolton's ex best friend walked into the pizzeria, and the bell chimed at the same time the door moved, warning us all. Leo, someone I haven't had much time with, announced to the group to stay cool. I knew he was only speaking to Nyx, the only hot head here.

I mentally prayed over and over again that he wouldn't come over.

Like all my other prayers, it went unanswered.

I studied his features as he sauntered over to the booth and stopped before us. His features were sharp, almost hard to take in entirely. His jet black hair only reminded me of a dark version of Bolton's, except his was villainously neat.

No villain ever had messy hair; think about it.

He wasn't much taller than me and was bulky like he worked out more than his body could handle. He was all American and the average kind of eye candy.

I could see his tricks safely harnessed behind his eyes, ready to attack at all times.

He looked directly at me, ignoring everyone else at the booth. "You're Bolton's girl, right? Where is he?"

"Excuse me? I'm not his keeper. I'm pretty sure he has a phone."

It came out without thinking first. I should have denied being his girl first and put sarcasm last. In any instance of feeling threatened, I lash out with very little thought process.

I could hear my dad's voice swell like the queued up soundtrack in a movie, each action perfectly paired with music.

You have to think before you speak. Count to five and then speak, my Little Archer.

He tried to teach me early but it was no use. I was ruined by my emotions.

I pushed my chin forward signaling Nyx to slide out of the booth so I could leave. As I stood up to breeze by Bolton's clear tormentor, Caellum stepped quickly in front of me, making me pause my storm out.

Things weren't the same without Bolton's presence lingering over everyone, hating that we could have fun and he wouldn't let himself even smile.

"Tell your boyfriend—"

I cut his words off before he could finish the sentence. "Are you deaf?"

I didn't even finish the comeback as I watched his face scrunch up in confusion at my left field question. After I waited long enough I finished, "I'm not his keeper. You wanna tell him anything? Find him yourself. By the way, *not* his girlfriend. We're enemies slowly working towards frenemies."

I slipped past him, reminiscing on the progress Bolton and I had made by seeing each other vulnerable. He had lost, only to have it rubbed in by this asshole, and he knew a sliver of me now that I wouldn't normally share with anyone. Somehow he lured it out of me effortlessly. I wasn't even completely sure how it happened.

The word "magic" came to mind.

Caellum didn't stop me; no one did. My storm out was complete when the cool air felt like relief from the tension Caellum dragged behind him.

The campus was a lot darker now, only illuminated by the lights hanging above the path between buildings. I squinted at almost every door, trying to place my own.

Note to architects: make buildings less similar on campuses.

Finally I found my building, after getting turned around a half dozen times. I pressed my fancy new keycard to the pad and watched the red light turn green.

Arbitrary, huh? Trust me, I'm on your side here. We are smarter than equating green to go and red to stop.

The door closing behind me was the only sound I could hear in the dark hallway. It was so quiet I heard myself shift from unfazed to paranoid easily. I wasn't afraid of the dark. I just knew that nothing cheerful ever came from the shadows and all that.

The dark, quiet, places were unsettling. I moved along the hallway, trying to find my room, closely looking at the room numbers and regretting leaving now.

"Arianna?"

I heard my name, but I hadn't recognized the voice saying it. No one used my actual name here. Not yet. I turned around slowly wanting to squeeze my eyes closed.

"What are you doing in the boys' dormitory?"

Bolton said my real name and his voice wasn't soaked in disdain. I didn't even know anyone knew my name, let alone him.

My brain wasn't catching up fast enough to speak when my eyes were boring into his shirtless chest. His illumined scantily white skin shone against the moonlight pouring in through the window. Every curve of his taut muscles made my mouth salivate.

"Boys' dormitory? Damn. I should have waited for Luna."

He stood there, leaning against the door, silently, like he refused to converse with anyone, hence not going for pizza.

I took a step closer, examining more of him when I saw the same type of scar as Luna. I could easily make out a ram's horns.

How could they not notice this? Maybe I was the only one to see him shirtless.

"Hey, your scar; it's a ram, like the sign Aries ... Luna has a weird scar on the back of her shoulder that looks like Cancer. What are you guys ... in some kind of secret society?"

He didn't laugh or even budge. "Never seen a birthmark? Born with it."

My eyes slanted down, and my tongue swiped against my teeth, like I was thinking with so much effort for a better excuse. If there was one, he wasn't giving it up.

"That's what she said too ... "

He changed the topic without me being done with it smoothly. "Hot date, or you prefer sneaking into designated boys' areas?"

I sarcastically, all monotone, pushed a "ha-ha" out. "Left without Luna. This place is creepy in the dark."

He laughed walking without me further down the hall, but he kept talking so I knew to keep the pace. "Why did you leave without Luna? She hitting on Nyx again?"

My eyes went wide, and I was thankful this hallway was almost too dark to see.

"What? No? Caellum came looking for you and I was over it. Gave him a heads up I'm not your girlfriend. You're welcome."

"I'm sure he did. You piqued his interest, New Girl."

I kept following him up a set of wide stairs to a second level without questioning where we were going or why. I simply kept putting one foot in front of the other and fed my own motivation to keep up with the school's king.

I refused to be deemed less than anyone, especially him.

"Not interested. The pretentious heartthrob vibe isn't my type." I didn't think before I spoke, once again.

He stopped at the top of the landing, looking down at me, as all kings do, and popped an eyebrow, like I meant to offend him directly.

"I beg to differ. You're the one still following me, aren't you?"

"You've got the pretentious, asshole part down to a T. Jury is still out on the rest."

A silence hit after he stopped responding and our back and forth faded. I let it, until he pushed open his door to a bedroom twice the size of my room I shared with Luna. I leaned in the doorway, completely aware that I was invited in.

"Nyx and Luna? Seriously?"

I watched him lay down on his bed, long and lean, starkly pale against his black sheets, and his hair still slightly wet. His blonde hair darkened from the water and stuck to his temples in a way I'd find annoying. The birth mark looked more like a scar in this light, and the edges were irritated with red.

"He's off limits. I know you're new and all, but maybe give it some time before you profess that you're into everyone."

My fingers curled under, lightly at first as I pushed my nails into my palm. He inflicted emotional pain, so I created physical pain, drawing connections between the two.

"I'm not into anyone here, so relax. Your posse is safe from my seduction."

He got off the bed in one motion, and his long legs took big steps. He leaned into the door, the thickness hitting him in the chest as he leaned into me. "More like claws."

Without even a goodnight, he pushed the door closed, forcing me out of its way before it sandwiched any part of me in its frame.

I scoffed at his all-so-fitting door: black, with no clue as to who lived behind it.

Ours had our names with a white board, like anyone would use that over sending a text message. It was very Luna. She believed people could be good but I knew better.

Statistically, I'd seen every corner of the United States, and everyone was just as selfish and rude as the next town. I knew better than anyone; no one was going to look out for anyone but themselves.

Why else did I wear sarcasm so well? Because if no one cares, at least it's funny.

Bolton

This was the death I loathed most.

Actually, I loathed them all, but today was cheerleading tryouts on our field at the same time as practice, and I wasn't in the mood to hear Kate and watch her wearing her fake crown today.

Her voice was always soaked in this "too good for everyone" tone that made it hard to hear what she was saying without hating her. It was especially annoying, because she insisted on doing tryouts on the field, claiming it gave "intensity" to the process.

Intensity she didn't need her surroundings for.

I tossed my pads on the ground as I walked up to Nyx, who was not so inconspicuously scanning the new crop of freshmen trying out.

Some of them looked so nervous I guessed they wouldn't last the first half hour, while others looked too confident.

I watched the opposite direction, at our newly formed team still trying to get our bearings this season. Everyone was learning their place and trying to settle back into playing consistently again.

"Luna should try out."

My arms folded over my chest as I watched the team get into formation I leaned back making sure my eyes connected with Nyx. "Excuse me?"

He coughed like he never meant to say it out loud, and I wasn't supposed to be caring enough to listen. "Yeah? She's cheerful and shit."

I patted his shoulder in pity and let the small laugh take over my expression, a rare feat.

We both knew he liked Luna, and she obviously liked him, but nothing would happen, not now or later. Nyx was in the category of using them and dumping them. Not even for sexual favors, but homework, coffee, someone to cheer him during games.

Luna wasn't the dump them type. We all knew that. She was made of sunshine, love for animals, and too many damn feelings.

Nyx was anti-feelings, anti-happy, and anti-sunshine.

If you're asking me? He thinks he's unlovable. There's too much depth and no one can swim.

The whole practice I could feel a thousand eyes on me, watching my every move, like I was some member of a boy band. Without looking, I could tell you their eyes were filled with lust and envy.

Every freshman assumed I must be dating Queen Bitch Kate just because of our repellant attitudes. Austin didn't care one bit. He swore by meditation and his fucking kombucha. Once I realized he didn't care, I stopped making a scene in order to set everyone right in one shot.

Austin looked at me as I caught a perfect spiral and our look exchanged it all. This kind of jealousy of Kate only secured her empire for another year amongst a sea of insecure girls.

I shouted to the team to do our typical drills while I slacked off. As a co-captain, I pretty much made the rules, and if I was being honest I didn't need the practice. I'd been doing this half as long as professionals in the NFL. I drank my water, while I casually looked on to the girls trying out, spotting one not like the other.

New Girl.

Arianna.

Wasn't this a curious development. In her Doc Martens, all black outfit, and opposite of spunky attitude, she was trying out? Now, I was interested. It would either be the death of our Queen Bitch or a blow up; either way, I wasn't missing this.

Upperclassman and myself decided practice was turning into being silent judges for the try out. We watched every girl do what was demanded of them, enthralled with calling dibs.

New Girl stepped up to Kate and the girls meant to be co-captains but they knew better. This wasn't even playing ground.

Kate demanded to know if she could tumble, and with a huge sigh moving her shoulders, she pushed her finger in her mouth to fish out her gum and flicked it in the trash, before preparing for her next move. Effortlessly, she tucked and flipped, shocking even me.

She outshined every girl, even while trying to snuff herself out in all that black.

I liked black.

I liked dulling the rest down to see what really mattered.

I like the honesty of black.

Arianna did everything almost as good as Kate, and I wondered if she used to be someone else.

Someone less herself.

Someone less filled with sass and snark.

I watched until she was less focused on the try out and scanned the field. I made a point to stop paying attention before she could catch me staring. Nyx threw the ball my direction from the center of the field at full speed right past my head. He had good aim; anyone else and the ball would have collided with my face.

After practice ended, I looked around the field, but the girls already finished and left with almost no trace. I shook off seeing her one last time for no reason other than to feed my own irritation.

I swiped my gear up off the ground and headed for the showers. The overcast of Seattle wasn't a saving grace today; the heat still boiled and blistered under all our padding.

I walked down the tunnel behind the team when I heard the immature noises of something catching their attention.

Arianna. Places she shouldn't be, again.

I walked right by her, not stopping for any extra second. "Never learn, huh?"

She pushed off the wall, with her arms folded against her chest. It was hard to look past her chest that she was clearly outlining without trying. "Don't pretend you weren't watching me out there."

That was all I needed to stop me in my tracks. I was caught hating her less.

I dropped my gear again, but this time the thud against the concrete echoed in the tunnel. "No one was watching you, sweetheart."

She didn't step closer to me or try to breach the gap between us. She was planted in her accusation. "Seriously? That's what you're going with?"

She was baiting me to confess, and I wasn't going to give her the satisfaction.

"Yes, Arianna, it's tradition. Upperclassmen claim their ... " I caught my own words as they formed, swallowing them whole, all the misogynistic edges. " ... territory for the season."

"Who claimed me?" I watched the smile tug at her lips when she asked.

"Not me, if that's what you're asking."

My response fizzled out the spark that twinkled inside her irises. I almost felt bad, but my desire to be honest always trumped anyone's feelings.

She didn't respond as I felt her eyes take inventory of me: all honesty, brutal, and no cracks for any doubt. She was still the new girl. She was a risk that no upper classman was going to take on.

They wanted safe, no push backs ... easy.

For the record? If we were choosing? I'd let our hate for each other simmer down into disdain if it meant choosing someone at Arcadia Prep.

She didn't need that kind of power in my real truth.

CHAPTER 10

Bolton

Another late night meeting brought us together, like it or not. I was avoiding going, even though I knew the boys would show up at my door beckoning me to lead the way.

I wanted to stop caring and stop trying. I tried to wrap my mind around being perpetually 18 forever but parts of me wouldn't budge.

Every part of me was stubborn, even my insides.

None of us would have chosen to be friends if it hadn't been for this fucking curse, for Pandora's stupid box, the gods dying—Pandora's most dangerous weapons.

I was the only one who remembered life before this loop. The gods would play their tricks, or punishments, on the mortals, and we would be banished to a Pandora's box so we couldn't influence humans like we were meant to do.

Without our influence, the humans worshipped many false gods, fell for everything, endured meaningless punishments, and didn't think for themselves.

Slavery was every color back then.

There was nothing we could do.

We went from being trapped in her box to trapped in a loop meant to keep us from the real world.

I was burdened with remembering for all of us.

I was jaded because of it.

Like clockwork, the boys showed up at my door and I opened it, pushing through them without a single syllable. I was in an especially cruel mood, paired with nothing but bad intentions.

I felt Nyx's hand land on my shoulder—a less personal attempt at comfort. No amount of comfort was going to fix me.

I snipped without turning my head behind me or in their direction, "Text Jasper. I want to have a party."

Austin's concerned and forever-even tone cascaded over me like a flu, poisoning my bad mood: "Doesn't everyone on campus have tests tomorrow? End of a unit."

I stopped at the exit, turning around to face him with so much anger pulsing through me I wasn't sure if I'd actually hurt him. That was normally what happened when Rage's claws dug into me deeply and drug me around like its own personal voodoo doll.

"I don't care what you call it, Austin. Make it a fucking study party." My fingers tapped my own temple in a version of sign language meant for him to use his head instead of his precious heart.

The meeting was no different, constant bickering that didn't quicken or slow down any progress. It was stagnant noise lulling me into a deep sleep; that's how bored of it I was.

I wasn't about to come clean with how much I felt she was different. I didn't know what that meant yet. It could just be hormones ... we had those now.

I sat in the circle completely uncaring, except for a possible party. I could blow off steam, find a distracting girl ... anything other than thinking of the past and present that wasn't changing any time soon.

The twins dominated these meetings. Omari was the voice of reason, and Cheyanne was cutthroat. Pure fucking balance. The twins often toyed with magic and rituals, making them easily the most qualified to make decisions around determining the one.

"I'm gonna need her hair," Cheyanne said, not necessarily to anyone in particular.

Leo and Beau both seemed horrified as they touched their perfectly manicured hair and even looked to each other as if they misheard her.

Cheyanne didn't joke, laugh, or even smile. She wore dark red lipstick and had obvious piercings instead of what girls labeled sexy (tongue, nipples, even further south). Cheyanne didn't ever shoot for sexy; she liked the toughness the nose and eyebrow rings gave her. Her stark pale skin and sleek, black bob only made her intimidation level rise.

I joked at her demands. "Right, we'll just let Nyx have at her. He likes pulling hair."

As soon as I said that, I wanted to squeeze my eyes shut and force Luna out of my vision. I didn't, but I wanted to. Nyx even playfully hit my ribs in her honor. All these feelings made my monstrous mood grow.

I looked straight at Luna interrupting small talk. "Unless you finally want to admit you have a crush on Nyx?"

I watched Luna squirm in her seat under the pressure of my calm as I asked. Her cheeks flushed a bright red and her eyes looked panicked as she looked to Nyx. She got up and ran out before any other words were said.

Guilty. Ashamed. Like an asshole. All the things I should have felt, but I didn't.

I was cutting through the bullshit with one question. And all I mustered up when all eyes were on me? "Oops."

I wasn't going to pretend to be someone I wasn't and feel bad just so everyone else felt better. They didn't need false hope.

The meeting didn't go much longer before everyone broke off and the guys told the rest of the group about the party later. I honestly didn't care if anyone showed up from the group. I was at a breaking point and needed to blow off steam before I did more damage.

Fucking hormones.

Nyx followed me back to the dorm; I guessed since he occupied the room down the same hallway. His pace, which kept up with mine, said differently. His strength was unmatched, and I was sure he wasn't using any real effort when I felt his hand shove me into the wall next to my door and hold me there.

"Don't ever involve her. I don't care how ruthless you feel."

I exhaled like I needed to get rid of the poisoned oxygen inside of me that wanted to hurt my best friend. Right now, no part of me cared who he was when he was threatening me.

I stayed planted. "Do you wanna admit you like her already? Or is this little act made up of friendship and delusions?"

The anger Nyx harbored was relentless and terrifying, if we're being honest. He had every reason to hate the world, shut us all out and crack his knuckles until it felt better. Hell, he even had the right to love Luna in secret. Whatever was coming my way for doubting his right to feel all that was justified.

His fist swiftly hit my lip, and I felt it swell around the crack that the force against my own teeth gave it. I slid down the wall, unmotivated to hit back.

Nyx leaned down, grabbing my shirt into his balled up fist and pulled me back up. "Delusions? Friendships? What do you know about either, Bolton? You're in denial about Arianna, and you forgot what loyalty is."

He released my shirt and left me there like some rag doll he was done playing with. I watched him slam his door, and

I slammed my own fist into the hardwood floor, surprised it didn't crack.

I pushed my head back, looking up at the ceiling as I ripped my phone from my pocket and texted Jasper.

There were already girls outside the abandoned building on campus all eyeing me like I was carbs and they had been on some stupid low carb diet.

I wasn't interested in the girls who arrived early. They arrived early for one of two reasons: desperation, or they didn't spend much time getting ready, because deep down they knew this was as good as it got.

I was vain on top of being an asshole. I know, real winner, right? When you wear a crown, winning isn't a concern.

I breezed past the desperation and moderate looks in search of Jasper. He'd be bossing the freshman on our team around somewhere.

I wondered if anyone ever questioned why they were following his orders. Guess not, since I found two guys lifting a keg, while Jasper went hands-free, watching them.

I recognized them from tryouts over the summer—freshies. I balled up my fist, letting my knuckles bump against his before I sat on the counter with my shoes hitting the island's sides carelessly.

"Who did you piss off?"

He noticed the split in my lip almost instantly and without thinking, I ran my tongue over it, making it sting all over again. Damn it.

"Nyx and his precious ego."

Jasper laughed, handling a football but not tossing it to anyone. He never stopped thinking about the game and winning, and it was apparent to everyone, even me—his less than dedicated co-captain.

That was Jasper's downfall: He was bossy but no one was following him anywhere. He wasn't a leader.

"Let me guess, you brought up his secret affection for the meek Luna."

I shrugged in annoyance at his accurate guess. Jasper could even guess without any information to go on.

So why does telling the truth out loud hurt so many people?

Jasper pulled the top off a beer and handed it to me. "Damn, Bolton. You needed tonight more than me."

I pushed the glass of beer against his, creating a high-pitched cling, before I pushed off the counter.

Substances was a check.

Now all I needed was to find a companion to drain these hormones and take my mind off the beast inside me that drove me to be so angry anyways.

People poured in as I walked around a large room that was once a classroom. There was a large open area for studying and a coffee cart now used to house Solo cups. I gave up finding anyone of interest when I stalked to the back of the building to the room we deemed off limits.

I heard footsteps long before I reached the door, alerting me someone was trespassing. Quietly I stood in the doorway, searching the room for the culprit, when I should have guessed:

Arianna. New Girl.

Her fingers danced on the surfaces as her curiosity took it all in. There was no way to tell anyone that I was in a dangerously ruthless mood so that they could warn her. It was too late now.

"You're gonna graduate from *New Girl* to felon if you don't start following the rules."

She laughed, and something about the casual attitude around the word "felon" made it seem like she knew trouble better than I did.

"Been there, done that … wasn't worth the t-shirt or the keychain."

I plopped down in the chair I put there years ago now. I had gotten tired of getting drunk and doing the same shit. I preferred to do it alone rather than with people I hardly liked. That's why this was *my* place to hide during parties.

She finally let her eyes gloss over me, and her face winced at the cut on my lip. I almost thought she physically got hurt; too bad suffering isn't transferable.

"What the fuck happened to you?"

That sounded like a real concern, in all its displaced glory. Stern, demanding, even judgment—-all there.

"Well, not that it's your business, but I finally got what I deserved for my mouth."

She fearlessly walked right over to me, standing between my legs, and leaned down to get a better look. Her deep blue eye, rimmed with violet to match her hair, reminded me of the sky when it got tie-dyed right before sundown. She inspected my wound that stopped hurting the more I pushed the beer bottle to my lips over and over.

Better than the golden hour, before the all the colors turned black and nothing was covered in the pretty filter. That summed up Arianna.

"Well-deserved doesn't make it hurt less."

She was wrong. It actually did.

"Are you gonna kiss it and make it all better?"

She actually half scoffed, half snorted with laughter, like I wasn't being serious. I was in a despicable and semi-diabolical mood, hellbent on the two B's that teenagers valued. Beers and Babes. The third B (bongs) was out, since I couldn't get caught with shit in my system during a pee test.

Arianna wasn't half bad looking, if I could get past her imma-turity and whatever tantrum led to her purple hair. Her skin shimmered like it was actually happy, and her lips were almost always smiling. In this moment, she was half goddess, but I couldn't forget she was always half hell.

My own personal hell.

I let my hand touch her thigh so she knew I was serious even though I was slumped down and perpetually bored.

"What are you doing? We hate each other remember?"

"Hate me tomorrow."

She suddenly got shy as she stood between my open legs and looked down, unsure of herself for the first time since she stormed into my life.

A world class bullshitter losing her touch in front of me. I wanted to be cruel and not so unusual, but I bit my tongue.

"How drunk are you? Your hate is lethal and you've never been nice to me."

"Not drunk enough for you to use it as an excuse. It's 2020; I know how to say no."

She swayed slightly between my legs, like she was thinking about my proposition. I sat up, making sure both my hands slid up her jeans to her ass. I still hated her but in this moment, all I could think about was how her ass was something you could bite into. She had a full ass that filled her jeans out in a way most girls would envy and guys would worship.

Why weren't guys worshiping her? Did they really need my okay or was it simply my disinterest?

"Bolton…" she countered.

"Arianna…" I rebutted.

I wasn't a dog and saying my name didn't kill my motivation. I was a teenager with my hands smoothing up the back of her thighs. Short of a cold shower or some relief, I wasn't planning on backing down.

"This isn't you."

She said it so matter-of-factly that I wanted to drop my hands and scream she didn't know me, know how royally fucked I was, or how much I really knew she was different but not in the way I needed.

I needed a savior when everyone was looking to me to do the saving.

"Maybe you don't know me very well."

I sat up, on the edge of the old chair, enticing her more by drawing her closer.

I was stronger than her, and she wasn't truly putting up our typical push/pull bullshit. I put a firmer grasp on her thighs to pull her into my lap, straddling me, as my hands grasped her hips.

"Is this how I get to know the King of Arcadia Prep?"

Even on top of me, she was still full of sass and attitude, and I wanted to seduce it out of her.

"You know more than most, thanks to your defiant behavior."

She didn't make any advances, she simply sat there comfortably, like I was her throne, and she had just been crowned queen, not of Arcadia Prep, of my heart.

"But do I know the real you? I wanna know the version of you that isn't king and aches as much as we all do." Her voice was like velvet on my skin when she spoke. It made parts of my awareness focus on what did ache, what really bothered me, none of which was my growing frustration to get laid.

This girl wrecked me in ways I didn't know possible.

I leaned up swiftly letting my fingers tangle into her hair as I pushed my lips onto hers too roughly. I was out of practice. She melted down into me, letting her hand land on my chest for balance. My hands grazed over her, exploring what I could, until I remembered why she was in this position to begin with.

Cheyanne needed her hair, and I was going to be the one to get it.

She deepened our kiss so much that my fingers in her hair almost forgot what they were doing and gave up, as I felt her tongue collide with mine. She wasn't shy or lazy; she knew exactly how to kiss. Every part of me got hungry for more of her, and the blood running through my veins felt thick with desire.

Jasper's anti-bulky body and height was enough to make him clumsy when buzzed. He bumped into the doorframe a few times before entering the room.

"Hey, guys! Kate made Jell-O sh- shit."

He turned the word shots easily into shit when he saw the position we were in. He drew our attention enough for the exchange or saliva to stop, and all I heard was our breath rattling in our chests, out of our control.

I sat back as I yanked two hairs from the back of her head as she yelped, still on top of me. She touched her neck like a mosquito bit her instead of throwing accusations.

I looked carefree, innocent, and comfortable.

These fucking hormones made me hyper aware that she was stretched into this perfect pin-up position, right on top of the parts of me that demanded attention.

On-the-way-to-drunk Jasper stumbled to the hard liquor we kept in this room, which was off limits to everyone else. I watched him pour shots before he attempted to carry them all over to us, while I waited for the cheers part of this.

He had no speech or witty comments or even the sobriety to say cheers before he gulped it back.

Arianna was next to throw it back, like a professional I noticed. Most girls didn't like Whiskey or hard alcohol. I was mildly impressed. I set mine down on the table, declining the liquid gold. I had two beers. If I had anymore, I couldn't be responsible for how rude or pushy I got with Arianna. That was my hard limit, two beers, and I was still in control.

She made no attempt to move or find her own chair, and the mind game of it all was getting to me. Parts of me loved whatever game she was playing, and I'm sure she felt that, while other parts of me despised that she could toy with me so easily.

She twisted her neck around, watching Jasper leave the room in his buzzed glory, one more shot away from drunk, before she looked back to me.

"He's a character."

"He's a party trick."

She looked at me confused with her eyebrows bowing along with her feelings.

"He's always proving something … always performing a trick."

She put her hands on my chest and her features softened into a clear lust. Even her lips were flirting with me as her tongue swiped her bottom lip.

"What was he proving tonight?"

My hands grasped her hips tightly to keep her from moving. She didn't need to know how easily I was turned on by her.

"That he's smart enough to not study, get drunk, and still make his marks. That he's better than everyone."

She unzipped her black hoodie slowly and discarded it like suddenly she wasn't cold at all. She pulled her bottom lip in and caged it with her teeth.

"He wants to be king?"

I felt my eyes slant down at her mention of a threat—one I wasn't actually worried about, but any threat made my alarms go off.

"No one will be me."

She took my calloused palm in her hand and dragged my hand along her body. She leaned back slightly, while slightly telling me what I knew was okay, to squeeze and grasp whatever I wanted in my hands.

I almost forgot about her strands of purple hair in my pocket, to either destroy her or make her one of us. I pushed away reason and the demands of the circle. Despite my reputation of being a

selfish man, I really spent every minute protecting everyone else. This was my moment to be my reputation.

I looked up at Arianna, who looked as starved as me. "Are you sure?"

Her eyes glowed in the dim lighting. The glint in her eye looked like the whiskey in the cup next to me—liquid gold with darker flecks. She nodded her head, and I watched her fingers delicately pull her tank top from her ribs.

My eyes were glued to her in a way that my attention was never demanded. I kept my relaxed position, just watching her, not advancing her in any way. I was content letting her lead. She finally dipped her head, and I sat up for my busted lips to meet hers again, while my arms wrapped around her, making sure to land on her full ass.

Hungry, our lips pushed into each other with aggression, the sting radiating off my lip was well worth it. Her tongue was soft inside my mouth. She even tasted sweet, despite her sour outside.

Her hands grazed my abs under my hoodie and shirt. She was motivated to see more of me. I didn't realize how willing I was to show her until I felt myself kissing her with more passion than a moment ago.

Nyx was hard to miss when he entered a room. He was harder to miss when he brought back up, Austin. My eyes drifted to them before I pulled away from Arianna.

She must have sensed them, because she pulled away and craned her neck to meet my gaze. She turned back towards me unashamed, completely calm.

"Guess that's my cue."

Arianna sat on me like a throne and suddenly I felt like her king. Not the bullshit title I earned with my bad attitude, being superior enough to be this school's leader, and the circle depending on me.

I earned this title differently tonight: A queen picked me to be her king, and it felt more fulfilling than anything I had ever done.

She zipped her hoodie again as we both stood, spinning her around I stood in front of her. The guys could probably read lips, but this was still private.

"I gotta deal with this. My room after?"

I saw her mulling it over and probably wondering what I meant by the vague "this." I may be her newly crowned king but those details were only going to be spilled after she proved her loyalty—and not one moment before. Good sex wasn't enough to pry the vaulted parts of me open.

"Find me after."

The back of her hand brushed mine as she exited the room, and I plopped down in the heavy chair with a thud.

Now they were cornering me?

Nyx didn't speak, he let Austin start the investigation that was pointless, because we were all there for the part that earned me a busted lip.

"We need to stick together, man ... " Austin wasn't comfortable with the hard conversations. He was too rooted in his emotions and feeding off how other people felt.

I stared at Nyx, yet I was talking to Austin.

"I didn't throw a fist, Austin. Talk to your boy."

His eyes were like knives when our stares finally connected. His arms were folded against his chest, and I could tell we needed more time for the dust to settle.

Austin was always fixing things without the gift of timing.

"We all know how special Luna is to him."

He didn't have to justify anything to me, we all knew how much Luna mattered to Nyx. He had been pining after her since he transferred in from Australia last year.

In my memories, he had always pined for her, for longer, centuries even, if I wanted to dig up the past, yet he did nothing about it. He was the toughest person I knew. He had the strength of the gods but little Luna scared him into silence?

"Does she know Nyx?"

I could be approaching this all wrong. I could be pushing him when I knew firsthand the avoidance of love. None of that mattered, being wrong was losing and being weak and I wasn't any of that. So I was going to blindly fight my position until he caved.

His anger was only mounting into diabolical.

He got a clean shot at me before. Next time, I was going to hit back, I wasn't above defending myself, even from my best friend.

I pushed past Nyx in the doorway with better things to do...like Arianna.

I found Arianna easily in the clumps of people; she stuck out like a sore fucking thumb. Purple hair matched her "don't care" attitude, and her smirk could catch someone on fire.

She was talking with Kate; mental note: Kate needed a new nickname. Queen was taken, and not by her anymore.) and Luna when I walked up behind her, bending down to whisper in her ear.

"My room. Let's go."

I wasn't pleasant or even asking her. I was demanding and brooding at all my edges, but it was who I was and Arianna didn't expect something different from me.

I was going to be a king regardless if I was her king.

She didn't even bother turning around, only twisting her neck in my direction.

"I'm being here for Luna right now. Want me to find you when I'm done?"

She just snubbed me in front of the girls and whatever gaze ended up on us.

She told me to wait like a dog who needed to learn patience before getting the treat.

Every part of me was set on fire and my hormones with it.

"Nah. Do your whole girl power moment. I'll find someone else."

She didn't even seem insulted as I walked away, only letting myself steal a quick glance behind me to see her reaction.

I knew I was fucked.

I knew she was going to be the death of me.

I knew with or without my consent she officially just crowned herself my queen.

There were plenty of girls to invite back to my room. Suddenly my narrow taste wasn't interested in anyone that didn't have purple hair. It was like a ton of bricks hitting only my heart and missing all other vital organs. One should have hit my head so we could all be on the same page.

Girls flirted with me, only the brave ones; the shy and meek needed not apply. Those quiet girls were afraid of us; the group was intimidating. If we're honest, they knew we were out of their league.

None had what Arianna did.

I felt trapped by my new-found devotion to Arianna. It was narrowing my already narrow sight and attitude.

There was only one girl I used for sex, Whitney, who we had been repeating senior year with for longer than I cared to think about. Every year we started over, and every year she forgot me.

Her attraction was unwavering though.

I knew I wasn't going to let our flirting get out of hand; I was making a point to Arianna. The point was for her to realize that me being king meant that I put zero effort into hookups, which also had the desired outcome of jealousy.

Whitney was giggling into her Solo cup that I stopped her from sipping as I pushed her hair back behind her ear. I whispered bullshit.

I wasn't trying and she was still swooning over my voice. We were in eye shot if she turned around. I'm sure Kate would point it out, after all she was "Queen Bitch" until I dethroned her.

Whitney's hand landed on my chest, and she pushed her ass off the wall towards my body.

See? Brave.

Arianna's head snapped in our direction and she quickly came over to where we were standing. I had to bite back a victorious smirk. I made sure my face looked bored with her antics and interruption.

I leaned against the wall firmly against Whitney folding my arms and dragging my eyeline up to hers. She didn't even look at me, only Whitney, when she spoke.

"Hi, I'm Arianna, I don't think we've met."

Whitney looked confused with her own transition from aroused to now scared of the girl in front of her. My ripped up soul tried not to enjoy this. Whitney pushed out a shaky hand and introduced herself.

"Now that we know each other, I just wanted to make sure you didn't forget who I was." There was a silence between her thoughts, probably for effect. "You see, we aren't into threesomes, so your services aren't needed any longer."

She stood there, regal, even though her words sounded filthy. I pushed my lips together, looked at Whitney without remorse to our quick death, and waited for her to leave without Arianna really driving it home.

The disapproving sigh was hard to ignore. I almost thought she'd stomp like a child too before walking away.

Shifting my body flat against the wall I looked at Arianna, waiting for her to make the first move. Arms still folded against me and still perpetually bored, I had no problem waiting for my explanation.

"I don't kiss and share."

I popped an eyebrow. "Don't you mean kiss and tell?"

She pushed my shoulder harder than I expected as her eyebrows got tense. "No, kiss and share. I'm not sharing. Period. It's me and only me, or you can run after Whitney."

I didn't dare move an inch, not even to breathe in a full breath. I wasn't giving her any reason to think Whitney mattered at all. I licked my lips trying to find the right words that didn't make me feel pussy whipped.

"Okay, no kissing and sharing. For your information, that was a lesson in waiting. I don't do that. Guess we both have hard limits."

I pushed myself off the wall and expected her to follow. I could feel her eyes roll behind me. She was truly an equal, never bowing down to anyone, not even me.

CHAPTER 11

Arianna

Bolton had a roadmap to all my weak spots.

Weak spot number one: sharing.

Weak spot number two: proving him wrong about me.

Weak spot number three: thinking he hated me but I'm smarter than that.

I could see how he thought he was sneaking those stares from across the room. Little did he know that I had been staring the whole time, trying to figure him out; no move went unnoticed.

Not much came of me basically stalking Bolton with my eyes. I learned he was quiet, calculated, and every other trait I could think of that basically drew a thick red line back to psychopaths. Yet, I found myself following him back to his room.

It screamed adventure, and I was in a desperate need of one.

His room was painted black; it wasn't a typical kind of dark that seemed endless or camouflaged space. This midnight kind of black was angry.

His room was a literal mess—clothes thrown around, his desk didn't have enough space for it to be used as an actual desk, and his bed wasn't even made.

I pinched my eyes closed just looking at it, I could feel my military dad reacting. I wasn't a neat freak but when you grow up as an army brat you are conditioned to not have many possessions and you make your bed according to military standards.

He sank onto his bed, that's how plush it seemed. I awkwardly stood in the middle of his room, waiting for his brash commands.

"Shy all of a sudden?"

His arm was behind his head, and his hoodie raised slightly, allowing me a peek at his ivory skin at his waist. It gave me chills that crept up my spine.

I had seen guys shirtless. Hell, I wasn't even a virgin, but looking at Bolton felt dangerous.

This trepidation was a sendoff to the most epic adventure I'd have yet.

"Shy? Me? I'm the opposite of shy."

He sat up, swinging his legs off the edge of his bed, and my heart started to beat slightly faster. He was unpredictable in every way. I was glued to his movements when I watched him tug at his hoodie until it was off.

His shirt got tugged up in the process, and he didn't bother to hold it down or keep it on him at all. His exposed, defined chest almost glowed in the dim lighting. Every muscle was on display, creating hills and valleys I was lost in.

I could see the ram's horns, which he insisted was certain was a birthmark, and almost every blue vein under his translucent skin.

He wasn't a king. He was a god above other men—one I was about to worship and apologize for later.

"Then let's finish what you started."

My hands on his shoulders, barely pushing him to sit back, was easier than I thought. He was doing what I was demanding for once, and the power was something addictions were made of.

I straddled his lap the same way I did earlier, except this time he wasn't leaning back, and there was no gap between my chest and his face.

"I'm not a throne you know."

I looked down, puzzled at his words.

"You can't just storm the castle, demand a crown, and sit on the king like a throne."

He was teasing me, and I was going to tease him right back. I unzipped my hoodie and shook out of the arms, letting it pollute his already trashed floor. A cropped tank top and strapless bra were the only material between us.

"Doesn't every king need a queen?"

He smirked at me before his hand pulled me by the neck into him even more. Our lips crashed together, and I swear I felt sparks crackle against my lips—sparks that I knew were a warning sign for something even more combustible.

His open mouth poured arousal into mine as our tongues laced together, trying to taste more of each other than possible. His hands dropped down to my waist keeping me stationary on his lap. We both knew every movement I made only spurred him on; that much I could feel below me, against the crotch of my jeans.

The sparks crackled along my lips as his pulled away. "No strings…just friends…okay?"

His words were full of strained breaths. Nothing matched, his words slowed down my motivation but his hands were grabbing at my hips in such a famished way.

I didn't know how to take what he said—compliment or insult?

Just friends? No strings? What was he really saying? No king makes rules without thought, normally to protect the people, but from what?

Even his lips against my neck and collarbones felt like raw energy tickling my surfaces that crackled even after his lips moved to a new patch of skin.

"Just friends?"

The words slipped out before I could catch them; the rest of me was distracted, basking in the energy. My question hung between us, heavy, as he ignored it.

His trailing kisses got lower, kissing my breasts through my bra and tank top. I repeated my question, and this time, I demanded an answer, instead of a shaky previous voice distracted by his full lips. This time I got creative while repeating myself: "Just friends …? What if I want more?"

I pushed him from lust to annoyance with one question, just like that. He pulled away fully, leaning back on his hands and looking bothered by the world, as he normally did.

"I don't do more. Hard limit."

Now I knew how to take it—insult.

If it hurt, then it was always insulting.

"I'm different."

I meant to sound confident, instead it just landed as cocky.

"Different doesn't prove shit, Arianna. It doesn't prove loyalty."

So he wanted loyalty. His rulings were to protect himself and promote loyalty. Good thing I grew up with American pride. That shit was poisonous and prideful.

Bolton's phone buzzed against the balled up, wrinkled, covers on the bed next to us. It lit up with another girl's name, and suddenly loyalty seemed like something he should learn to practice before he preached.

I got off of his lap. The mood was passing, and my panties were drying up.

His fingers typed away, replying to the mystery girl with the name I wouldn't forget now.

I fetched my hoodie out of the sea of black fabric on his floor and headed for the door without warning. The worst part was that he didn't stop me. I pulled the door open only to be met with a girl I hadn't officially met yet.

I remembered her from Austin's introductions and had seen her face in our history class.

Cheyanne. One half of the twins.

All goth.

All sour.

All intimidation.

She looked like someone you shouldn't piss off, and I knew when to be quiet. I slithered by her, hoping she'd ignore me all together. The strong judgment in her eyes didn't ignore me; it burned like holy water on a demon.

Maybe there was more to Bolton than I realized. I only looked back once to witness their exchange. He handed her his hoodie, and my uncertainty rang even louder in my ears.

Why his hoodie? Who was she to him? I made it clear I don't kiss and share.

I purposely walked slowly, hoping I would catch another glimpse of the mystery girl with mean features and meaner mannerisms. She didn't need the fishnet and piercings to look hard; it was more obvious than her choice of jewelry.

I kept walking slowly with no reason to rush. Bolton didn't come after me, and apparently she wasn't leaving anytime soon. I gave up at the same time I arrived at the girls' dorms.

I had a habit of holding out hope for longer than it was healthy.

When my mom passed away, I was convinced it was a cruel joke and held out hope for some miraculous return. It's embarrassing to admit I held onto that same hope until I hit high school before I realized hope didn't change shit.

Hope was a pipe dream, a placebo, a castle in the sky ... one hundred percent fake.

No matter how real you were, hope seemed unavoidable. Desires grew from hope; crushes grew from hope; all the good emotions we craved came from the counterfeit feeling named hope.

It made me wonder what was real and what wasn't. Is hate really all that bad? At least it's real, authentic, more tangible than a castle in the sky...

Hate was a throne in hell.

Still a throne.

I lost hope for Bolton. Every ounce of hope that I had almost let grow again quickly turned into hate for him. I hated Bolton and his games.

Kate, Luna, and I were sitting in the quad, which was basically a huge patch of grass with benches and a willow tree that provided a type of ambience I praised. All my textbooks were sprawled out around me, all open to chapters I still needed to catch up on. Transferring a few months into a school and learning at a college level made my brain pulse with frustration. I was so studied out that everything looked German.

I let my body fall back onto the grass, arms spread wide, and the temptation to make a dirty snow angel crossed my mind. I hadn't been anywhere with snow yet. Dirt angels were the next best thing.

Kate was reapplying her lip gloss, like she did every ten minutes. "So you and Bolton..."

She wasn't asking anything specific, so I kept ignoring her until she grew claws long enough to sink into the truth—the awful truth she wanted to know.

Luna playfully shunned her, even though I'm sure she wanted to know too. Her good girl charm and big heart couldn't stomp out good gossip.

Kate's eyes widened, and her voice made a strained type of sound meant to capture how annoyed she was. "Well, Arianna, what happened with Bolton? He never hooks up."

I didn't bother to sit up, keeping my gaze on the willow tree now upside down. "He's kind of a dream but there's something about him that makes me hate him."

Luna laughed, clearly well versed in assholes who you tend to love anyways. She had personal experience with Nyx, at least that's what the gossip pointed to.

"That's why no one tries to get with him."

"Thanks for the warning, guys. He should come with labels."

Kate sipped her overpriced coffee and scrolled through social media, no doubt, when she spoke. "He does. His face is angry and filled with hate. He wouldn't selfie very well."

I couldn't help her observation making me laugh so hard I felt my stomach clench into an abdominal workout and not let go.

She wasn't wrong; it was obvious he wasn't the happy type. Shame, the anti-happy type just happened to be exactly what drew me to him.

I sat up, making eye contact with Kate—the one girl I knew wouldn't lie. Kate was brutally honest and took pride in whatever reaction that got as long as her truth was spoken. "Tell me about Cheyanne?"

Luna's once carefree face turned instantly worried at just her name.

Damn, who was this girl? Did she strike fear into everyone?

Kate put down her phone with a huff. "She's kind of our friend. She's all types of weird and very intimidating."

"Okay … what's her connection to Bolton?"

Luna looked at Kate like she was trying to measure out mentally how honest she'd be.

"They never dated or anything crazy like that, why?"

I swear I saw her eyes actually roll when she said "why."

Kate was straight out of the movie *Clueless*, and none of her minded one bit how not politically correct that was anymore.

I hesitated to share how I ran into her. I didn't want them to think I was easy or worse think I actually liked him when I was now dead set on hating him. "I ran into her in the boys' dorm. She was there to see Bolton. Gotta know the competition, right?"

The girls looked mortified before they locked eyes with each other and burst with laughter. My eyebrows raised and eyes widened, while I tried to pretend to go back to reading, between gasps for air.

Kate touched my leg, still trying to contain her laughter. "Oh, sweetie. Cheyanne isn't competition, and you aren't completely helpless in the looks department. I know Bolton isn't hitting that. I only ever heard about Whitney, and you pretty much took care of that at the party."

She's not competition, yet she picked up his hoodie in the middle of the night? Never mind the blow to my ego when he stopped kissing me to respond to her text. I begged the jealousy inside of me to stay a slow simmering burn.

I knew myself. I tipped towards hate instead of hope, and my punishment was emotions like jealousy.

I let my body fall back down into the plush grass and tried to want to study some more. No amount of green tea matcha was going to dig me out of my self-loathing slump today.

CHAPTER 12

Arianna

Today was the first day I wasn't late for history class. Somewhere, my parents were celebrating—one in heaven and the other on some secret retreat, fighting even more secret wars.

I stopped in the hallway to pluck my phone from inside my jacket pocket of the mandatory blazer to text my dad. He hadn't texted me in a week, and more than three days made me hyper aware of the possibility of losing him.

> ↗ Me: *Text me when you can. Ignoring the three day rule?*
> *Punishable by death—by me, not terrorists.*

I waited a few moments in case the even more anxiety triggering dots appeared. My head dropped, and I slipped my phone back into my pocket.

"Arianna. Late. Again."

I looked up at the clock and couldn't even argue; I was late by two minutes. Dr. Alba was no joke in his old school glory.

He was anti-talking and anti-phones but I enjoyed his class the most. He didn't speak at us, and he wasn't so hands-off that it felt like a pointless study hall, like I was used to.

I sat down in the only seat available, next to Bolton.

No one dared to sit next to him in the back. Half the time he used the other desks to prop up his own feet.

Thank god this was the only class I had with him.

"Now that everyone is here, we can get started. Halloween is coming up. Does anyone know the dark history of Arcadia?"

I perked up in my seat interested. Nyx and Bolton were whispering like they typically did instead of listening.

It looked like gloating most of the time. Sometimes I'd hear Nyx say Luna–rarely.

"Nyx, what's the history of Arcadia?"

He twisted back around to face the front of the class and made a lazy attempt to make eye contact with Alba.

I wasn't a suck up but I couldn't afford to not pay attention in class either. I actually had to study, while guys like these ones simply showed up and the rest worked itself out.

"It's rumored Arcadia is on sacred ground. Witches used to summon the gods, and this was their doorway into the mortal world. But we know that's all bullshit, right, Alba? Fairytales."

Alba snaked through the aisle of desks, scanning the room for his neck victim. "Why does it have to be a fairytale? Our library has books from the covens, ledgers, all the proof one wants."

Bolton spoke out of turn, and it made Alba spin towards him on his heel.

"Proof? The Bible isn't even proof that Jesus walked the earth, and you want us to believe this school is special because of some fucked up folklore?"

Alba waved a finger in the air towards him. "The best things are the ones we can't prove, Mr. Cadoc."

Leo and his boyfriend, Beau, sat on the opposite side of the room, and both giggled to themselves, until a harsh glance from Dr. Alba made them spit it out.

Leo, sounding completely factual, said, "Bolton doesn't believe in anything. Proof or not."

I looked down at my unopened notebook and wondered why the campus was so big and why half the buildings were closed or off limits. I even wondered for a moment about why we weren't allowed off campus on the weekends or why we never had away games.

It was starting to feel like a sentence, and none of us knew what we were being punished for.

I hadn't realized how caged I felt until I was forced to look at Arcadia more critically.

Austin raised his hand and even waited to be called on before talking. "It's said that a wealthy family, considered royalty, lived here in the 1600's."

Dr. Alba nodded, like he was learning something too. "Yes, Austin, good. The Arcadia compound is known for its roots in royalty. Just as any balance would have it, the campus is also known for magic. Since there are so many theories on the history of the campus, let's make this your homework."

The chalk scratched across the blackboard as he outlined the homework I now had from this class too. I was slowly drowning in homework, upcoming tests, and catching up on the material everyone else already seemed to know.

No one even cracked a book or notebook in class. I was out of my league here.

For the rest of the class, I zoned out, until Bolton hit me with a balled up piece of paper, purely for effect, because he spoke in a hushed tone instead of writing anything down.

"Why did you run out of my room like it was on fire?"

His question tempted my new hatred of him to skip from simmering straight to boiling.

"I told you I don't kiss and share. Kind of awkward when girl number two shows up before you're done with girl one."

He sat back from leaning over his desk's edge just to get my attention. His wicked smirk was kerosene on my anger, all cruel and relentless.

I threw the small crumpled up paper back at him before he sat up again.

"Cheyanne? That Cheyanne?" He pointed two desks away at the twisted soul I now called "bitch" in my head, sitting next to her twin brother, who couldn't be more opposite.

He was bright, fresh faced, blonde, and had bright blue eyes that resembled sea foam instead of a true blue. It was hard to hate someone who seemed so approachable.

I settled for not lumping him in with her.

Bolton dragged my staring away from the twins. "It's not like that. Never will be. I don't fuck my friends—hard limit."

My features felt sharp when his contradicting sentence spewed out. "You told me just *friends.*"

He sat back in his seat, facing forward, as Dr. Alba shifted, trying to find the whispers in the room. "I'm not boyfriend material. Don't need you being clingy."

Did he just call me clingy? It's the equivalent of telling someone to calm down mid rage attack.

Before I was dropped at Arcadia, I was the queen of not unpacking and collector of goodbyes.

"I don't want a boyfriend. How's this for clingy?"

I got up from my desk, gripping my unused supplies to my chest and ambled to the exit. My heart raced from the cocktail of emotions—worried for my dad, pissed off at Bolton, and still slightly jealous that Cheyanne could command his attention while I was on top of him.

Really taking blows all around.

My sense of direction still limited to my routine, I wandered down spare hallways until I found a name plate next to a big oak door labeled "Library."

Finally, somewhere I could get some peace and quiet.

In every place I've lived, there was always one solace—a quiet place with no interruptions or outside noise. It was my getaway. I pushed open the door, and memories of my last home flooded me, pulled me under water, and kidnapped all the fresh air in my lungs.

My last solace was a man-made dam with a bright "no trespassing" sign on every fence closing it in. It was mine, only mine, until I let *him* into my depths.

I opened myself up to him, and the result was Arcadia Prep.

He was made up of hope and dreams, while I reveled in hate.

I never even had the chance to confront him after we were put in the back of a cop car and escorted back home from trespassing.

There was one main road to our homes, and the whole town buzzed with seeing his face scorned with regret next to mine in the back seat.

Son of the mayor, handcuffed, and no longer to my heart, with his tarnished reputation.

After that, the school kindly declined having me return, exiled from the only high school in the small town.

My aunt also decided it was best if I found a new foster home while my dad fought for this country. Guess that's how he landed on a boarding school.

I threaded through the aisles of books in the pure, unsoiled, silence. I found desks off the rows of books and larger desks in eye shot of the librarian. I settled for a large table by the large windows, light pouring through and warming the wood. I dropped my stuff down without thinking about being quiet until I heard a harsh "shhh" in the distance.

She was slumped down in the chair, almost hiding, and I stomped my way towards the Librarian's desk in the center of the library.

She was the woman who showed me to my room on my first day. Tall, slender, pasty pale skin, like she never saw the sunlight directly, and she moved like gravity and air had no effect on her. Her bun was piled so tightly on her head it looked like it hurt, as I got closer.

"Excuse me? I need to find books on the school's history for a project."

She didn't look up or even try to make eye contact with me, instead she pointed to where I came from and scribbled down a number associated to my request.

I took the paper sighing extra loud for effect, annoyed everyone has the social skills of goldfish. They were all scared of interaction, manners, social cues we all learned in kindergarten.

I got lost in books with spines all resembling each other—thick, old, fragile things. I was scared to touch them. Even my gaze seemed to paramount.

Each spine had a date range, and I chose a random book, before making my way back to the desk where I had dropped my stuff.

Bolton was sitting at the head of the table with the chair backwards, thumbing through my notebook when I coughed, subtly, letting him know I could see him.

"Guess who you're stuck with for this project."

I rolled my eyes, taking a seat in front of my stuff and trying my best to ignore his presence.

"That book isn't going to teach you anything about Arcadia."

Slamming the book shut, another loud noise eliciting another "shhh" my direction. "And what will? You? Because you're just so helpful and nice?"

"Ouch. That almost hurt ... if I had feelings. I know more about this school than those damn books."

Slanted eyes, still full of hate, peered at him with so much judgment I felt like Cheyanne for a moment. "I don't need a partner. Go choose someone else."

He sat back, eyes on his phone. "Alba's rules not mine. Besides, you said it yourself every king needs a queen."

If I kept rolling my eyes with this much conviction, they might actually get stuck the wrong way.

He was using my own words against me now. What a *plagiarist.*

"I take it back, okay? You're just an asshole in an aluminum crown."

A quick chuckle turned into a cough, and it seemed unexpected even to himself. I smirked in the glory of catching him off guard. That had to be a record.

"Asshole or not, I'm still your partner for the project. Get used to me."

He was hard to get rid of, just like a king.

Without slaughtering him, we were all forced under his reign.

I refused to acknowledge him the rest of the time I was in the library, jotting down notes and trying to find enough information on one topic to be able to write a paper.

Bolton sat there quietly, with his fingers laced around his phone, perfectly ignoring me too. All of me seethed with hate for him, except for my lips, which wanted to collide with his again.

I could easily feel the rush of a quick spark still lingering on my lips even a day later. Hating him, while my body craved him, was going to be the best challenge I ever took on.

Bolton

She made hating her the hardest thing I'd ever done. She was the only girl to say every unfiltered insult, not afraid to ignore me, and she certainly had parts of me reacting that normally preferred the comfort of a warm mouth not a cold blooded bitch.

I had to keep my eyes glued on my phone, just to keep myself focused on why I was supposed to be interested in her: the circle and whatever Cheyanne was doing with her hair.

She was keeping us in the dark, even though I handed over my hoodie mid make out session.

It reminded me to find her at lunch and demand some answers.

I left the library without a word to Arianna before I did, and I headed straight to the dining hall to find the twins.

If you spotted one, then the other wasn't ever far; they were inseparable.

When my mind would escape its routined cage, I would think about how that must be a type of true love. Being forced together, so opposite, yet having an unbreakable connection.

It was my only idea of love I had, and it had to do. I had no plans to sacrifice my heart, or my crown, to anyone.

The dining hall buzzed with chatter I sliced through; when I walked by, it was hard to ignore the gawking and chatter coming to a silence. I never knew if it was because I was king or because of my constant miserable grimace that I wore proudly. I gave up wondering.

I used to shout, act out, let the misery feed off their gossip, but their gossip made my throne. It raised me high above the other men around me.

I found the twins sitting with Austin on the stairs we always occupied. I didn't even wait to be an acceptable proximity from her to talk. My deep voice sounded boosted, "When are you gonna give me an update? I've texted you."

Cheyanne looked up from her phone with a glare that was made to turn people to stone, except me. "Relax, Bolton. I'm working on it. It's not that easy. It takes time."

Impatiently I asked, "What part takes time? Just do your witch shit and tell me if she's one of us."

Omari, her twin, who never spoke unless it was gravely necessary, added to our conversation. "Worried she may not be one of us? You know what happens if she isn't Bolton. Be careful what you share with her."

Her cult vibes disrupted his angel features.

I carefully didn't share anything, not to protect her but myself. Sharing wasn't a priority. Neither was venting enough to let anyone in our little secret we all shared.

"I don't share shit. We all know that."

Cheyanne sat back, enjoying the exchange. She enjoyed anything with an edge enough to cut, and our words were vicious.

Omari was suddenly a talker. "I see how you look at her, Bolton. It's trouble. If she is one of us, good luck convincing her you aren't crazy, and if she's not, then you know what happens. We can't stop the ritual; you know that."

Annoyed, I looked away from him and the truth I avoided at all costs.

I always avoided the reality of how many times we had been wrong in the past, how many people we buried in the woods behind the school, and how many lies we came up with to protect our asses from questions. I could even name every person that wasn't the one.

Raven.

Darren.

Harold.

Francesca.

Samantha.

Tom.

Lucille.

Norman.

Scott.

Brittany.

Simone.

Anthony.

And last year, Ryan.

We were all so sure about him until we arrived at the altar and the way it all felt wrong. It was pure bile swimming in my stomach threatening my lunch to come up, because I couldn't bear to put any dinner down my throat.

The real person wrecked was Cheyanne, who fell for Ryan's charm as soon as he stepped foot on campus.

She tried to protect him, but at that point, we were so desperate to get out of our own hell that anyone attracted to us became the center of a witch hunt.

Cheyanne may seem cold on the outside but her insides were as warm as anyone's. Her first love had been ripped from her arms in the hopes he'd set us free.

Boy, were we wrong.

After sending Cheyanne into a full personality change, we put a lot more caution into the ritual then we did before.

She used to be normal, piercing-free, even *nice* .

Now she was this hard shell that terrified even me sometimes. There was no more guilt, shame, or even fear of the repercussions; she was unapologetically looking for an escape, no matter what it cost.

She stared up at me, like she resented how much I saw her as broken now. Really, I just saw how much I was about to be her if Arianna wasn't in fact the one.

"You let me know when you're done doing your little magic show and have some fucking answers," I practically growled at her, before I stormed out of the dining hall, more pissed off than ever.

My mind was still stuck on Arianna, the ritual, and all the trouble she was creating in my life. On the way out, I crashed into her like my thoughts conjured her up right in front of me.

"Jesus fucking Christ, Arianna. Watch where you're going!"

I stepped away from all her books, papers, and phone, which clearly cracked when it fell. I wasn't about to help, so the least I could do was move out of the way.

She kneeled down, looking up at me. "You don't have to be such an asshole. Are you shooting for some kind of award?"

I stood above her, exactly where I liked to be, above everyone, looking down at her only to prove a point.

She can sit on me like a throne but I will always be king.

"I have my reasons. What are yours for being so clumsy?"

I didn't expect her to answer me. I was being more asshole than normal.

"Well, you don't have to keep being an asshole to me."

She actually thought she was different, held some meaning, all because I took her back to my room. That didn't win her any brownie points. I leaned down, eye level, while she picked up her stuff defeatedly.

"Prove it, and I'll stop being an asshole."

I made sure she looked at me when I said it before I got up and ambled down the hallway away from her, the mess, as the pain in my chest filled with doubt that she wasn't the one.

Anyone on the football team was excused from our last two classes on days we had games.

It wasn't really a luxury if you knew our coach.

He was permanently dressed in Arcadia pride, all navy and maroon, all the time. He was a cliché if we were being honest. He blew his knee out a few months into going pro, and it never healed right for him to get a second shot at his dream.

Coaching a private school's team? Probably wasn't even Plan B for this guy.

I changed into my under armor, leaving my pads alone until actual game time. On game days, we didn't actually run plays or get to hit anyone until the other team stepped onto the field. No, instead we did cardio, which normally meant laps until someone either threw up or passed out. I had seen both happen, even in the shadow of Seattle.

I arrived on the field, pushing myself between Austin and Nyx, trying to find what their gaze was stuck on. On the other side of the field was the team we would play in two hours and their cheerleaders in smaller outfits than our own wore.

They were early, by hours, and I was aware they didn't come from that far. Our coach came up next to us, arms folded against his chest, eyes squinting in their direction.

"Their field is under construction, and they needed a place to practice. I never told them we'd be welcoming. You're welcome, boys."

Nyx reached over me to slap Austin's hand in excitement, completely ignoring me and going right for my runner up. I watched a brunette cheerleader smile and look down when our eyes met out of embarrassment of getting caught.

"Still mad at me?"

Nyx bulldozed into me when he walked around me and onto the field, clearly making a point. Yep, still mad.

I followed him, throwing my hands out in a clear defeat.

"Everyone knows you two like each other. It was a bad joke, okay?"

He turned around, rushing towards me, until his face was an alarming distance from mine. "It wasn't yours to joke about. You're just mad, because no one is ever gonna love an asshole like you. You wanted to be king? Now you are. Lonely, huh?"

I wanted to fight back. I wanted to push him out of my space. I wanted to do a lot of things that would make him my enemy but I didn't.

Instead, I shouted right into his good looks: "I didn't want any of this, and I didn't ask to be anything. I stepped up because no one else was."

Nyx started chuckling, like anything I said was actually funny. He even pinched the bridge of his nose, trying to force it to die down into a more controllable state.

He patted my shoulder before he walked backwards shouting so effortlessly. "Keep me, my feelings, and Luna out of your mouth. Oh, and Bolton? Next time? Just apologize."

Practice sucked more than usual. Coach was showing off, which really just meant we were working twice as hard to back up his shit-talking.

We had an hour break to eat between practice ending and the game beginning. Every guy on the team knew weighing yourself down was the worst thing you could do for yourself.

I didn't even bother changing out of my under armor, it was going to stay on under my gear anyways.

I walked right by the cheerleader playing coy with me earlier, throwing a smile her way, and making sure I brushed past her enough to get her attention.

I wasn't actually interested.

Hell, she didn't have purple hair and an attitude problem, so my dick really counted himself out. It was worth having her smile at me again, the rival, a small confidence boost.

The coffee cart outside was almost always open and stocked. If I couldn't have food before a game, at least I could pour some acidic coffee into my empty stomach.

The guy wouldn't even take the money I pushed forward. Instead, he told me, "Just win tonight."

And yet, they wondered why my ego was bullet proof, and I wore an invisible crown.

No one ever stopped to think they elected me. They built me up, and the monster I am was really because of them.

I was avoiding Nyx, like a bitch, and using my hour to walk around campus, far from the field and my teammates. It was eerily quiet.

The cheerleaders were most likely warming up, and the rest of campus was gearing up for the game. Everyone always attended, even if you didn't care for football. It was the blue and maroon running through their veins, the school pride.

I walked past the girls' dormitory when Arianna flew out in a hurry, and I took a big step back moving out of the way of her clumsiness.

Her legs were bare. She wore socks that landed at her ankles and a cheerleading skirt more modest than our rivals but by no means long, which landed mid-thigh.

Her arms were covered with white spandex and her purple hair was pulled into a high ponytail with a big bow hiding the fact that it was purple.

I couldn't rip my eyes from her. This was the most I'd seen of her, and it felt like a move on her part.

Teasing me.

"Why aren't you on the field?" she asked me, while smoothing down her skirt, like that would magically make it longer.

"We always have an hour break between same day practice and the game."

Shocking her and even myself, my voice wasn't rude or condescending. It was void of all the dark feelings that transformed my words into jabs.

I searched her legs for any obvious marks. The same kind we each had and the light bulb in my head went off.

Fuck waiting for Cheyanne's voodoo magic bullshit. I made sure to circle her catch the back side of her thighs with my gaze as I sat down on the steps, hiding my real objective.

She probably just assumed I was objectifying her; that part was true too. Arianna had the best pair of unblemished legs I had ever seen. Minus her Doc Martens, I could actually appreciate their length, their perfect cappuccino colored skin, and how much I was dying to have them wrapped around me—to be her throne again.

"I'm not fulfilling some cheerleader fantasy if you win tonight." She definitely felt my eyes glaze over her skin.

"You sure about that? I'll even put my phone on silent."

She folded her arms under her chest, not having the effect she wanted. I was busy making this my new personal favorite fantasy. "I don't make the same mistakes twice, Bolton."

"Mistakes are just obstacles. Thought you were a fighter, Arianna."

I got up, walking away from my words, which I was sure held the weight I wanted them to. I didn't get far before she caught up completely. We were both headed to the field for the game.

I knew a shortcut that led right to the boys' locker room. I knew all the shortcuts. She was babbling on about our project, when I stopped listening.

Right outside the entrance to the guys' locker room, my hand quickly caught her hip and gently pushed her against the wall. Her lips were parted, and her eyes begged me for what I was about to do next. I leaned down into her space, tilted my head to the right, and let her soft lips press against mine innocently.

I pulled away only enough to throw in her face: "Anyone tell you that you talk too much?"

Her palm hit my chest but I didn't move. Compared to on the field, that was a light breeze on a fall day. My forearm was still against the wall, and I was still leaning into her.

"What was that for?"

I pushed off the wall leaving her devoid of an answer altogether, and I pulled open the door to make my way down the hallway to the locker room. I didn't notice that she followed me, until I heard her footsteps—light taps behind me.

I didn't turn around or speak, hiding my smirk, as I tasted her still on my lips. Peaches, Chapstick, and all the spark that crackled against my lips like the unused body parts they were.

"Just because we made out one time doesn't mean you can do whatever you want."

I pushed open the big double doors and quickly came to the conclusion that while I was stuck on her taste, she just walked into the guys' locker room.

I debated turning her around and pushing her out the doors.

Instead, I was gonna stay true to who I was: an asshole, who, as Arianna put it, wore an aluminum crown. She was in for the answer to the questions that she was begging me for: Why.

Simply put, she was mine, and no one was going to challenge the king.

Most of the guys were shirtless still, changing from their cardio soaked under gear to dry under armor. It was pointless.

I walked over to my locker, and she followed blissfully ignoring the concerned stares. I was forced to pay attention to her when she leaned next to my locker, only staring at me, expecting a reply.

"Sorry to break it to you, sweetheart, but you're in the guys' locker room."

Her eyes turned a darker hue, and her arms folded again in discontent. "And? Nowhere I haven't been before."

I smirked down to the floor, avoiding giving her a victory over me. "Remember all the places you aren't supposed to be? This is one of them. We can talk all you want later."

I pulled my padding up to my waist and secured it against my abs before I closed my locker.

The shoulder pads were all in a bin closest to the wall. She actually stayed next to my locker, probably because of the fear of seeing someone naked without wanting to.

Austin fell out of the formation of guys close to their lockers, padding up, to shoot her direction: "This is a guys' locker room. Girls' is across the hall."

I laughed, grabbing pads and suiting up. I waved her over and pointed to the ties on the side for her to at least make herself useful if she wasn't going to take the warnings.

Nyx shot me a look of concern, before his eyes bobbed to one side, and I saw the coach coming. A girl in the guys' locker room wouldn't be overlooked—Not even for me.

I grabbed her arm, keeping her in front of me as I snuck her out the door. She didn't like being manhandled, and her frustrated features said it without her having to.

I pulled her into me, letting her knock into my pads before I repeated our kiss from earlier, except this one was stimulated by her attitude. Our tongues touched gently before I pulled away, leaving her still frozen in our kiss.

I whispered between us, "It's called a good luck kiss. If you think I can't kiss you, then storm back in there and watch everyone avert their eyes." I leaned down into her neck, placing a light kiss below her ear, whispering, "Because I'm king, they won't disobey me, and you're mine."

I didn't leave any time for her to respond, turning back into the locker room, leaving her still swooning from the stagnant attraction between us.

Once I crossed the threshold and the door closed in front of my face, I could already feel their taunting coming. All the guys jeered with their mocking.

I ignored them, going back to my locker and wrapping my fingers in the way I made a habit more than a need at this point.

Nyx bumped into me without any words, just a solid look that warranted thanks for looking out.

I nodded back in my own silent way. That was the thing that was irreplaceable about Nyx; we both hated talking and didn't actually need to.

The game was physically taxing, and every muscle in my body wrenched with ache, even the water pressure pouring out of the shower felt like torture.

Jasper was in the shower next to me, almost inconceivable, celebrating the win. He was dancing under the water when he turned towards me leaning over the shorter partition. "We celebrating tonight? Pizza shop? I'm fucking starving."

For the record, he was always hungry, and I never celebrated.

Arianna

The whole game I felt distracted by Bolton, not him physically playing, but the way he felt on my lips long after the kiss was over.

The feeling was all consuming, and I nearly tripped on myself more than once. Kate shot me draggers with her eyes each time.

Other than the slight malfunctions, my first game wasn't terrible. I forgot some of the chants and ended up mouthing them. That went noticed by our captain and proclaimed "Queen Bitch."

After the game, the girls headed to the locker room to shower and get changed, while Kate's hand wrapped around my forearm pulling me back from the double doors.

"Is he gonna be a problem for you? I don't let girls use the team to get some football ass."

I looked at her, half petrified and half concerned with what people thought. I still hated him, no matter how much I liked his mouth on mine. I knew how crazy that would be to explain ... to anyone.

"No, no. He's not a problem."

I couldn't even bring myself to say his name to her. That would only solidify that there was a thin line between hate and love; if I wasn't careful, I'd fall one way more than I was willing to.

She grilled me, waiting for the faintest reaction or slip up. I was unflinching; I was good in a crisis.

"Go shower, then Pizza Palace … Telling, not asking." She slapped my ass playfully and forced me forward, switching gears from fearless leader to friend effortlessly.

I was impressed.

Girls like her, at least from my past experiences of being the new kid, didn't have dimension. They were 2D, all bitch, and no apologies.

Kate may be dubbed "Queen Bitch," but she was so much more.

Pizza Palace was crawling with students—footballers, cheerleaders, supporters, even some facility all blending together in a sea of maroon and navy pride. Without a second thought, I searched the room for Bolton.

What was wrong with me?

I chanted, silently and in my mind, "you hate him … you hate him … you hate him … " hoping it was enough to keep the fine line from swallowing me whole.

Leo and Beau waved me over to the booth we sat in the last time I was here. This time, I contemplated not sliding in; last time, I nearly had to hop over a few bodies to escape.

I made up an excuse that I was going to the counter for a milkshake. I waited in the line with no real commitment to an actual milkshake, even though my stomach was twisting in envy of the thought.

Austin cut the line, leaning against the counter, waving me down, and asking, "What's it gonna be?"

My stomach convulsed, pushing me to say a chocolate shake and fries. I liked to dip them, mixing salty and sweet into one treat.

Austin ordered a burger and fries but quickly added a veggie burger and fries with no salt to the end of his order. No doubt that part was for Kate.

He twisted around, now back against the counter, and he was suddenly serious. "It's not a good idea ... you know that, right?"

With effort, I kept my features placid, almost innocent. I could never give you fully innocent; that never looked right on me. "The milkshake? Oh, I'm not lactose intolerant. No worries."

He didn't even crack a smile. "Bolton. Bad idea."

Austin was Bolton's friend, making his statement all the more confusing. The waitress slid over my milkshake, as I contemplated not even engaging, my silver tongue had other plans, like it always did.

"Bad ideas are kind of my thing."

My hair bounced in a too bubbly way when I spun around, leaving Austin to judge what was good and bad for me without my blessing.

He shouted from behind me: "He's not coming!"

I spun around again with quizzical eyes, hoping he'd get to the point quicker.

"He never shows up here, so don't hold your breath."

I watched him grab the tray of food, when I noticed the mark inside his wrist, similar to Luna's and Bolton's, but a different sign.

Taking a step to the right, I blocked his path and planted myself in front of him. "What's that? Tattoo? Birthmark?"

He stuttered around it, like he couldn't think on his toes. He finally spat out, "It's a burn from years ago, Nancy Drew."

I was fishing for reactions, glitches in his facade, answers that were honest instead of the bullshit he was feeding me.

"Luna and Bolton have them too. What are you guys ... ? A cult?"

Austin pulled down the sleeve of his flannel that he had over his black shirt in hopes to cover up what I already saw.

Pointless. I was ruthless type of relentless when it came to information I wanted.

"A cult? This is 2020, Arianna."

He pushed past me, and I already found it boring without Bolton.

I headed for the door, when Jasper came in. (He was the jester, if we were still playing by royal titles.) He was loud and cocky, and if he wasn't laughing himself, he was making others hold their sides and flick away the tears. He was fun but he wasn't living on the edge enough for me.

I needed a dangerous element to feel alive.

It all started when my mom died … I just kept finding new ways to feel the rush I'd get, and before I knew it, I wasn't just chasing danger; I was dangerous.

I waited for Jasper to commandeer the attention of everyone in the room so that I could slip out unnoticed, when as if appearing out of nowhere, Bolton stood against the doorway looking at me.

"Everyone said you don't show up here."

I leaned against the opposite wall, where we were blocking any traffic from coming or going.

"I was forced against my will."

I squinted at him. "Austin has the same mark/tattoo/thing you and Luna have."

I wanted to catch him off guard and assess the damage it would do, if any at all. His features stayed in place—calm, cool, collected—in a way I had never seen someone maintain all day, every day.

It was my new favorite kind of danger, being kept in the dark from everything he felt. "And? Any new conclusions?"

He toyed with my desire to figure this place out and its occupants that were connected somehow but I didn't know how deep that actually went or what the marks meant.

I shook my head in an obvious no, when he tilted his head towards the door. The cool air pinched my skin compared to the stale air inside the too crowded Pizza Palace.

I walked further away from the pizza shop, when he shouted, "Hold on!" from the door and went back inside. Drinking my milkshake I walked on the skinny ledge alongside another building, waiting and working out theories as to the marks.

Friendship tattoos? Too sentimental.

Actual birth marks? Too coincidental.

An actual burn? In the shape of astrology signs?

Definitely a cult.

Bolton breezed past me with two plates with two slices of pizzas piled on top. My milkshake was nearly gone and somehow he knew the hunger pains in my abdomen had moved on from twisting to a stabbing sensation to get my attention.

I didn't even ask where we were walking as I bit into a slice of pizza. A small piece of heaven broke through the dark vibes this school gave off when I moaned in pleasure.

He turned towards me all of a sudden, mid bite. "Are you religious or anything?"

I was too invested in feeding my hunger pains to truly be caught off guard by his deep question. "I think something up there is looking out for us but I don't know what it is. I don't think anyone does."

Facing forward and scanning his badge to enter the boys' dorm, he spoke again freely. "I'll tell you what the marks are in my room. Not here."

In his room, I leaned against his desk, polishing off my pizza and completely ready to hear him confess the truth.

I egged him on, tortured with waiting, and anxious to know, "Well? Tell me already."

He stood in front of me after dropping his phone and keycard on top of his bed, probably never to be seen again.

His room was a tornado of things flung around just like the last time I was granted permission inside.

He was stoic, giving consideration to take back the offer. Maybe he was just like everyone else and had moments of weakness.

"First, take your clothes off."

Every part of my body was stunned, and my eyes widened. I wasn't sure the truth was worth being that vulnerable.

"What does that have to do with anything? I don't think I want to know if it requires being naked."

He started taking his shirt off in some solidarity pact to make me feel more comfortable. It didn't work.

"Can you for once listen to me? I need to check you for any marks. It's the only way to be sure."

My eyes pinched like I had missed a chunk of this conversation that led to me being examined for a mark. "Hold up. Rewind. I don't have any marks."

"I'm not taking any chances. Use my bathroom then but check everywhere."

I let my jean jacket drop down my shoulders to show him my bare arms to prove it to him. "See? Nothing. I'm not part of your weird cult but I still want to know. Start talking."

He sat back down on his bed defeated and his bored expression was taken hostage by a look of pure worry.

Seeing someone so strong, tough even, seem so incurably bleak, I could tell how serious he was.

It put my joking to rest when my mouth collapsed into a frown, and I gave in to his demands one article of clothing at a time.

I started with my boots and socks, "You better spill while I do this." Next I unbuttoned my jeans and pushed them down my legs, exposing my unblemished complexion and black panties.

"We're not from here, okay? Now we're stuck on campus, and every time someone new comes they think they're the one."

I rolled my eyes with a huff before pulling my shirt off. I knew it wasn't a ploy when his eyes stayed connected with mine, not even breaking eye contact for a peek at my panties or bra.

"The one? One for what?"

He stood up and, with one big step, ended up in my space. His hand reached out to touch my arm, stopping me from unclipping my bra. "You don't have to take off more."

I unclipped my bra anyways letting the straps fall off my shoulders and down my chest between us. He didn't look down but something told me he wanted to.

"Weren't you taking your clothes off in solidarity?"

I pushed down my black boy-short panties down to my knees before I stepped out of them and handed them to him. I was naked in front of Bolton—the man I both despised and, yet, felt so aroused around.

I watched him push down his jeans while maintaining eye contact. He left his boxers on—something I noticed when I looked down. I couldn't help myself.

"Am I the one? Any marks?"

His eyes hadn't even looked me over yet, and it felt like respect more than a rejection. "Bolton, you'd have to look at me first."

"Turn around, face the mirror."

I slowly turned around feeling his hand scrape across my midriff while I did so. I stared at myself in the mirror completely naked and probably in the best shape I'd ever be in.

From what I understood about aging, it was directly linked to growing more dissatisfied with your body. I was going to soak up loving it, for now.

Bolton stood directly behind me, not enough to feel his dick against my ass but close enough to watch him move my hair to one side while he spoke into the nape of my neck.

"It can be small like Luna's or big like mine. It depends on the person." His gaze dropped down to my rib cage, "Why do you have a bow and arrow tattoo?"

It felt more awkward as my dad came to mind. "That's what my dad used to call me. His 'Little Archer.' I shot words without thinking."

Bolton's fingers traced it lightly while he mulled something over in his mind. I could see the wheels turning as my arms crossed over my chest, trying to cover my breasts at least.

"Turn around," he demanded, with such authority that my body listened before my attitude did.

Turning to face him, I kept my arms in place, shielding some of me, at least. I looked between us, letting my eyes stare at his bare chest and fall downward slowly.

"That's not really fair. I'm *completely* naked."

He was still sporting black boxer briefs with some kind of Italian looking symbol on the band. It was on the tip of the tongue, but honestly, his protruding package looked impressive. When I was impressed, it had the effect of shutting me up.

I watched his hand cup himself, while not breaking eye contact. "This is business. Not pleasure."

I sulked, like a child who wasn't getting their way, complete with a popped hip and brow.

"For fuck's sake ... " His fingers hooked into the band of his underwear, and in one swift push, his boxer briefs were on the floor as he stepped out of them. "Happy now?"

My mouth gaped open in complete shock at how comfortable he was, standing in front of me, stark naked. He wasn't even cracking a smirk at how impressed I was; he must have been used to this reaction.

He kneeled down on one knee, taking a closer look between my legs for whatever illusion he was looking for.

I tried to make small talk, as I looked at the ceiling, which was the furthest my eyes could go from what he was doing. "Where's everyone else's marks? You said everything depends on the person ... "

He stood up, checking under my arms, before he answered. "Austin's is the only other one I've seen as a tattoo. Like your bow and arrow. Everyone has them scattered around: hips, behind the ear, hands, biceps, top of the foot."

I laughed out loud that he actually thought my rebellious tattoo from freshman year really meant something to his theory.

I reached for my hoodie and panties, covering myself up before I demanded that he explain what he promised, as I sat Indian style on his bed.

"This would be the time you either tell me the theory, or I get disappointed that you're really after sex."

He walked over to the window, leaning against the small lip that hung off the edge. "You're not gonna believe me ... after last time ... " He trailed off like his thought vaporized between bad memories. I fake coughed, trying to pull his attention back, when he faced me before continuing: "I'm not human."

My stoic face waited for him to say he killed someone, and they were all guilty by association or something but it quickly melted into a robust laugh. I slapped my hand over my mouth and started laughing hysterically, until there were tears in my eyes.

I had to choke out, "You aren't serious? I mean, what are you then, Edward Cullen or Jacob?"

He wasn't laughing when I finally tried to make eye contact. He wasn't even smiling or smirking. No part of him found my joke funny, and I put him in the category of vampire.

Wolves seemed like they might have a better sense of humor—definitely not Bolton. His fair skin and dark hair made him practically a Photoshop's dream, easily blended into the background.

"Can you take this serious? The last person we told ended up dead, Arianna."

My laugh became stale in my mouth. I could tell he wasn't kidding, and whatever I was about to hear wasn't going to be funny.

"We're from Olympus. We're all descendants of gods and god-desses. Fourteen years ago, we were released to find the ones who slipped away. We woke up here, at Arcadia, trapped."

I felt like he was speaking another language, making it hard to keep up with all the syllables and sounds pouring from his lips.

"What do you mean trapped?"

He inhaled and exhaled sharply, "We can't leave Arcadia."

The edge of his bed felt like the tallest cliff all of a sudden. I was teetering on the edge, and all the information I was taking in felt like a swift push.

I stood up, frustrated and confused but wanting more pieces for the puzzle I was putting together. "What does that have to do with me?"

My anxiety was hard to summon, I lived for the unknown, this kind of unknown felt like drowning in foreign waters.

His answer wouldn't be a life raft; I knew that, while I waited for him to breach the space between us.

"You're the one we've been waiting for."

I wasn't just drowning anymore. I sank straight down and felt the weight of everything he was saying hold me under, while I gasped for any type of oxygen to hit my lungs.

In a state of panic, I jumped up and grabbed my jeans and boots, while the only color left on me was my manufactured purple hair; the rest of me was as white as a sheet of blank paper.

"I don't know what kind of game you're playing, but I'm not some desperate new girl who will take any friendship over honesty."

I slammed his bedroom door behind me and practically flew down the stairs, like I had motorized wings, until I bumped into a laughing Nyx, who was coming in the same door I was exiting through. He held up his hands, trying to create some kind of visible boundary of his personal space.

He analyzed my panic, anger, and deprived oxygen state as an alarm he couldn't ignore. "What happened?"

There was no comfort in his question; it was all business and to the point like he was. "Nothing. I don't wanna be part of whatever game y'all are playing."

I stepped back, making my point by creating more space, before I spun around and headed for the girls' dormitory.

Nyx didn't try to stop me.

All I heard was a mumbled "fuck" under his breath.

Arianna

Luna wasn't in our room when I got back from bolting from the boys' dorms.

The silence was nice, and it let the loudness of my panic fill the space without her nurturing. Twisting the shower handle of the small stand up shower we had in our room was always tricky.

You had to pull and twist at the same time in order for the water to come out of the shower head.

I stripped down, once again, staring at my tattoo along my ribs, wondering why my dad landed on "Little Archer" as my nickname.

Why not trigger finger or something easier to relate to not thinking before I spoke? And did he realize my astrological sign was an actual archer?

There were too many what ifs.

I stepped under the water letting the heavy water pressure rain down on me like a storm.

Luna still wasn't back when I dried off and crawled into bed. I may not have wanted her before, but now I was ready to pick her brain and connect some dots. Instead, I pulled out my phone and googled Bolton's enemy's school, along with his enemy on Instagram.

Caellum's name yielded thousands of searches; I was impressed.

I opened his Instagram profile to find nothing but life after Arcadia. I was pretty sure it aligned with life before: football, girls, parties, just minus the circle of freaks who tried to recruit me into their fucked up club.

Maybe they were a cult; I hadn't stayed to get the details.

There was no doubt that Caellum was handsome and confident, just like the boys at Arcadia. He would have blended in effortlessly.

I stopped scrolling when I got to a shirtless selfie of him in a dirty mirror. I couldn't help but admire the hottie from Bolton's hell. Caellum had abs I wanted to lick, even though they weren't magically flavored. He had almost white blonde hair parted in the center, thick brows, and a smile that looked divine.

He was a heartthrob on his way to making other parts of your anatomy ache too.

Before I couldn't stop myself, my finger hovered over the message button, and I was typing:

↗ *Sorry, this is random but do you have a tattoo related to astrology?*

I pushed "Send" immediately after I was done typing, not giving myself a chance to second guess myself. I was a serial type-and-delete kind of gal.

I would type something sarcastic first, second guess myself, type how I really felt, third guess myself, and then become even more sarcastic.

I hid behind it, where it was safe. Real feelings meant really losing people instead of just the idea of them.

I knew every time we moved to some crappy apartment that it wasn't the last time. Keeping people at a distance allowed me to make up these great possibilities of who they could be.

It was easier to miss the idea of someone than the actual person.

I scrolled without really thinking, trying to pass time, until my eyelids screamed for sleep. They were fluttering shut and open again on their own, when I finally fell asleep with my phone in my hand.

The next morning, Luna was leaning over me with wide eyes, whispering my name. I jumped, clutching my phone to my chest.

"Jesus, Luna! You can't wake people up like that. I'm too young for a heart attack."

Luna giggled the small way she always did when something amused her. She stood up tall, announcing her reasoning for waking me up on a Saturday.

"The library opens earlier on weekends, and no one goes there on Saturdays."

I cut her off with my hearty service of sarcasm, "Shocker."

She rolled her eyes, like she expected my tone, even half awake.

"It's the best time to work on our history of Arcadia project, duh."

I had forgotten about that project, and now I wished she didn't remind me. It was worth taking a zero if it meant ex-communication.

"Of course you wanna go to a library on a Saturday morning…"

I sat up, letting my phone fall into my lap, before I saw my screen illuminate my notifications, several private messages on Instagram. I ignored Luna's voice in favor of swiping on Caellum's messages. I wanted answers; no, I wanted validation.

> Caellum: *haha that's random.*
> Caellum: *making a fan club for me? Guess that deserves some deets.*
> Caellum: *Yeah, I do. Why?*

I squinted, like I could read between the lines of his messages with just a stern look. It was a complete shocker when I couldn't. My fingers tapped fiercely against the glass screen of my phone, typing my response.

> ↗ Me: *I don't do fan clubs, cults, or anything that requires me to play well with others.*

All smirks, I locked my phone and drew my attention to Luna, who was pulling on a knit sweater in a dusty rose color that didn't clash with her strawberry blonde hair. It complimented her.

It took me a minute to realize her eyes were wide, and I had missed something. She rolled her eyes, not bothering to repeat herself.

"Just get dressed. I'll meet you at the coffee cart downstairs."

I pushed myself out of bed and just threw on my signature jean jacket. Changing for a library visit wasn't needed; my joggers and tank were fancy enough to browse dusty old books.

I grabbed my bag and stomped down the stairs, only motivated by the sunny outlook of coffee.

Luna held out a small hot coffee, while she leaned against the railing, waiting for me, before we made the trek across campus to the library.

Libraries were always quiet at this time on Saturday morning, it was creepy. We found a table warmed up by the sun and perfectly tucked behind shelves of books.

Luna took off as soon as her bag hit a chair. She was laser focused, and I was hitting a wall, while yawning into my to-go coffee cup.

I took my coffee with me into the same aisle of books I was in the last time I was in the library. I pulled the only book off the shelf that caught my eye—the only black book among the faded colors. I thumbed through the fragile pages, not sure what I was even looking for, when a drawing of a forest made me stop and stare. It was a simple drawing, not much detail, but I analyzed every corner of the page.

The candles on the stump in the center of the tall trees, the footprints in the dirt, and the feeling I got from just the picture without reading any of the words.

It was a sinking feeling, similar to when Bolton blurted out his insanities to me, hoping I'd jump on board.

I skimmed the words on the adjacent page, only stopping at the highlighted words: sacrifice, coven, curse on the town, and the number fourteen.

I don't know why those words jumped off the page, seemingly bold, underlined, and italicized.

The sinking feeling only climbed a mountain as I thumbed further into the book.

"Something worse than witches, a kind of power that couldn't be trapped by their human forms. They moved like us, spoke like us, felt just like us, except their purpose in Arcadia was greater than fulfilling God's Word.

One of the thirteen fell into the Devil's lust one winter. Their love only grew with the trees blooming in the spring. It wasn't until Pastor Oscar questioned his intentions with young Rosalie that we saw his dark side.

The thirteenth member of their unnamed coven stumbled over his words, and we caught his mark of evil on his neck, hidden under his collar.

I stopped reading, wondering why it all felt so familiar to me, when I had never heard of Arcadia before my dad dropped me off here. I sat down between the bookshelves in the small space, still holding the book and my coffee. I folded my legs together, reading more of the legend.

> *The devilish mark was burned into him with the fiery depths of hell.*
>
> *He called himself Phrixus, a name as foreign as his tongue.*
>
> *The council met on the full moon after the blanket of black weighed heavily on everyone's eyelids. Our order and laws needed to be upheld, even among the Devil.*
>
> *That night, Phrixus walked into my office demanding our ear.*
>
> *"You are wise to fear me. I walk among mortals in this form, yet I do not blend in. I require the girl, as payment, and I will leave your fates to my gods, instead of at my own blade."*
>
> *The buckles on my men's boots shook with fear but I wasn't ready to accept defeat at the Devil's hands. I was a holy man bound by my Bible and spirit that lifted me from my bed every morn. I placed my hand at my sword and steadied my gaze on the man. He looked as young as Rosalia but the Devil can take many shapes.*

I stopped again to contemplate the words I soaked up and how much those words fed the feeling in the bottom of my stomach. Sinking further into familiarity and despair at what transpired so long ago.

I closed the book and pulled the ones next to it off the shelf without inspection before making my way back to the table.

"Find material for your project?"

I sat down with a hard, loud thud against the wood, and then I looked up, like I expected the librarian to elicit some loud shhh from the desk centrally located.

"Did you know in the 1600's there was a group of people with burned marks that scared the town shitless?"

Luna twisted the book towards her, reading the spine and immediately pulling them towards her. "You can't use these. They're artifacts. Fragile."

I laughed at her; none of that sounded like a good enough excuse to me.

"What are you talking about? They were on the shelf. If they were so off limits, wouldn't they be under lock and key?"

She looked uncomfortable and tense all of a sudden. Even the thought of someone near her breaking the rules sent Miss Innocent into a silent meltdown.

I ignored her aversion to breaking the rules and took notes on the urban legend I chose for the project, leaving Bolton with no choice.

He wasn't here or helping, so I became a dictator, the queen he let me be. Crown but no throne.

It felt like hours later, when the sun was sitting higher in the sky and beaming down on the wood even harder. I pushed myself inch by inch closer to the warmth, craving it after all the gloomy weather I had experienced so far here.

The laughter of males nearby caught my attention quickly. I was looking for any excuse to stop studying these old books for a project I didn't want to do to begin with. It was a welcome distraction, until I lined up faces with the laughter: Bolton and Nyx.

They breezed through the library, disregarding the quiet signs and even the librarian eyeing them. They ran this school, and everyone knew it.

King and the baron, with the good looks and abhorrent personality.

I didn't know what Luna saw in him. He barely spoke, and when he did, it was threatening. I was shocked he even knew how to laugh; it had to be at someone's expense. Those two didn't enjoy anything but aches and pains—the kind that turned souls black and hearts to stone.

I dipped my head down into my book, hoping not to be seen. Maybe they were here for some quick errand, and I could be spared. Bolton's fingers tugged down my book, as he leaned over, waiting for our eyes to meet.

Great, my king had found my hiding spot. Here came the torture.

But, we didn't become queens by sipping tea and keeping our gloves white. The snarky tone in my voice was saturated to the highest limit possible: "Can I help you, Bolton?"

I didn't let my eyes find his; instead, I kept them low and stuck to the pages of my new favorite book. Rosalia was a queen in disguise, and I was committed to finding out what happened to her, once the unnamed coven showed up at Arcadia.

Bolton grabbed the entire book from the table and thumbed the pages without any delicacy in his touch.

He was rough and cruel, even down to his fingertips. "What's this? Some light reading?"

I didn't even have a chance to speak before Luna's tone shifted from sweet and innocent to annoyed and pissed off. "She found it on the shelf, which is weird, because I thought those books were removed."

What was her problem with this damn book?

It's an old book; none of the people were alive; and the jibber jabber of an old man wasn't relevant now.

Bolton sat on top of the table, instead in one of the twelve chairs surrounding the table, and kicked his feet up on an empty chair with his back toward me. He completely cut me out of the conversation, and I was sure it was an uncalculated move.

I would leave but now I wanted to know what the fuss was with this stupid book. No, I *had* to know now.

"I put it there." His deep voice was smooth with no lumps of rudeness to be seen. He was simply factual.

Why did he have this book? Why would he hide it in plain sight?

Luna's pissed off switch just blew, and she tossed all of her colorful pens and the rest of her supplies in her bag, before she stopped between the boys.

"You're playing with fire."

Coming from Luna, her words were more ominous and threatening. Whatever this was really about had her panties twisted, causing a type of seriously uncomfortable chub rub.

Nyx went after her; I'm sure all this was a great opening for him to comfort her without revealing how much he felt for her.

I didn't understand their relationship at all. It was clear to the deaf and blind that they had this magnetism that couldn't conceal how much love was really there.

I couldn't help wondering if they tried and it didn't work, or if maybe something else happened that kept them from trying.

Bolton swiveled around, facing me with one leg on the table with him now. "And … ? Still think I'm crazy?"

It wasn't until he asked me that I was forced to analyze my thoughts and take inventory of my sanity after last night. Thankfully, it was still holding up.

The book wasn't a legend or myth. The unknown cover was the marked ones; the town was terrified of the sociopathic rage that came after a declaration like that; and I was the girl that the Devil had his sight set on.

Damn it, if I only got to read further. I might know my aligning fate with Rosalia.

"You still sound crazy. I have a project to do. Are we done here?"

My phone buzzed against the mahogany table with so much force the librarian leaned over her desk's edge just to shush me with eye contact and a curt, "No cell phones." I picked it up off the table, quickly reading the response from Bolton's enemy right in front of him without him knowing it.

I was plotting his downfall right in my hands, and his unknow-ingness was what I was going to drop my new crown in.

Opening my direct messages I read Caellum's response: *I got it now, foot fetish? What school do you go to?*

The green active icon attached to his profile photo made replying right away easy. I quickly typed Arcadia into the box and hit send.

I was just hoping that didn't deem me untouchable, a warning sign he could just ignore if it meant giving Bolton a taste of his own medicine.

Bolton grew irritated with waiting his turn, while my whole attention was clearly elsewhere. He snatched my phone from my hands. He read the messages and clenched his fist around my phone in an alarming way, before he brought it to his mouth in a silent scream.

He was exactly the kind of angry I envisioned—the same kind he made me feel between kisses. "Why are you messaging Caellum? You don't know him."

"Exactly, he hates you, so he has no reason to lie."

He stood up, dropping my phone with a thud against wood, before drilling his closed fists into the tabletop. "I put that book there so you'd put shit together yourself, not run for help. He can't be trusted."

I felt like challenging for no reason other than I could. "Why can't he be trusted? He had a mark, just like you said."

His expression was pinched everywhere that he had a sharp feature: eyes, lips, nose, even his jaw. All were tight with anger and getting more severe with every word I spoke.

"He's not part of the circle anymore."

He paused, standing up straighter and making every intention of walking away, when he pivoted towards one last time. "For some-one smart enough to take me as your throne, you're not thinking like a royal. Instead, you wanna sleep with the enemy."

He walked away with a look of disgust, and I swiped the book back, pulling it close to me and keeping its legacy safe.

I opened to the page with a drawing of Rosalia and continued my reading where I had left off.

> Henry Jon
>
> He demanded her as a sacrifice but promised to not hurt her if he could prove she was the one. His words were a snake in the tall grass, unseen and venomous. The Devil explained how sure he was that our innocent Rosalia was the essence of his lover from his world.
>
> His world... he described it with so much beauty that I wondered if Hell was meant to draw us in and betray us after death with fiery pits.
>
> He needed to sacrifice her human body, so his unknown cover could return home. Her essence would live on with him, and her human form would die in its place, as an offering for desire.
>
> Rosalia was my sweet daughter, my youngest and most able bodied. She was bright in a way the other village young envied her and followed her everywhere. She was a leader, cursed with the female anatomy. She would never be able to take my place, and it brought so much sorrow that I almost believed death was a better fate.

I focused on every detail of Rosalia's portrait on the adjacent page. She was young, maybe fifteen at the most but her age wasn't yet disclosed.

Her skin was flawless, and her eyes were much wider than average with an almond shape to them. The curls she wore almost made a crown, like she knew her purpose all along. She was beautiful and strong.

I read more of the book before I pulled up Google on my computer to search a combination of her name, Arcadia, and key words like sacrifice. There were millions of results, and I didn't have time to search them all.

I knew just by the lack of sun that the library was most likely closing soon. I let myself get lost down the deep, dark hole of internet searching until the librarian pranced over and lifted an eyebrow at my things still sprawled on the table.

"We are closing in ten minutes, Arianna."

Why did adults do that?

Say your name like you needed to be reminded? We both knew my name without it being mentioned.

I rolled my eyes without noticing, until the sigh left my mouth, volunteering my dedication to this story and validating its highlights.

I was coming off full bookworm, and it seemed like a gateway drug to a long reading list.

I threw all my stuff in my bag, including the book Bolton hid in plain sight, and now determined that ownership was transferred to me.

CHAPTER 16

Arianna

The sky was a watercolor painting: oranges, reds, and even some purple. The sky was as undecided as I was about everything. Unlike me, eventually the clouds and stars would let a dark haze blur out the color landing on a nightshade.

I wasn't going to land anywhere. There was too much still unknown, and that feeling of sinking wasn't going away.

I walked by the faculty building to not see a single light on, except for one small window behind a bush was illuminated.

Why would someone be in the basement? What was in the basement?

I mocked the torturous king when I made him question my loyalty. I betrayed him by reaching out to his enemy and plotting his overflowing anger. Now, he pushed me right into some modern version of Nancy-fucking-Drew.

It's official: You can hate someone so much it changes you into someone you don't even recognize anymore.

I stalked the perimeter of the building, keeping a distance, while collecting clues. *Is that what she did? Collect clues?* I couldn't remember how Nancy Drew ever solved any mysteries, only that they always had some happy ending.

"What do you think you're doing?" Kate's dumb blonde impression was perfect, minus the blonde locks. She scared the shit out of me, though.

Nearly jumping out of my Doc Martens, I slowly turned around to see her in a pink jogger set, with her arms folded against her and one foot pushed out, even though it wasn't tapping. I searched for a reply that kept me innocent.

"I got lost ... ?"

Her still popped hip and eyebrow didn't melt into believing me. I was caught.

"Sure, New Girl, whatever you say. This building is off limits."

I watched her slowly climb the stairs to the front door as she spoke—a contradiction wrapped in pink and bitch. She stopped to look over her shoulder; she knew I didn't care about mundane rules like "off limits" or "don't touch."

That was where I lived, my happy place: the danger zone.

"Seriously, Bolton would kill me and not, like, metaphorically. Like real dead, gone, cease to exist."

I tried not to smile at her attempt at severe threats. I bet she was molten chocolate underneath, hot and sticky.

"I know what 'off limits' means, Kate."

She rolled her eyes and climbed the stairs again, disappearing behind the heavy door. I kicked some rocks, hoping she'd take pity on me and piss off Bolton, but no one came or went for the few minutes I waited. I finally gave up and went back to my room.

When Luna wasn't there, I was able to piece it all together more and more. I had the book open, my notepad full of scribbles, and my laptop open to Google. I was still Nancy Drew even in the solitude of my bedroom.

The passages were long winded, but it basically boiled down to Henry Jon, Rosalia's dad, ended up giving her as sacrifice to spare the lives of Arcadia's residents.

He went mad searching for her and even put a bell next to her coffin in case she woke. He met the demands. I guess he had never heard of the saying, "We don't negotiate with terrorists."

Rosalia died, and there was no way of knowing if anything the unbanned coven said was true. There was no evidence other than this damn book.

Did Bolton think that was enough to convince me? Was I missing something?

I tore out the pages in the front where Henry Jon drew a map and labeled everything down to details, like how many steps were between fixtures on the map. He wasn't playing around, and neither was I.

I grabbed my phone and swapped out my jean jacket for a hoodie, since the chill was almost unbearable after 8 PM. I headed outside in search of the forest, where he had met the coven and where the sacrifice had happened in hopes that there would be something more to find on the walk there.

I was desperate and grasping for clues.

The ground crunched under my Doc Martens with every step—small and calculated, big and reckless.

There was no way to be quiet in these words. I used my flashlight to illuminate where I stepped, and that's about all it illuminated. Everything looked like a carbon copy of each other; every tree was similar and no real defining factors to help me keep my direction certain.

I came across the clearing after counting my steps carefully, like Henry Jon did when they blind folded him and escorted him out to their altar. He may have lost his mind after her death but he was sharp as a whip before.

I was focused on looking down when I tripped over something against the tree trunk. I fell right on my ass and slammed my fists down against the dirt, dropping the map and my phone in the fall.

I patted the ground around me for the map without any kind of light, which was the most important part, if I wanted to make it back alive.

I found my phone and sent a quick text to Luna:

> ↗ *I'm in the woods following a hunch. If I'm not back by midnight, then panic.*

After it sent it, I tucked my phone between my chin and shoulder pointing it in the direction of what I had tripped over. There rested a small box, and slowly, I opened it. I stopped inhaling just in case something was dead in there. I even pushed myself back, unsure of what was inside and protecting my face from the possibilities.

Raising the lid, I laughed to myself at the random items inside. There was nothing scary or threatening. It was a memory box; it was just more creepy because it was abandoned in the woods behind the school.

I fingered the items: a lighter, a hair tie, a photo clipped from a yearbook, a ring, a fake eyelash strip, lipstick, a pin, a fortune cookie fortune, a bookmark, dice, and car keys.

It was a random assortment of items that didn't fit into the image I was building in my head.

I closed the box with the items carefully tucked inside and turned around to inspect the rest of the clearing. There was a stump filled with candles melted down into each other. I let my fingers smooth over the hard wax that tears rolled down the length of once. I looked at the items surrounding the candles, like the items were praising the candles standing above them. Feathers, a mason jar of dirty water, seashells, and a small pot of dirt, making up all four elements.

None of this looked old enough to be from when Henry Jon visited this clearing. Everything seemed an untouched kind of new.

I jumped out of my skin when I heard an ominous voice from behind me. "What do you think you're doing?"

I clasped my phone to my chest and tried to grasp my breath, when I saw the figure still draped in shadows. "Who's there?"

Oh my god … what a basic-ass reply that practically splattered from my mouth.

"I'm hurt. You don't know my voice by now?"

Instinctually, I rolled my eyes, realizing it was none other than my torturous king, Bolton, himself. "What do you want?"

He laughed, moving around in the dark, like it was second nature to him. The flashlight on my phone had a hard time keeping up with his crass movements.

"A little bird told me you were out here snooping around."

"Seems like your court is infested with rats."

His fingers smoothed the exterior of the candles before standing in front of me, jarring my stoic expression. "Don't confuse loyalty for treachery."

I didn't flinch when his warm breath licked my skin. I was committed to staying still and being the type of queen who didn't tear her eyes away from bloodshed. And there was going to be bloodshed if he thought I was going to back down.

"1600's called and wants their vocab back."

He took another step closer to me, "Seems like you didn't learn anything from Henry Jon today."

The hand holding my flashlight dropped to my waist and naturally a hip popped, adding to my like armor sass.

"If you want me to know something, then just spit it out, Bolton. Team Edward or Jacob?"

I could see his casualty turn into my own personal casualty as his features got tight and fists curled. "This isn't a game. I'm telling you so I can protect you."

I backed away, finally breaking the tension growing between us. I stepped back slowly and carefully but only enough to breathe fresh air instead of the oxygen only exchanged between us. "From who? Protect me from who? Everyone in that book is dead!"

He kneeled down, level with the stump, producing a lighter and giving the candles a job to do.

The glow was soft and yellow, at least I could see more beyond the flashlight on my phone. He stood tall, less angry, but still tense, like I pissed him off.

"Not everyone, Arianna."

I didn't speak. There was no use. There was nothing I could say that was going to fill the gaps or ask the right questions to get the answers I wanted.

"I'm still alive … That book took me a long time to find. I'm the only one who remembers before here."

Convenient, is what I call that. No one to validate your parking in a lying zone.

"So you're telling me you're the one with the Devil mark who sacrificed Rosalia? Halloween is in two weeks … "

He pulled his phone out, disrupting my amazing jab, deflected by a damn phone. "I gotta go. Do you know your way back?"

Within a few long strides, he disappeared into the darkness, leaving me there holding my makeshift flashlight and still wondering how to piece the puzzle together. I was just as confused as before, if not more so now.

I threw my head backwards and looked up at the sky, like it would answer all the silent questions in my head. I gave up after my fingernails sunk into my palm and stung enough to unclench.

I only made it a few feet forward, touching every tree for extra stability with every step. It wasn't until my fingers grazed over the trunk I felt something odd. I wasn't even sure what felt different about the bark a few trees away from the clearing.

Something tugged at everything inside me to investigate.

Goddamn it … I had Nancy Drew senses now too.

I patted the trunk trying to investigate the urge in complete darkness, juggling my phone, while patting a tree down is harder than it seems. Trust me, try it.

I finally found what seemed like fake bark. When I tugged at the seams, it slid to the side, opening up its secret cave. I got on the tips of my toes and flashed my light inside the cave, waiting for spiders or a family of rats to be very pissed off at me for disrupting their home.

With a heavy sigh, I found a small black box. It was simple and had a crest stamped on the lid. I turned the box over each way, looking for clues on the outside before I dove inside.

I breathed a clean inhale trying to push down the adrenaline and anxiety. The last box I opened out here was full of random shit that made no sense.

The latch seemed fragile and worn out as I lifted the lid to see a velvet baggy, like when you buy cheap jewelry. I plucked the bag out and gave it a small squeeze, trying to feel the shapes of the objects and make some assumption of the contents. It made a crunching effect with every squeeze, driving me closer off the edge of reason. I finally opened the bag, where the velvet was pulled close it was stiff and almost immobile, not wanting to be opened.

I dove my fingers inside, pulling out papers folded expertly into smaller versions and unfolding them carefully. Something old that had braved the Seattle elements wasn't going to be fragile, they would be close to rigor mortis. The pages were almost glued to the creases that I tried to flatten out.

The same pen and ink writing screamed Henry Jon at me without further investigation. I tucked the pages into my back pocket before I closed the hiding spot up all over again.

The woods were coated in a type of black that made your eyes adjust and heart race for no reason. I managed to not fall once on the way back to campus.

As soon as the streetlamps illuminated the sidewalks between the buildings I took an extra-long breath to make up for the short ones I pushed down the whole time I was in the woods.

I almost ran up the stairs to my room, and when I saw Kate and Luna on her bed talking, my adrenaline turned to anger.

Luna was the only one who knew I was out there, and she had told Bolton, who came running to inflict more torture on my poor soul.

I let the book fall down on my bed, and I gave her a glare that was meant to melt off all the innocent bullshit she wore like make up. You can't be innocent and rat someone out at the same time, not in my book.

"Thanks for snitching."

Kate didn't even mistake my tone, and her shocked expression twisted towards Luna next to her. Luna let it seep in and didn't even look guilty.

She didn't explain right away or have an excuse ready. She was graceful and understanding like she always was. "Arianna, I get you are upset. It's not safe to be alone in the woods. I was worried about you. We all know you can get over your head ... "

There was a part of me on reserve, constantly on ice, waiting until the right amount of heat inside me melted the ice and that part of me spoke without thinking.

"Excuse me? Over my head?"

This was the fire licking the ice and melting the reserve I kept far from others. After my mother died, I tucked it safely inside. Now and again, I still spoke without thinking, slinging my arrows at anyone and everyone, but that was a kid's game compared to what Luna was awakening.

"Yes, sometimes you act without rational thinking and don't consider the consequences. Isn't that why you're here? Sometimes you talk in your sleep. Begging your dad to let you stay if you change."

There wasn't a degree of cold left in my body when she spoke all this into reality, in front of Kate.

"At least I'm brave enough to be myself, Luna. I'm reckless and impatient but I'm never gonna be the innocent twat who is too scared to be loved."

I grabbed my towel off the door, with my shower caddy, and didn't wait for her oh-so-shocked at my behavior attitude. It wasn't shocking. Not my insult, not my attitude, not my cutthroat on reserve.

I was me all the time, leaving no shock-worthy element to my personality.

We had a private bathroom in our room, all the seniors did, but I needed out of our shoebox room and away from her assumptions about me that she was putting on display.

The hallway was old and had a certain musty smell you couldn't escape, but right then, it still felt refreshing. I swallowed the fire down, trying to cool my icy reserve again before it lashed out at anyone and everyone around me.

CHAPTER 17

Bolton

I had a reason to leave our little get together and that reason dissolved when my phone wouldn't stop buzzing in my pocket. Alba called me over and over again, making stealing my attention easy.

I had bolted from the annual meeting at a pivotal time: Caellum, the book I left Arianna, and the twins being close to ready with their ritual bullshit. It was easier not being present to hear the same argument over and over again.

It was the same song on repeat, boring into my brain and becoming my own personal theme song that I loathed.

Do we need Caellum to go home? For the ritual?

Is Arianna the one? What makes me so sure?

What if the ritual doesn't work?

All I heard was their drowned out voices while I stopped giving a shit about ten times ago.

They were all desperate to go home but none of them remembered home. They were suffocating all their resources to find a cure for being a teenage dream. This was what everyone wanted, and we were trying to throw it away.

Don't get me wrong, I didn't want to be a fucking teenager. I was the essence of a god stuck in a skin suit that's sole purpose was to rebel, make a mess of girl's panties, and find a less serial killer way of getting my aggression out.

Home wasn't home anymore. All our gods were dead, and this world was being pulled along by something much worse than their games.

I stomped my way into his office like a fucking superhero who saw the distress signal. "What's the emergency?"

He turned from the book shelf he was pawing at, meeting my gaze, and being dramatic as always. "A book is missing from my shelf. Do you know anything about that?"

I leaned against the door frame, crossing my arms and making sure I wasn't giving anything away. Not even pleasantries.

"Nope. Is that it?"

Alba moved around his desk with a book in his hand and perched on its edge. "It doesn't matter how much you tell her, Bolton. She won't remember. It's written in her sign to be disconnected from the celestial bodies."

I got tense, even though I forced my body to stay relaxed as much as possible.

Something about Alba always managed to put me on edge. Something about him creeped me out, and I couldn't tell if it was my teenage body or me rubbing his Virgo ass wrong.

"She's different. She's curious. She can survive it."

He laughed, standing up from his desk like he was done explaining it to me while I threw a tantrum. "Stop forcing it. You think Cheyanne didn't think the same way you are right now?"

"I'm smarter than Cheyanne."

He slapped his hands down on the desk, equal parts annoyed and frustrated with me. His head dipped below his shoulders, and his silence felt thick in the air.

"Finding the one takes patience. You're human, and human error accounts for emotions, feelings, hormones ... You have to stay level-headed."

"I don't think anything based on fucking feelings, and I'm better than human error. I'm nearly a god."

I wasn't sticking around for the rest of his pointless lecture. No one could decide if I was team Arianna or team throw her to the wolves and see if she's our ticket home.

I was deceitful and misleading on purpose. How I felt was mine and mine alone. I didn't need validation.

The entire way back to my room my mind was a flood gate to last year when Cheyanne tried to convince me her new lover was the one. I had never seen someone fall so hard for someone else. She wasn't swimming in the iris of his love; she was drowning with no signs of the coast guard to pluck her out of that kind of storm.

Every day she begged and pleaded with me to do the ritual because of how sure she was. I didn't have any proof, nothing solid, except her devotion-sheathed eyes.

No one made a move without my say so, no matter how sure they seemed to be.

My instincts were right when Omari drove the blade through his chest, and we were all there still, left to gawk at the lifeless body and realize this was the price of being wrong.

I should have done more to stop the ritual but the human part of me ached for Cheyanne falling for her first time.

I wasn't making that mistake again. I was going to exhaust every possible way to prove she was our ticket home or prepare her for the worst.

Either way, I was doing everything in my power so when I buried her body, I'd hurry the guilt too.

Classes resumed; time didn't care how we felt or the drama separating our minutes; it moved regardless. I slammed my locker, already pissed off that Ivy Prep forfeited the game tonight and now Caellum's team was getting a second chance to rub winning in my face.

We were good enough to beat him but not without enough practice time. It wasn't even the practice time, not really. My team needed to barb with each other, crack jokes at other's expenses, and build up some confidence.

They were too scared of not being good enough that it seeped deeper into the confident parts of themselves too.

"What's your problem today?"

Jasper specified "today" because every day I had a problem. If it wasn't the circle, it was the fucking ritual, or Alba, or the Luna and Nyx drama... It was always something just out of my control.

I gritted my teeth through a curt answer: "Nothing."

Jasper laughed as he leaned against the lockers with his bag dangling from his shoulder. I didn't bother carrying shit, whatever books my arms could hold, they did. I had done this year over so much I had everything pretty much memorized.

Jasper was relentless, dry, touchy, and uptight. So he pretty much fit in with the rest of the guys, minus Beau and Leo.

We weren't against them being together or anything but their personalities were more vibrant compared to our dark hues. They were sunshine, while we were moody motherfuckers bringing the rain.

"Okay, but 'nothing' sure seems to have you in a mood."

I glared at him, halting his ignorant thoughts from being silent inner monologues to whatever kind of concern this was.

He gave up quickly; his relentlessness wasn't any real match for me. I held everyone's secrets, all the answers, as the only one who remembered home. I was invaluable. It didn't help deflate my ego.

I turned around quickly, for a clean getaway, when I collided with none other than my favorite purple-haired girl.

Arianna.

I gritted my teeth, already tipping over the edge, and it didn't matter that I had a soft spot for her under my mound of hate. She put another vex in my scale for me to weigh. My scale was broken, and only tipped one way.

"Watch where you're going," she almost hissed.

I could hear Nyx and Jasper sneering behind me at my rage brewing.

"You're the one not looking where you're going. Pay more attention."

Was this for leaving her in the woods?

Was she in just as bad of a mood?

Isn't anger part of acceptance?

Maybe she finally figured it all out.

I looked around the hallway, like she couldn't be talking to me, but I was the only person her gaze was locked on.

Her and I.

Hate and more hate.

King and queen.

I stayed quiet, and my silence wore her down after just sixty seconds.

"What's your problem? You hate me. I get it. Don't worry, it's reciprocated."

I grabbed her elbow with too much force, sometimes the anger was hard to bite back, as I walked forward into her until she had no choice but to move backwards.

Now against the lockers I breathed her in; she smelled fresh laundry and morning dew. She was intoxicating, and it almost made me lose focus of my bad mood.

I barked into her, regaining composure. My fingers pushed her inked strands behind her ear, and my hot breath gave her goosebumps on her arm that I felt raise against my fingers. "You want me to like you? Try being loyal."

The color didn't fade from her face, instead she became more animated: blushing cheeks, eyes glossed over, her mouth stuck open. It was almost comical watching her choke out any words at all. "I'm loyal. Maybe I'm just not to you."

Did Arianna Weston officially declare her my enemy? Not just the new girl I loathed–my enemy.

My betraying queen was aiming for blood on her hands: mine.

The warning bell rang, making everyone move with gumption from their place of gawking. I didn't move, and neither did Arianna.

We stood in the hallway, with my body weight pushing her back into the lockers, and our hate clashing. I looked down at her, concluding her hate was all bullshit but that mischief in her smile made this so much more fun to play along.

Leaning down, I pushed my lips to hers, and the palm of my hand snuck into her open blazer to find the waistband of her skirt. I squeezed her side when I opened my mouth and my tongue slithered into her mouth. She tasted like honey: warm, wet, smooth...She was everything a kiss should be, hungry and wanting more.

Some girls gave it all away too soon, shoving their tongues down your throat while their hips swayed to meet yours and their hands tugged at anything they could grasp. It was sensory overload. I liked to experience each step before combining anything. Different fuels caught fire at different temperatures.

Arianna was slow and even.

Her arms slung around my neck but didn't pull me closer. She kept me intrigued, even though I knew it was time to pull away before it became difficult to do anything about it before homeroom.

I pulled away and she groaned in an offended tone. "No...why did you stop?"

I smirked with so much pride I wanted to slap myself. "I'm kissing a traitor."

"You know what I've learned about being the new girl so many times?"

I popped an eyebrow, wondering what this new girl considered wisdom to someone of my caliber.

"The only traitors are yourself." Her words slapped me across the face without any actual contact.

Traitors were only what you made of them, and most of the time, I demonized myself. She was a traitor for hearing my secret, running away, and reaching out for the evil worse than me: Caellum.

"Tell Caellum I say hi, traitor."

I bit my lip, looking down at her lips, which were now a brighter red from our kissing—used and abused. The part of me that called her my queen didn't want to stop, but my fury side always won, silently working behind the scenes to keep me focused and unhappy.

I left Arianna to regain composure against the lockers, only looking over my shoulder once briefly to see her fingertips caressing her own lips, rubbing me in, saving me for later.

I kicked my feet up in math class on the empty desk next to me. I only had Jasper in this class with me, while the rest of us were spread around in civics, English, and French. I would have traded Jasper for Nyx or Austin.

Jasper was the more vocal version of Nyx, always talking and resembling a dog with a bone when he found a subject matter he liked. Don't get me wrong, he blended in with us and was part of the circle bearing the mark of the Capricorn but it didn't mean I like him best.

As soon as I sat down, he leaned over, pushing his phone in my face to show me some Instagram posts of Caellum's school. They were on the field running passes when Caellum showed up in the camera frame, moving his fingers along his neck, slicing his own throat as though it was meant to piss me off.

It worked.

If you wanted to get under my skin and evoke a god-like response, threaten me. It'll earn you an enraged version of myself, one I'm even scared of.

I got up abruptly making the teacher stutter around her last words. I didn't turn around to yell Jasper's name summoning him to follow me; I didn't need to. He followed me anyway.

As soon as we were in the hallway, I told him round up the team and meet me on the field. His eyebrows caved in even though he didn't bother asking me anything.

I had my own mission: get us all excused by Alba so that this wasn't some staged walk out when half the class left class to go practice.

Caellum wasn't getting the best of us again. We were gonna practice until everyone's fingers hurt against the leather and their pads felt too heavy to bare.

Tomorrow night, we would be ready to win.

Arianna

Hate and Luna were gossiping as to why Bolton was extra himself today in French when I tried to eavesdrop. I was great at listening and becoming almost invisible, even with purple hair. It was part of my new girl arsenal.

"Caellum is back on campus tomorrow."

Luna's sympathetic face frowned while Kate's eye roll didn't put up with drama from boys. Unlikely friends but I rarely saw them apart.

Kate saw me listening in when her features scrunched up and glared at me. She was always catching me, seeing me, when most didn't. I wasn't sure what to make of her all-seeing eyes.

"Do you have something to add?"

Her voice was saturated in annoyance, and I didn't blame her. She kept catching me at my worst.

"I don't get their beef. Caellum seems nice."

She pretty much scoffed at me as soon as the pause created a period to my thoughts.

Luna jumped in, defending me, even after my verbal lashing. "She doesn't know. You can't blame her for it."

I smiled sweetly at her, and my poisonous arrow that I had shot before thinking felt a lot like regret instead of the anger it was born from.

Kate, on the other hand, didn't care as she leaned forward with her snarky expression. "You can't crush on him and not take his side, *princess*."

I wanted to correct her; it was "queen"—his queen actually. She was dethroned and overruled the minute I took my seat on his lap. I was never a princess—not before Bolton and certainly not now.

I wasn't next in line, and I wasn't waiting for someone to crown me.

I twisted at my desk, turning to completely face her with ease. "First of all, I'm no princess. I can slay dragons too. Second, what do you plan to do about Caellum then?"

She suddenly looked confused, and I couldn't tell by which part—how much she doubted me being a queen or not having a plan for Caellum since she claimed loyalty five minutes ago.

This is who they crowned queen before me? She didn't even have a plan for their "enemy."

The only thing Kate had right was her loyalty being in the correct bed, so to speak, of course. This coronation was teaching me a lot, mainly that Bolton appreciated undying and unquestioning loyalty.

I twisted back, swinging my legs under my desk again. "Meet me tonight after the bells in front of the library."

She may have had loyalty but she didn't have the balls to get dirty and do what needed to be done for the king.

We waited for the last bells to ring before we even attempted to leave our room. The same bells rang every night at 8 PM, alerting the students to the curfew that required us to be safely in our rooms.

Of course, this didn't apply on game nights; the double standard was screaming so loud I was deaf.

Luna was in all black, borrowed from me, and I donned the same colors head to toe. I swapped out my white Doc Martens for my older black pair—the pair I normally wore when trouble disguised itself as fun, before a wrong turn was made on moral code street.

We all met outside the library with one extra body; that was the first red flag I missed.

Austin was firmly by Kate's side, with his arms wrapped around her from behind and his face nuzzled into her neck. He wanted to be anywhere, but here, that much was obvious. He made other plans involving Kate.

No, I wasn't jealous.

I had a crown to keep straight.

I was focused on revenge and the familiar fluttering feeling inside my stomach that I missed so much while I was swearing off trouble.

Luna and I walked together to the edge of campus, letting the love birds follow behind us. I knew I had to apologize for being a bitch but my tongue suddenly weighed a thousand pounds. The guilt felt easier to carry.

She looked at me like she could read my mind. "Arianna, it's okay. We all get angry and say things we don't mean."

I whispered in a low tone, making sure there was enough distance between the love birds and us before I spoke. "Is that like … your superpower?"

Her laugh was all genuine, pouring out of her mouth, and her fingertips rubbed her eyes in order to catch the happy tears.

What else was I supposed to call it? I was barely believing all this, and now I was asking ridiculous questions I wasn't sure I wanted the answers to.

"I'd never heard someone call it superpowers. That is really funny."

I looked at her with my head tilted to one side. "What do you call what you guys can do then?"

She stopped walking to stare at me very seriously to make her point. "Control, Arianna."

I should have dropped it then but I wanted Bolton to come up more in this conversation. What better way was there than to bring him up myself. "So what's Bolton super power?"

She looked behind us, since Kate's only superpower lately was busting me when things got good.

What a rent a cop.

"Major douche? Incredible asshole? Beats me."

I looked at her with my head tilted to one side. How could they not know or care what his superpowers were? It was like living next to Harry Potter World and you simply shrug when someone asks if you want to go. It wasn't acceptable behavior.

"Excuse me? No one knows?"

She laughed, like it was shocking he held his own secrets with a firm grip. I rolled my eyes at myself for even asking.

Dumb move, Arianna.

Her hand landed on my arm just as we stopped at the opening of the mouth of the hidden path—the same one outlined by Henry Jon. This time we wouldn't be following his ghost into the woods, we were going the other direction to end up behind the boys' locker room.

"You're the only person he's let close in a long time. It's a privilege we don't get afforded."

Her words made me smile, and I quickly wondered if Nyx offered that on his menu of services.

I felt protective of Luna, my roommate and only ally here, and the possibility of her heart hurting made me want to launch a war the size of the battle they once had for Helen of Troy. She deserved for someone to take care of her the way she did all of us.

We all stood still, checking for anyone around us. The coast was clear but Kate refused to set one Gucci shoe on the dirt path overgrown with vegetation.

"Austin," she whined in her too prissy voice. "I *cannot* go in there."

She stressed the word with so much emphasis I watched her face crinkle in disgust at the thought of being forced to blaze that trail. I didn't understand her objection to adventure.

Who plans adventure? Who cares if your shoes get dirty and your hair gets messed up?

I dove into the unknown with no safety net, no back-up plan, and no fear. I wanted every day to be a mystery that I had to unravel.

Kate was the opposite: perfectly armed for every day, every ounce of fun, and planning it all was the adventure for her.

Luna, to my left, was mentally assessing everyone with her deep blue eyes, while I shined the light on the overgrown pathway leading to the boys' locker room and taking the first steps into the wilderness. I was determined to prove my worth, with some good, old-fashioned sabotage.

Luna just wanted everyone to be happy, fed, and hydrated. She was in touch with her feelings, too much for my liking. She coddled everyone like the mother I lost too young, and ironically, I hated the reminder instead of letting her tendencies extend to me too.

I hadn't dragged anyone out here. I was capable of riding out my own plan and enjoying the typical trouble that came right after. I didn't need them to follow me.

I stomped out every ounce of needing anyone the further I got down the path. I looked over my shoulder slightly, not obviously, when I saw Austin following along with Luna. Kate was thrown over his shoulder and being well-preserved from the adventure.

A smile crept up to my mouth from the pit of my stomach, knowing that people followed me, without pressure or force but because they wanted to. I knew I wasn't a princess–now I had two feet firmly placed under me and my crown. There wasn't any doubt left now that I had an army.

The path was a shortcut to behind the building, and it landed us right in front of the emergency exit to the boys' guest locker room.

The guest and home team were firmly separated by a long hallway. Even the girls' locker room was across from the boys', while the guests were down the hall just to create a buffer of loyalty.

Probably Bolton's idea.

I yanked the door open, expecting an alarm that would pump the adrenaline building inside my blood but the quiet was even more eerie. I slipped into the complete darkness, holding the door for Luna behind me. I shined my flashlight onto the surfaces, making sure it was empty—devoid of gear and people.

I dropped my heavy duffle bag on the bench and tucked my phone into my bra strap so it could shine on and I could become hands free.

I packed shaving cream, dish soap, extra laces, even fart canisters to ruin the crisp air in here. Kate scoffed at my bag full of pranks. "That's your sabotage plan? Do you know Caellum? He probably has one of his goons check the room before anyone enters."

Her inability to share all this information before we planned to come here with a bag full of useless pranks would have been nice. Clearly her reign as queen wasn't a gracious one.

"Kate, why don't you share your plans then?"

Luna was between us, and Austin across from her, all circling the bag, as tension became a hot, sticky mess between us. My blue irises had to be dripping in resentment, and as I became all kinds of pissed off, the shade got darker. They always did get a mucky mud color when I was pissed off.

Kate's arms were folded, and her hip popped in an obvious expression of not caring, even if she did. Neither of us were backing down or even arguing with words.

This was all glares—queen against queen.

Austin, being the sympathetic and empathic person he was, suggested we bail on the whole mission. Luna quickly agreed when she realized we still didn't speak though our gritted teeth and pensive eyes.

Finally, I spoke, remembering queens don't need to rule with an iron fist or lace gloves. I could be a new kind of queen. "Comprise? Whatever you're thinking and some pranks."

Kate popped an eyebrow to match every other part of her that was popped too. "I'm not sure you can handle what I have in mind if this is what you brought. I expected more from the troubled girl."

The tension sitting on shoulders felt even more heavy as I kept myself from shooting any more arrows without thinking. I waited patiently for her to continue.

"You're gonna text Caellum. He doesn't know you, and we're gonna ambush him as soon as he steps foot on campus."

She was putting my adventure to death and resurrecting planned revenge.

"He knows who I am," my voice was weak and almost fit into a whisper.

I shouldn't be admitting I reached out to Caellum, let alone that we had some kind of private message rapport.

Everyone looked equally shocked and displaced with their immediate anger. I forced myself to keep my gaze up and shoulders back; I wasn't going to crumble.

"Does Bolton know? You know loyalty to him is, like, required."

Kate didn't say required for what exactly but I got the point. Bolton and loyalty were synonymous. Got it. I shook my head trying to let it soak in further, down deeper, to a spot that would brand my memory.

I didn't want to justify her with a response. Of course Bolton knew, there wasn't much he didn't know.

I wasn't keen on keeping anything from him after how he reacted so similarly as Kate just had. I was actively avoiding telling him about the pages I found after he left the woods.

I knew I needed to show him before he found out on his own.

Kate ripped my phone from my hand, pulled up the app I messaged Caellum on, and bypassed all my password locks without a single hesitation. She typed exhaustively as she spoke out loud each word under her fingers.

Every time she mashed me and effort together, she came out on the other end, seeming so vexed to even be bothered.

It made me cringe.

 Text: *Hey, do you want to meet before the game tomorrow? Little pre-game celebration?*

She smirked at my phone, almost letting her cheeks tint a slight pink, and I knew that meant he replied.

They crowded my phone like it was magic, while I pretended to be bored.

Being the new kid fourteen times really drove home the lesson of not showing people when you care. Showing you care gave you away, and in a snap, that one moment of weakness could be used against you. If I didn't care, then no one else did either.

Win, win.

She read his response out loud: "Switching teams? I'm happy to steal anything belonging to Bolton."

I rolled my eyes in such disappointment. He didn't suspect anything. Bolton wouldn't choose an opponent that wasn't worthy, and this guy was stupid. He was thinking with his dick instead of strategy.

I needed more time to get to know our enemy but Kate moved the timeline up to tomorrow.

She knew her castle was on fire, her crown chipped, and her reign over; that's when moves become messy instead of calculated.

The walk back to the dorms was quiet and slow. The adrenaline was fading, and my thirst for adventure wasn't even close to quenched.

Luna ripped off her black bulky clothes quickly and let her strawberry curls fall down from the pony tail.

She was beautiful in this innocent way, like nothing bad had ever happened to her and everything was still well intact.

She gathered her shower supplies and headed into our cozy bathroom to shower, while I carefully opened my bedside table drawer to the pages I hadn't fully inspected yet. I hid them in plain sight, holding the tradition both Bolton and Henry Jon held, between the pages of the book it was once ripped from.

My fingers ran over the creases carefully, smoothing them down and looking over his penmanship.

> *Henry Jon*
>
> *With Pastor Cotton, Blacksmith Samuel, and Ranger Charles, we were determined to exhaust ourselves with finding their weakness. Our days were numbered, until I had to hold up my end of the bargain. We needed a deicide, the killer of false gods. I prayed every night for guidance from the one and only true God. Right when we were defeated most, after we called upon everyone but the Devil himself to call back his children, we were given a holy sign.*
>
> *My sweet daughter would sleep walk on occasion, for this reason I strung a bell to her door handle that alerted me she*

was scampering off. We had gone months without her waking in the darkness, until the Devil, who lived on the edge of town, taunted her faith.

I tied my robe around my midsection and grabbed my gun, standing at attention next to my lamp. I followed behind her, far enough to not wake her but close enough to see without a lamp. She walked into the woods, like she had known every twig, pebble, and curve of the land by heart. I stopped behind a thick tree when she stopped, peering slightly, watching her kneel down onto the thick grass.

I had never seen my sweet girl speak in tongues when she woke in the night. Her voice was smooth, like she was almost singing, when she spoke the word Ophiotaurus. She was speaking the Devil's language, and it shook my faith in my God. My pure, innocent Rosalia was being dragged deeper into the grasp of the Devil.

I waited, watching her hands feel the grass around her, like she was blind, until I heard the grass moving. I couldn't spot the culprit of the movements but I heard it coming as I aimed my gun to shoot right past her ear if I saw a threat. I froze when I saw a bull emerge his head from the bushes. I allowed my breath to even out as I steadied my hands again. Rosalia got up from her knees and presented sugar cubes to the animal, like it was her pet horse. I watched the bull push forward, and I saw the rest of its body was a serpent.

The door to the bathroom creeped open, scaring the shit out of me as I read along, feeling every tang of anxiety Henry Jon did.

She casually asked after glaring at the old book in my lap, "Working on your project?"

I should have been but I was captive to Rosalia's story. I needed to know what had happened to her like I needed to breathe.

Something inside me felt connected to her more than someone who was just relating to the character; she was changing something inside me, awakening a cosmic struggle.

I retired from my book after Luna snuggled up into bed and clearly was getting ready to sleep. Not willing to disrupt her sleep, I flicked my lamp off and closed the book with the new pages still unread.

CHAPTER 19

Arianna

On game days, campus seemed less gloomy and more alive. I was the displaced dark cloud in the perfect sky today. I had a date with revenge that didn't feel right, and it was stirring my thoughts all day.

Bolton didn't even come to class, and the loyalty branded in my mind was churning with guilt, more and more, with every class change and saunter down the hallway without him there.

Kate was giddy in French, like she couldn't wait for the moment Caellum was alone, even though I was in the dark about what was actually going to transpire after that.

I get him alone, and then what? I talk him to death? Great plan, Kate.

I leaned over my desk during our quiz to gain her attention, while I watched her pink pen glide from question to question effortlessly, especially for someone who talked instead of learning.

I was trying to decipher any of the gibberish on my quiz, having never taken French, and I had paid attention as much as I could, just to get further lost.

"We need to talk about the plan."

She didn't even look up from her paper. "Don't worry about it. I've got it."

I was being kept in the dark without even a lighter—a stupid little lighter that would barely illuminate anything.

Going to class, I looked for Bolton, or even Nyx. My conscience wanted me to come clean to him before I found out what Kate's plan really was.

Something clawed its way from the bottom of my stomach to my throat, and it brought the threat to drag up breakfast with it.

Up until my last class around 3 PM, there still wasn't any Bolton, any of the boys, or even breakfast regurgitated.

The game wasn't until 7, so I had time to hide out in my room with Henry Jon's pages.

I dragged myself up the stairs forcefully, lacking even the energy to take the next step. I was burned out, and I didn't understand why. I had stayed clear of any adventure, not for a lack of trying. Just being at Arcadia was exhausting.

I let my bag fall off my shoulder in the middle of our empty room before I crawled into bed, completely clothed in my uniform that wasn't wrinkle free before this decision, so I determined it didn't matter.

Yanking the covers up to my chin finally, a yawn forced my jaw into a stretch. I was forcing my eyes open and the wheels to turn in my mind enough to prepare for whatever Kate had up her sleeve. My eyelids, at half-mast, closed anyways, while I begged my mind to keep trying until a deep sleep snatched all of my efforts.

It was a kind of sleep I hadn't had in years. I had been functioning on four hours a night since I could remember.

I was probably an insomniac at this point. Not even coffee elicited the slightest buzz. Nothing but an entire bottle of NyQuil really put me on my ass.

The severity of four hours a night only hit my bones once in a while.

Bolton's voice tumbled against my ear drums, and fear seeped into my soul. "Run."

Wherever I was, it was too dark to even see my own hand in front of my face. I looked down, trying to listen to the ground against my Doc Martens carefully for clues but I came up empty. Everything was put on mute, except Bolton's voice, echoing for me to run.

I felt a sharp pain in my lower back, and it made my breath hitch and freeze. I tensed around a foreign object lodged into my back that my hands couldn't reach, and my vision was robbed by the heavy black of night.

His hot breath caressed my ear without feeling him touch me anywhere else, expertly touching everyone he came into contact with while keeping a distance I envied. Nothing touched him, not me sitting on his throne, not me wearing an invisible crown, not our moments my mind constantly replayed.

Bolton was untouchable.

"I told you to run. Still not listening."

I still couldn't find my breath, as a painful groan escaped my lips, hoping if something came out that the pain would ease.

"Do you want me to hurt you, Arianna? Hurting you isn't some trophy. It will end us both."

The sarcasm that ran through my veins wanted to smirk through the pain and taunt him with how strong I could be but the pain brought me to my knees. I heard the dead leaves crunch under my bones. I was left speechless by the pain, something so rare it shocked even me.

"I will burn the world down, the end of us, if you make me hurt you."

Slowly I felt myself bleed in and out of consciousness. It was hard to tell when my eyes were closed or not, both dark, but one held Bolton's voice.

I woke up choking on my breath and the dream being the last thing on my mind. A cold sweat covered the back of my neck, chest, and back, like a fingerprint of my dream, all the affected areas.

I sat up in our empty and dark room, trying to regain composure. I touched everything around me, trying to convince myself that this was reality, tangible, while that dream was a version of Bolton's betrayal that didn't exist.

Turning over, I saw that my phone read 5:30 PM, and it was hard to be mad. I wanted to casually sleep through Kate's plans.

She hijacked my adventure and now my revenge too.

I leaned over, tugging the drawer open that kept Henry Jon's pages safely hidden in the pages between the old binding.

I opened where I had left off last night. After the half serpent/half bull appeared for Rosalia, and Henry Jon was made a believer in something beyond good and evil.

Something, or someone, like Bolton, playing both sides and making it look easy.

When Bolton was good, he almost glowed, and the hard edges seemed personable.

When Bolton was bad, he made me question what real torture was when he had your body aching but begging for more.

He was an enigma wrapped up in beauty and pain.

By the time I dragged my still heavy body out of bed, it was almost time for her "plan" to kick off amateur hour. Everything about Kate was meant to irritate your patience.

She was a typical mean girl, without the two-faced jabs. If she had a jab, she didn't pretend to be anything but herself—one face, one girl (typically in pink), and no filter for her attitude.

My phone kept buzzing against the wood of the bedside table, while I threw on whatever my greedy hands pulled out of my drawer. It didn't really matter what I chose, as long as it wasn't this stiff uniform, which got me nothing, except for detention for the unique spin I constantly put on it. I wore thigh highs instead of tights, Doc Martens instead of loafers, and none of my uniform was ever as pristine as the other girls.

Tonight, some leggings, a crop top, and flannel tied around my waist would have to do. Nothing designer or ironed, just all me.

The field was starting to become flooded with people ready to cheer on the players, for both sides.

Exeter was a rival of Arcadia in every sport, and picking a side was half the fun. Their rival had everyone in the stands involved, invested, and intrigued.

After seeing the game myself last time they played, I was in shock at the push and pull. All my other schools were firmly either the loser or winner. There was no push or pull.

Arcadia wasn't anything like my other schools. The prestige practically assaulted you with just a glance, never mind attending here.

I got to the girls' locker room to change, since I went against my better judgment and tried out for the team. That wasn't even the shocking part. That part was that my name sat comfortably on the short list of girls who made the team.

My earbuds blared PVRIS's angsty ballads, which really sounded like poetry to my ears, when I walked in and went straight to my locker. So far, I was unscathed by Kate's watchful eye.

I spoke too soon. I opened my locker to yank my cheer uniform off the hanger, closed my locker, and was scared shitless by her standing there.

"You're late. Get ready quick. We have boys to make drool."

I let my head hang as I plucked my earbuds out of my ears and cursed myself for changing. I shouldn't have bothered. What a waste of being awake. I didn't bother giving her shit. I got changed and pulled my purple hair into a half up ponytail—the best I could manage with my medium length hair.

I smoothed out the crimson red and navy blue uniform in the mirror before I shifted my eyes up to see myself looking more polished than I had since my mom died.

It was an easy marker to my life: before my mom died or after. Two very different versions of myself, the same person, but a hell of a lot more tricks up my sleeves now.

She wouldn't approve of my love for vengeance, adventure, and danger. She wouldn't even approve of my words becoming arrows and piercing all the fragile skin I had.

I smiled big in the mirror, pretending to be someone I didn't know for a second—someone who didn't have so many defense mechanisms and so many people that she had fallen in love with just to vanish into a new town.

The smile faded quickly into my content straight lip. I gripped the porcelain sink so hard my hands flared up with red in every crease. I wasn't going to let myself be another person who judged me.

Stop being a little bitch. You don't need fake smiles and a mom. You wear a goddamn crown, and you need to act like it.

I guess I had a thing for affirmations. My straight lip curled into a smirk, and my eyes got muddy with deception, as I pushed out a huff to fog up the mirror before I drew a crown above my head. I stared at it until it bled. See? Even the royal bleed the same kind of fleeting defeat.

I walked away from my doodle on the mirror with my head held higher, letting the smirk act as armor.

Kate told the girls to start sideline cheers and waited for them to leave before unfolding her arms like her guard was down.

"You. Don't you have someone to meet? I'll be right outside the door. Make sure to get him outside. I have the cuffs."

"Do I wanna know why you own handcuffs?"

She smiled to herself, looking down then back up to look me in the eye. "Cops and robbers, duh."

I felt the game had different rules or was code for something. It explained a lot.

I wasn't interested in being a cop or robber. I didn't want to break the rules or follow them, I wanted to create them.

"The kid's game?"

She popped an eyebrow at me. "Not how Austin plays it. Everyone likes being the bad girl."

I grabbed the cuffs from her hands trying to erase the images of Kate being a type of bad he could punish.

Ew.

I pivoted on the ball of my foot just how Kate taught me during practices. Throwing it in her face felt good, and I walked away with more sass in my step than normal.

I inched closer and closer to the guest locker room, while I messaged Caellum to meet me by the emergency exit sign glowing above me. I prayed he wouldn't respond but when my phone buzzed in my hand, I knew it was him.

♑ Caellum: *I don't celebrate before I win.*

♐ Me: *I'm worth it.*

♑ Caellum: *Oh, I know that. Bolton shoots higher than the normal standards. I wouldn't expect anything less.*

I tried not to blush at his assumption. I wouldn't expect Bolton to choose anyone less worthy than someone royal enough to fit a crown.

♐ Me: *A little pregame fun. Come on.*

♑ Caellum: *I can't take the begging. Okay, exit sign in five.*

It wasn't five minutes later, when the locker room door opened, and he paraded down the short hallway to me and the exit. I gripped the cuffs behind me, not making any moves for him to hear the metal clank together and give me away.

He came closer, slowly, like I was his thunder, and his flames would cause a combustion big enough to burn even us. It made me uneasy, and his green eyes were intensifying the closer he got. I wanted to look away before my fake smile melted down my face.

Instead, I was pinned against the door with his piercing eyes.

He didn't leave much space between us, and he licked his lips as he looked down at me. Fire and thunder, dangerously close. I swallowed back kneeing him in the crotch. I didn't have any other reason, except for his smug-ass face being too close to mine.

What was the only thing keeping me from driving my knee into the only parts he was thinking with?

Bolton.

He deserved this win, my loyalty, and revenge for whatever this loser did to him that made his soul hate like he created the emotion.

His fingers manipulated strands falling out of my ponytail behind my ear as he leaned down, and I held my breath.

"Do you think I'm stupid, bitch? I wouldn't waste a victory on Bolton's sloppy seconds … who, actually, really looks like thirds."

The metal cuffs dug into my grip, leaving impressions I knew would be there when I let go. I let one hand go, rising in a motion to slap him and catch him off guard so I could cuff him to anything. He wasn't going to make it out the door to Kate if I didn't sell it enough here.

Before I could move any further, his strong arms closed around me, and he fished the cuffs from my grip. With one hard yank, he practically left a burn from the metal on my palms. He was stronger than he looked and acted, and way more than I could handle.

In a quick move, he had me handcuffed but only one wrist. I laughed thinking he messed up, when I pulled my arm and realized I was cuffed to the door handle of the emergency exit.

Kate's plan was used against us.

I should have been on the outside, away from any kind of help I could shout for but if he wasn't smart enough to think of that, then I wasn't offering to adjust myself to the outside instead.

"You really thought you could play me? Bolton knows better. No, I'm guessing you went rogue. Wanna win over his black little heart?"

I gathered all the moisture in my mouth and spit so hard I tasted the sour aftertaste. He leaned into me but not enough to let my free hand get ahold of him. "You're gonna regret that. Hope your little boyfriend is ready to get crushed without his little cheerleader providing false hope. Gimme a 'F'…" he leaned forward even more, like he couldn't hear me chant with him. "Gimme an 'A'. Gimme an 'I' and a 'L'. What's that spell?"

He taunted me over and over by spelling "fail" and thinking I'd actually give him the answers. This plan was dumb, not me.

His face was close enough for me to contemplate more hideous evils worse than spitting. "Fail… hope the Black Heart Prince appreciates the valiant efforts."

I twisted my wrist until it was sore and contorted myself every way I could think of to release me, while I watched him walk away.

Not only did the plan not work but it fed the monster living in Caellum. It wasn't hard to see why they hated each other now.

Two different kinds of kings at war for the throne.

The hallway I was now stuck in was the opposite direction the teams would take to the field. I was stuck here until Kate realized I wasn't slow but royally fucked—literally.

It wasn't until the game started and the cheers echoed into the locker rooms that Kate tanked the exit door open to find me dragged along with it. "You were supposed to handcuff him, not him handcuff you. Duh."

"Just give me the key." I was too annoyed to put up with her duh's and omg's. She fished into her cheerleading top to pull out a small key like a damn magic trick.

"Who would have thought? I'm saving your ass."

I unchained myself from the handcuffs and rubbed my wrist where I had metal burn. I always imagined breaking out some cuffs in the bedroom but those fantasies were ruined when I felt the aftermath.

She walked ahead of me with so much pep in her step she could have been a one woman cheer team.

As soon as we walked out of the tunnel, the first half was moments away from ending and the crowd roared with raw energy. I searched for Bolton's number on the field. I found him quickly, when every collision on the field jarred my eyes.

He was throwing the ball when another player collided into him, taking him to the ground as the ball flew from his fingers.

I knew the other player was Caellum, as soon as he popped back up, only to lean down again. I couldn't hear what he was saying to Bolton but I was sure it wasn't sportsman-like.

Bolton shot up, and his gloved hand yanked the mouth guard on Caellum's helmet, before their respective teams formed sides. It was an all-out war on the field, and the ref was slow to actually stop anything. He was willing to let them kill each other.

The ref finally called a timeout, and I caught up to Kate, who was directing the cheerleaders in their sideline cheers. I watched Bolton walk to the sideline after his coach shouted his name.

I didn't dare break formation, even though I hadn't even really started trying but Kate's wrath would outlast Bolton's. She was the lesser evil.

He walked right past the bench, the water, and towels for the team went straight to the tunnel entrance.

My eyes collided with Kate's, who was already looking at me intensely. I let my brows collapse, and my face turned into a physical apology for what I was about to do as the girls kept cheering around me.

I broke formation and jogged lightly to the tunnel to Bolton. I knew he probably didn't want to see me but I had this nagging need to try.

The tunnel wasn't cute, it was just a concrete tunnel leading to the locker rooms. It wasn't anywhere people wanted to be; it was a funnel for the anxious nerves, excited rage-to-be on the field, and the emotions that couldn't be trapped within these walls. Without those feelings swirling in the air, the tunnel felt barren and empty—dead, even.

I heard his helmet fly against the concrete floor creating an echoing bang that made me jump.

I should be used to this feeling. Every time I was around Bolton, my bones jumped and my functioning normally wasn't as seamless as it should be.

"Bolton?"

He roared so loudly I thought it was meant to deafen me to any other should but his vocals.

"I was just checking on you … "

It was an on-the-spot lie that had as many holes as Swiss cheese. I was there to beg for forgiveness if Caellum had told him anything.

My plan to prove my loyalty was hijacked by Kate's plan to prove peasants shouldn't be crowned queen.

"Check on me, huh? After you pissed off Caellum enough to reward us with another loss? We actually had a chance this time."

The guilt sunk in and paralyzed me head to toe. Everything about me stilled; even as he walked forward, coated in pads, making him seem even bigger, I still couldn't move. The navy blue jersey bounced off his eyes, making them darker—villainous. I should

be scared of him, and maybe somewhere in the back of my mind, behind lust and envy, I was.

"I ... I was trying to help."

He was right in my face now, so close I could see the sweat beaded up along his hairline and even the ends were wet. He didn't push the rebellious pieces of his hair away that fell into his eyes. "By giving him ammunition? You don't know him. You might as well have danced on his fucking grave."

I stood so still I felt like a sore muscle, tight and quivering from the excess tension.

"I was trying to prove my loyalty."

I was too close to actually see if he got closer but I noticed his lips more than before. I swallowed the lump of desire in my throat. I wanted to keep hating him: his attitude, his good looks, his ability to always be right, and malfunctions I experienced every time he was close.

Wanted to, was easier said than done when need took priority.

His tone was soaked with disapproval: "Next time don't prove anything, Arianna."

My mouth collapsed as I ran through my on-cue sarcastic responses that I could have given him.

He moved around me, like he could slither instead of walk now. His still gloved hand reached around my waist and pulled me back into his pads. He was touching me just how I ached for him and now there was football equipment wedged between us.

I melted into his touch when my head fell to one side, begging for his skin to touch mine. I felt his lips move against my neck, as he spoke in a less disappointed tone.

"Queens don't have to prove anything."

The air I was holding in was hot and bitter. I was desperate for the guy I hated to do more than whisper against my neck.

I regretted my next moves with so much angst I could have stomped my foot. "If I'm such a queen, why do you refuse to be my king?"

It wasn't until my question hung in the air, unanswered, that I understood the error of shooting off the arrows of my words without permission. I never regretted my unfiltered thoughts … until this one.

No one wanted to be the needy one, the one who made the first confession, or the one who admitted something unreturned.

Yet, here I was, in a tunnel during a game break, being a type of extra hated.

"I'm not going to be anyone's anything, Arianna. Stop trying to make me not *hate* you."

I knew the feeling.

I wanted to hate him the same way I did when I met him but now I hated him for not giving into me, his temperament, his ability to hate me, when I could return the favor.

His voice didn't get louder until the word "hate." That word felt more powerful, louder, exactly how it sounded. It ate at my soul.

Why wouldn't he stop hating me? I was prepared to call a truce.

I pushed past him, making sure my shoulder connected with his padding, which hurt me more than him. I wasn't going to stop hating him until he stopped hating me.

I rolled my eyes for fun. I had just pissed off his mortal enemy without trying. I could hold a grudge.

Back on the field, I kept my eyes anywhere he wasn't, even though I could feel the anger behind his orbs trying to burn me from afar. The only time his gaze sacrificed me was when he was on the field or arguing with Nyx.

It wasn't hard to miss something was going on with Nyx every time Bolton's hand pushed against his chest like he was holding him back.

The curiosity had its claws deep in my motivation, and now I had to know what was happening.

The whole game I was mouthing cheers and half-assing my way to the edge closest to the team, even though they were masters at low tones in their husky voices and keeping whatever it was private. It didn't stop me from trying.

Kate barked my direction, "Arianna! Are you on cheer or the football team?"

Bolton

The dark gray sky airbrushed with smoky clouds opened up into a downpour. I could barely feel it until my glove slipped against the ball, and I had to readjust my grip, before I soared it to Nyx half a field away in a perfect spiral.

I may not have felt it through my jersey and pads but the field became softer than I was used to, and my vision became tainted by the sheet of rain.

Every sense was paralyzed, and the home field advantage lost any real value when Caellum's team already beat us once this season.

I was just living through the replay at this point.

My muscles screamed with ache, the lack of morale felt heavy instead of light, and I wanted to give up. Giving up wasn't an option, it wasn't part of my make-up.

I glanced up at the clock, draining down to seconds in the last quarter, and I rushed into the hoard of oversized defensive line-backers. The clash of my pads against theirs sounded like thunder without the lightning.

No, my lightning was on the sidelines being the all-consuming distraction she knew she was.

I was pushed down to the ground with one heavy shove, no matter how much I felt rooted into the ground.

With the same force, I fell against the soaked field, rattling in my cage of pads, until my body went limp and somber.

I stared right into the rain, watching the angry drops create some kind of illusion that I was still moving when I wasn't.

I knew the clock hadn't run out of seconds, because everyone was still moving and the crowd was trying to motivate whoever had the ball on my team with their sheer screams.

If that shit works for you. It doesn't get my dick hard like purple hair. She wasn't cheering.

I knew she wasn't cheering. My head dropped to my left side, and her expression, through the drops, was troubled—a kind of troubled I didn't know she could conjure since she was always creating trouble in my life.

For a split second, I thought of the edges of my organs, how far they'd expand, and what my kindness towards her could do to me. If she was the one, she would die, and if she wasn't, she would still die.

Loving her was a dooming fate that I wasn't ready to accept, so until then, my heart was going to stay small and my kindness limited.

I heard the buzzer go off, and I still felt unmotivated to get up, to be anything vertical. I pushed my helmet off and let my arm fall back down, not caring where the helmet went.

We had lost for the second time in the season to Exeter, and our chances of being in the finale was slimmer than Kate's waistline.

Nyx offered his hand, dangling it lazily, unmotivated like me. We weren't losers; we didn't know how to lose gracefully.

"They didn't play by the rules. You should have let me break them too."

I could hear the anger in his voice. It wasn't directed at me, so I didn't care. The whole game, Nyx wanted to use the parts of him that weren't human, the parts the circle hid, and the parts that were unexplainable. His strength wasn't something that the crowd on both sides of us were going to overlook, but he was convinced the pounding we took was at the hands of Caellum's abilities.

"You know the rules. I'm not dealing with Alba's shit."

I slapped his hand away, finally getting up, and when I did, my eyes locked on Arianna.

Looking away wasn't an option, she wasn't some girl or a quick fuck.

She was a queen that I hadn't taken as my own yet, but she still demanded the respect of royalty.

I wasn't in the mood for the troubled expression she wore the whole game or the questions I knew she wanted to ask but didn't know how.

Henry Jon's journal begged more questions than answers–at least it was historic and proved I wasn't a crock of shit if she wasn't going to believe me.

I couldn't believe how much control she was hosting in her rebellious tongue. She hadn't asked me one stupid question or made one stupid remark. She was all intimacy, open wounds, and emotions that I wouldn't understand in the same way people around me did.

Instead of intimacy, I saw sex.

Instead of open wounds, I saw fear.

Instead of emotions, I saw annoyance.

I was, in essence, in a teenage body made of things that didn't belong here.

I pushed right by Arianna, leaving her wanting things I couldn't give her—not on my highest high or even this crippling fucking low.

I heard her voice beg for attention: "Bolton, are you—"

It was smart of her to cut herself off from finishing that sentence. The answer wouldn't have been pleasant.

I didn't shower until everyone left the locker room, wearing our loss longer than anyone else. I threw my pads in the bin in the corner on top of the pile and let my jersey pollute the floor, just like I would have in my room.

My body was covered in moisture, rain, and sweat dancing on my skin, as I walked to the showers naked. I wasn't shy. My body was a temple, a host, and one I took pride in.

Perfect was a way to be as close to my true form as possible.

Twisting the knob all the way to the right, I didn't even wait for it to heat up when I pushed myself under its unforgiving spray. It lashed my skin in a punishing way that I let myself deserve—not for long, just enough to get a grip and move on.

There was nothing I could do now. None of us controlled time.

As soon as I twisted the water off, the dripping showerhead echoed against someone else in the room. Shaking my head, I pushed my palms back squeezing the excess moisture from my hair.

It was a locker room—no locks, no privacy. Whoever was there wasn't going to possibly make my mood worse … unless you had purple hair, pretended to hate me, and was now making risky decisions in order to please me.

She was bowing to me as king, and if we hadn't just lost, I would have been laughing at her subordinate behavior.

I rounded the corner, leaving the shower stalls behind me, when I saw Arianna straddling the long bench taking up the only space between the rows of lockers. Her legs were as wide apart as could be and her arms straight with her palms flat against the wood, the only thing blocking the view of her panties.

"Can I help you?"

I had to pretend to not care she was there or that I was now thinking of her panties.

"I wanted to check on you."

She was looking down the whole time the sentence fell out of her mouth, like she wouldn't admit to worrying about me. When she finally looked up, her cheeks turned a deep red, like she had just ran a mile in under seven minutes, when she realized that I was only in a towel.

"Checked on. Done. Anything else, Arianna? I kind of need to change."

She didn't move, except for her eyes, which looked down again. My once tough-as-nails, firecracker, queen material looked a lot like average instead.

She had questions floating around in her head, so many I could clearly sense them battling for space.

"I dreamed you killed me."

She stood up slowly, still trying to not make eye contact after staring at me for two hours straight on the field.

"Did you learn anything from Henry Jon?"

I wasn't waiting for her to leave to tug my towel off and change. I had been naked and in a towel long enough.

I was done wearing the loss. I stayed facing my locker, trying to be modest, as I stood there completely naked in front of an already blushing girl. I pulled my boxers on first, making sure I didn't kill her here and now.

"A lot of useless things. Things that don't explain you … or us."

I pushed past, her zipping up my black hoodie and pulling the hood up to cover my still wet hair. "That book is us."

I could tell by the look on her face that I was confusing her, and she didn't like being toyed with that way.

"What does that mean? Why can't you ever just say what you mean? I don't need a riddle."

I walked past her enough to lean over and let my low tone hit her ear, "What's the fun in dying, if I tell you when and where?"

Leaving her there to ponder more riddles was an asshole move, I know. I should just come clean but I already said enough—enough to get me in trouble with the wrong people, like the circle.

I wanted to tell her everything: about the ritual, about the circle, explain Henry Jon was our love story's first documentation, and explain this probably wouldn't be the last time she forgot and I had to force her to remember.

Luckily, everyone else in the circle got a turn, so I didn't have to repeat our history being reenacted over and over each year.

I was always prepared. I wasn't expecting to relive her anytime soon. Once Rosalia, Clementine, Isabella, Florence ... she had had many different names but only one person was brave enough to transcribe our encounters: Henry Jon.

It took me years to find that book and to have something to hold onto in her absence.

There was no pizza after this game, not that I would be caught dead rewarding myself with anything after a game like that. Even the wins, I would celebrate alone in my room, contemplating how many more times I'd be forced to do senior year over.

The good didn't outweigh the bad in this scenario.

The circle had their annual Wednesday meeting to discuss Arianna and the ritual. I should be whatever version of excited I could manage but anyone discussing her meant discussing her death—her sacrifice. I wasn't 100% positive she was my Rosalia reborn without her memories or simply my loneliness finally catching up to me.

Nyx was outside, smoking off the loss, when I crept up the stairs to the faculty building. "How much did you tell her?"

He didn't shift his eyes to me in a violent way that I would have expected, when he finally asked me the question. Nyx didn't play by the rules any more than I did, yet his tone was all judgment and no rebellion.

"Enough."

We had slipped right into the role of best friends when he transferred into Arcadia but this was a two way street.

If you wanted information, then you had to give it.

Everyone was already there when we walked downstairs to the candlelit basement where we kept our secrets. Some of us were forced to wear them instead, like me—the curse of being an awful king. I had to protect us, put the circle first, while everyone acted "normal" for the fourteenth time.

I didn't bother sitting; I knew I wasn't staying long enough to hear any bullshit. Arianna had just poked the bear; we just lost another game to Caellum's team; and now I had to hear everyone plan to sacrifice Arianna during the ritual.

Cheyanne dropped a Ziplock bag on the table, like it spoke for itself when witchcraft wasn't any of our native tongues. It was the connection to home for her—focusing on the abilities that no one else had in contrast to the mortals surrounding us here.

With a huge sigh, she sat back and explained, "I did the spell. It's her. I nearly set fire to the dorms."

Cheyanne did some kind of spell with the few strands of hair I managed to steal. I was helping them kill her. I didn't have much choice.

Kate was the first to react. "Seriously? Are you sure?"

She was used to life semi-human. She enjoyed it, actually. Going home wasn't on her priority list. She had Austin, and that's all she needed.

Human emotions came with the body: hormones, loneliness, jealousy, belonging, or in Kate's case, love.

In this form, the emotions were like thunder rumbling through your bones, demanding every ounce of your damn attention and bleeding into everything else with ease.

"It means she can do the ritual, Kate. Keep up."

I spoke to her without even looking in her direction, while I thumbed Arianna's file sitting between books in a stack.

Why was it down here? What was Alba planning? What was in the basically empty file before he knew I was going to thumb through student files?

I wasn't in the habit of asking pointless questions without answers, which meant I better figure it out.

Glancing over my shoulder, I watched them all enthusiastically entranced with a possible way out of this.

A graduation from this purgatory.

That was all I needed. Enough hope created a flame, and everyone was drawn to the flame. Rolling up the bulkier file, I shoved it under my shirt and halfway down my pants, trying to conceal what I was going to take without permission.

She was mine, so by extension, her file was mine too. Now all I needed was a quick getaway.

Creeping out of the room was easy, except when it came to Nyx. I glanced over the group one last time before I climbed the stairs, and his eyes were trying to pierce through me, tacking me to the wall and demanding answers. I didn't have any. I didn't know why I was protecting Arianna in one breath and serving her up to the circle in the next. My heart and head were in a constant battle.

One was going to win—either the knife of logic or my bleeding heart.

My body couldn't keep up with my desire to get back to my dorm room to crack open whatever news was in her file.

This was a time I really wished for abilities–wishing didn't make some bullshit abilities suddenly appear.

I was the only one cursed with even more normalcy.

Bolton

I was still in the hallway on the wrong side of my door, when I opened the file and thumbed through the information, including a police report and restraining order marked with McAllen, Texas Police Department at the top of both.

I really couldn't be surprised someone else felt like Arianna wasn't their cup of tea either but to this degree? Police and restraining orders?

I guess she had as many secrets as I did.

Now I didn't feel as bad for being an asshole to protect mine.

I read the report more closely, even though the information just gave case numbers and files to reference beyond this sheet. This was a placeholder stating she was a minor, and it was sealed up for her own protection.

This world separates mistakes as an adult and adolescent like it will determine your character. They can't send you off into the adult world already stained.

In my world, all mistakes are punishable, and the severity depended which god you pissed off.

Zeus was the one you didn't piss off... ever.

I should know. He was my king, and I was one of his subjects. We all were. We were created from anger, honor, lust, desperation, need, respect, despair... all written in the stars for a reason.

I was immortalized for saving a family when Zeus honored my sacrifice with a constellation forever in the sky. That was my first death I outlived. I thought that it would be the only death.

Our essences, who we truly were, are immortalized, reborn with each death. And when lost, only the circle could take us home, at least that's what the legends have told us before our gods died.

Now, I was pretty sure the magic of them was going to die with us too.

The file gave me enough to go on without any real facts. The rest would be easy to pry from Arianna. At first, her hate was real; now, it was her playing pretend. I was pretending too—not to protect my heart like she was but to protect her from a certain death.

If it meant going home, then the circle would do whatever that took. Fourteen people came before and died, just for us to see the desperation in our eyes while they bled out, and we were still stuck here like some bad joke.

Clearly, we didn't learn our lesson. We convinced each other it was a fluke and not the right person, even after carefully vetting them.

I had fourteen different people's blood on my hands—blood I couldn't wash away. I fell from honor and grace, pretty quickly.

I was going to hide the file in my room before I decided to use it against Arianna when I pushed her for the missing answers.

I texted her, while I still stood in my hallway on the wrong side of my door.

♈ Me: *Meet me in the library. Come alone.*

⤴ Arianna: *Why, so you can blow me off again? I'm not in the mood to be Nancy Drew tonight. Role play with someone else.*

↑ Me: *Truce?*

It was the only way I could justify gaining her answers, by giving her something in return: a truce. I knew she wouldn't let that slip by her. Henry Jon was teasing her with every page, and there was no real conclusion in sight. He went crazy, leading every witch hunt and losing everyone's trust, trying to find Rosalia. No one believed him, and all he had were the pages of his journal, hoping to save someone's favorite.

The library closed every night at 9 PM, our keycards worked no matter what time it was. Clearly a weak spot in their security. I slipped inside, even closing the door behind me slowly and carefully, just in case security was doing rounds.

He was only ever here on the weekends when the student body was sure to get themselves into more trouble. He was middle-aged, overweight, and wore headphones on patrol—so not smart. He was easy to trick and avoid.

I climbed the stairs to the second level like I was on autopilot for more privacy in a dark, closed library. I sat on the edge of the thick cherry wood table waiting to hear the door marking her arrival.

↑ Me: *Upstairs.*

⤴ Arianna: *Not creepy at all…*

I smirked, pressing my tongue to the inside of my lip distorting it from growing bigger. She was a smart ass 24/7, in-person and in-text. Every time her attitude transferred to her tongue, I swear my dick jumped into action, reminding me my taste pool became smaller and smaller, down to one person, named Arianna.

She walked along the railing, letting her fingers slide behind her against the chunky wood banister, making me notice his journal in her hand. We were both armed with evidence, ready to throw it at each other, and eventually call a truce.

"So I'm here. You ready to spill some secrets, King of Arcadia Prep?"

Her fierce tone didn't make me want to do anything but fuck her against the banister while she called me king.

I waved the folder in front of me, out from being rolled up in my back pocket of my jeans. "Why did you really leave your last school?"

Her composure shattered as soon as she saw the ugly blue folder that hid everything for her, sealed up and states away. She didn't even have to carry it around unless her subconscious was weaker than she wanted to seem.

"Where did you get that?"

"That's not an answer. Who's the kid with the restraining order?"

She looked like she wanted to run away, she forced herself still, shaking slightly, as her face tried to regain her normal composure again. "What are you? How does Henry Jon know about you?"

"I'm not answering anything until you do. Eye for an eye."

Her eyes looked down, contemplating if I was tricking her. I wanted to but Arianna was in even more danger now. The circle was ready to sacrifice her, and she was still in the dark.

I was being forced to show my hand before I was ready. I stepped closer to her, leaving the folder on the table and letting my hand take hers. She felt warm compared to my constant cold, and she tingled against my palm, trying to melt my heart in the process.

Her eyes snapped up to mine.

"I'm not tricking you. I can't protect you if you aren't honest with me," I did my best to keep my tone even.

She scoffed, like everything I said was a lie that she couldn't believe. "That's rich, coming from the guy who's done nothing but lie to me."

I searched my memories trying to find a lie in our timeline and came up empty. If anything, I was brutally honest.

She saw my confusion bubbling to the surface. She pushed past me to lean against one of the bookshelves, taking the warmth away from our interlaced fingers.

"I don't need more lying, Bolton. My mom died when I was younger, and all I heard was nothing but lying: how it would get better, it'd hurt less, how I'd feel her with me no matter what... All lies. Then my dad said he'd be around more and take different positions for work. More lies. I don't even know where he is in the world. Top secret, even from his daughter. I haven't heard from him in weeks. So, don't be another person lying to me."

I watched her sit on the table and leave me by the banister like she took my upper hand from me. Crossing her legs, she looked comfortable, waiting for everything to unravel, and confident she'd get what she wanted.

I was about to storm her castle and claim her comfort and confidence as my rewards.

"I'm not just lying to you. I'm lying to myself, Arianna. Do you think I want to be this guy? Bound to a human form, soaked in hormones and angst, and chasing after you? I'm a fucking god. I don't belong here."

"Makes two of us, yet, here we are stuck together at Arcadia Prep."

I let my hand manipulate her knee off the other and my palms held them apart long enough for me to push myself between them. I wasn't just storming her castle; I was winning now. I pulled her knees towards me, forcing us closer. I could see her pulse quicken on her neck. Her lips collapsed, and her chest expanded and deflated quicker.

"What happened in Texas, Arianna?"

Her response sounded like a moan, breathy and low: "I can't explain it. It's not that easy…"

"Something happened to that boy because of you?" I made sure my hands smoothed up the outside of her thighs and stuck to her ass. She wasn't fighting me; she had no reason to. She didn't even see me winning the battle.

Everything about her hesitated, even her lungs expanding into my own chest. I was so close that I could smell her minty gum from her puffs of breath escaping. . She was pouring out the warmth of her heart against my cold.

"It happened so fast. I didn't… he just started having a seizure. I didn't give him anything. We weren't drinking. He just grabbed my arm."

She didn't look at me while she spoke, like it'd change how I looked at her when I was sure the blood on my hands were going to trump whatever happened in Texas.

I pushed her obnoxious purple hair behind her ear, like I was pulling back the curtain to her glassy eyes, which welled up instantly as her sentence finished.

With my thumb catching her chin, I pulled her face up to mine, and she whispered between us, "I don't want to hurt you. That's all I do, hurt people, make them love me just to leave them."

She wasn't going to hurt me; she was going to be hurt by me.

"You aren't going to hurt me. Impossible."

"I hurt him without even trying."

"I'm not him. I'm your king and—"

Arianna cut me off before I could finish when I realized she finished my thoughts for me. "…and I'm your queen."

Without any answers, I pushed my lips onto her minty mouth, as my hand snaked up to her throat with a loose grip, waiting for her to react. Her tension melted into my hand as my grip got tighter, and I forced my tongue into her mouth. I wasn't weak, and neither was she. We could endure the pain, the suffering, the chasing, even the hating, and still be bound to each other for lifetimes beyond this one.

Her legs wrapped around the back of my thighs pulling me closer and pushing my now obvious hard on into her accessible crotch. She was testing my self-control that was non-existent right now.

While my mouth opened for her tongue, my hands slipped between us and unzipped her hoodie to expose just a black bra under the fabric. She was prepared to storm my castle and hit me right in the hormones.

She arched her back, pushing herself further into me, when my fingers danced along her bra clasp. She was oozing a kind of experience I didn't want to think about right now, even though it danced in the back of my mind, reminding me that our time apart was only getting more and more sinful with each lifetime.

"Bolton, I'm not … you don't need to be so gentle."

I pushed the hoodie down her arms and left her exposed in nothing but the small amount of fabric that covered her breasts. I produced a small switchblade between us. She begged me for anything but gentle, so that was exactly what I was going to give her.

"Oh, I won't be."

The sound of the blade springing into action made her jump, and that reaction alone had me grinning, while the ache below my zipper demanded more than this teasing.

I dragged the knife along her warm skin up to the center of her bra, where it looked most fragile and stressed. With one quick motion, I had pulled the blade towards me cutting between the cups and leaving her even more exposed.

Her breasts weren't anything but perfect: dusted in bronze, her nipples a shade of dark pink that complimented her tan. I couldn't help myself when my hand grasped her tits from underneath forcing them into an even more perky state, while my mouth closed around one.

Arianna shifted under my tight grip, I was listening for her to change her mind. Her voice stayed silent, only producing small whimpers and moans, because of my lips tugging her nipple between my teeth.

She was an old wound, the lifetimes of losing her, that I was healing in this moment.

Her hand dipped between us pushing her chest further into my mouth when I switched nipples. Her hand put pressure on my hard ridge outlined in my sweats, running her palm against my length, testing any more resolve left in me.

My hands followed her lead, dropping down to her crotch and pushing the inseam of her jeans right into her clit.

I knew everything about my Sagittarius—what made her moan, what made her squirm under my gaze, where her sensitive spots hid from the world. I knew exactly how to make her submit to me.

I could feel the tension between us becoming unbearable. It was stiffening the air, making it hard to see or focus on anything but the tension.

My teeth gritted against her unblemished skin, further and further, not helping to alleviate any of the hormones.

Her exacerbated voice hummed, "I thought you hated me."

"Who says I stopped?"

Now wasn't the time to exploit my inner monologues and let her know just how much I considered love to be a razor sharp, fine line separating love and hate.

Her thinking I hate her only spurred her on when her hand became absent from my hard on and she rustled with the button on her jeans instead. She was impatient.

Her ex-boyfriend in Texas must have been inexperienced and the opposite of a lasting impression. She was damn near desperate to get her pants off to grant me access to where I really wanted to be.

Our determined mouths clashed, consuming each other, and our hands tried to keep up the same pace.

Nothing could keep our pace after her fingers scraped down my sides, pushing at the waistband of my sweats. Instinctively, I wrapped my hand around her throat putting all the attention back on her.

"You first."

She stood up from off the table, still completely calm, like my hand was a goddamn accessory she didn't mind. I tightened my grip, and she struggled to stay upright and shake her pants down at the same time, leaving her exposed, naked, but beautifully strong.

Not one vulnerable spot I could exploit.

In a quick motion, I stepped forward, leaving her no room to escape, forcing her back to her original position, legs open for me to get comfortable between. I couldn't drag my eyes up from her body, memorizing every curve and dip on her frame. She was the right amount of comfortable, not too much or lacking, and she moved her body like she knew exactly what I wanted to see when she laid back, taunting me.

Suddenly, her legs collapsed together with force, making it hard to see her glistening for me anymore. "I completed my round of show and tell. Your turn."

"What do you want to know?"

She sat up, and the mood didn't change. The tension still hung as heavy as I was. My hand clasped around my length just to ease the ache, while she got off on my truths instead.

"Explain. What are you then?"

"Zeus is my king. I'm not supposed to be here, none of us are. We were released and got stuck here."

I was hoping it was good enough but I could see her wheels turning, spinning right into how crazy what I was saying sounded. I wasn't an idiot. I knew what I was saying was incomprehensible, but it was the truth, one I hadn't planned on ever sharing with anyone, until her.

Keeping crazy to yourself is a lot easier.

Her eyes were at half-mast, and her hands ran up under my shirt, her nails scraping down me after. "Henry Jon? Rosalia?"

"That was the first time we were released, the Victorian Era. We were meant to influence the people, propel evolution forward, inspire change—"

She cut me off too impatiently. "Influence? How?"

"As I was saying... our signs, all the traits based on us, influence people around us. Each of us is different. When you're around Luna, you feel more patient and aware of others, when you're around Nyx, you feel more intense and competitive."

"What am I when I'm around you?"

"What you should be: motivated and relentless."

I shrugged my hoodie off, letting it fall down my arms, and the zipper made a small sound when it hit the floor below me. She didn't waste any time ripping my shirt from me aggressively, motivated, relentlessly.

I was happy to oblige.

I watched her eyes scan my body hungrily, moving from one defined muscle to the next, thanks to football. All of them started to ache from the hits I took not even a couple hours ago.

The heat still poured off my body in waves; my heart still pumped with leftover adrenaline; and now I felt shaky under the pressure of the hormones mixed with everything else.

She slowly opened her legs for me, like it was meant to be cherished. I didn't break eye contact when I jerked her legs forward, making sure I was between them this time, changing the tone she set easily.

She arched her back, pushing her growing need onto me, while my hands were busy tugging my sweats down, only enough to expose what I needed.

Pressing my balled up fists onto the table and leaning into her, meeting halfway, like any king would do for his queen. I searched the ocean in her eyes rimmed with violet hues to see if any hesitation was there but I found not even one sliver of doubt.

She was all in.

She was comfortably wrapped around me.

"Bolton ... Just fuck me already ... enough games."

My queen reborn, she wasn't sweet and naive anymore; she was demanding and impatient. This version of her, modernized from the 1600's, complimented who I was more than ever.

We were unstoppable, and no one would think to dethrone us.

I pushed my hips forward shifting my alignment easily when I felt my thick crown slip inside her warmth. She took my breath away, forcing my knuckles to push into the solid table even more, creating the opposite of white knuckles. Instead mine were red and bruised, exactly how I was going to leave Arianna, after letting me cross this line.

My hand snaked up between us, and my fingers wrapped around her throat, picking up the pace of my thrusts. She wanted to be fucked, not loved or treated like some virgin she wasn't.

That was something I already took; she just didn't remember all of our past. I knew she loved the roughness. I knew every inch of her desires, because I had known her for lifetimes.

Her small hands clasped around my forearm, letting me know it was too tight. I knew she needed to focus on how good she felt inside of the oxygen I was cutting in half now.

She just needed to remember, and this seemed like a promising way. She tried to choke out my name but my fingers on her vocal cords wouldn't allow it.

She was going to drown in either the pleasure or the pain.

"Do you remember me yet?"

I saw the panic wash over her face, pairing well with the lack of oxygen. Nothing about my confessions or me were sinking in. I kept my focus on the human instincts, like satisfying my hormones when I realized I couldn't fuck her into remembering our past.

Maybe she isn't the one. Maybe I wanted her to be so badly I fabricated every piece of evidence claiming she was.

I felt every part of our truce, all the progress, fall away with every motion of sinking between her legs. I was hate fucking her. Every thrust was more powerful, and the scowl on my face refused to let her see that I liked any of this.

She wasn't Rosalia reborn; she wasn't the one who was going to help us get home. Now I hated her even more for it.

Her lips nipped at my neck trying to reach me. "Bolton, slow down." She was out of breath, and her legs were shaking against my waist. Her whole body shook its way into coming, and I had to force my face to stay angry. She was coming undone, and this provoked a grin I was pushing away.

"Just come already, Arianna," my voice growled, sounding desperate for her to finish. I didn't care about coming; I wanted her to remember and that ship sailed. My hand even let go of her throat and resumed its position on the table, knuckles buried into the lacquer and chips of the table.

"What?" she hissed out, like I directly offended her. I stopped my hips from burying my length inside her, defeated, and let my head hang low between us.

"I can't do this. Not with *you*."

I felt her legs fall from being pinned up against my hips, and she scrambled to cover herself up.

Her eyes looked betrayed and polished in wetness that I knew I didn't want to stick around for.

Girls crying was always uncomfortable, and I never seemed to know what to say to make it stop. I always made sure I was out of

Arianna

"Was this some kind of prank? Get the new girl alone, get her talking, and fuck me until you couldn't even follow through on your own bullshit? You didn't hate me enough for hallways anymore?"

Bolton didn't even pull away from me after telling me how much of a mistake cutting my bra off was.

I pushed my palms into his chest to gain back control of my space, and the same feeling I got in Texas crawled up my spine—a charge of energy and rush that I didn't know what to do with.

As soon as I felt my palms land against his bare chest, I felt the same sparks I did when I touched anyone in his dumb circle of friends.

When I touched my ex before, he had a seizure in trespassing territory that got us caught by security.

These were the only times I felt this kind of *power*.

Without any warning, Bolton pulled away too quickly but not before making a face of complete anguish and pain gripping his chest where my palms were. My eyes wanted to roll, and I wanted to let the word "pussy" slip off my tongue.

A little static electricity, and you too can turn the bad boy into a wuss.

"Motherfucker. Is that what happened in Texas?" His head was down, trying to assess any damage to his still bare chest, while his eyes shifted up finding me.

I pulled up my panties and kept adjusting myself until I looked at least a little closer to how I arrived, even with my now useless bra.

"It was some static electricity... get over yourself."

Not so tough now, huh, pussy?

I started to walk away, and I snatched my phone off the ground where it fell. As soon as I shot up, Bolton's hand was wrapped around my arm, holding me in place.

"It doesn't work on me; you can't hurt anyone else in the circle. Your ex? You probably gave him a heart attack. How many times has this happened?"

I was hearing him but my head spun out of control and my body shook from all the emotions building up without having anywhere to go. I felt drained from his betrayal, drained from the power I felt to defend myself, and now I was remembering him explaining how much of a god he was.

Everything was out of control and sounded like lies I could believe, which made it so hard to decide what was real.

"I don't know, Bolton. I don't keep track of the friction in my life. Didn't you humiliate me enough back there? Pity fucked me into hating you just as much as you hate me?"

He actually looked confused, like my words hurt him more than how he had just hurt me.

"Pity fuck? Humiliate you? I couldn't fuck you when you don't remember me. I couldn't hurt you like that. Queens don't let men tell them how to feel. Decide for yourself, Arianna."

He let go of my arm and brushed past me, down the stairs, to the exit, before I could even get my thoughts together.

Decided for myself? If I'm crazy? If I'm powerful? If Bolton is still messing with me? Crown or not, navigating Arcadia Prep was proving to be more difficult.

I followed behind him, even though he was out of sight already, pondering every exchange we had up until now and his clues about who he was.

He kept asking me if I remembered him but I had never met him in my life, which ate away at me like cancer for the rest of the night.

By the time I made it to the girls' dorms, everything was dark and quite like not a soul was there. When I pushed open my door, the lights were off, and Luna's bed was flat. She wasn't here. I was thankful. I needed to shower off every part of me that I didn't understand and hope it only left what made sense.

I spent longer than I really meant to in the shower, taking my time, because once Luna got back, I knew she'd be tired, leaving me to be mindful of how loud I was. Downside of having a roommate your senior year of high school: a lack of freedom.

The only things that felt better after my long shower were my muscles; nothing else seemed resolved enough to relax.

I yanked out Henry Jon's journal from my bedside table, before glancing at the time on my phone: 12:12 AM Curfew was 11 on game nights and weekends so we could all bask in the glory.

Luna would never be caught missing curfew; she was practically the mom of her friends and so innocent that I thought even the Devil would shy away.

Arcadia Prep kept track of our keycards and swipes, meaning every missed curfew was a mark against you. I was pretty sure I never made curfew and was still waiting for my punishment.

I smiled to myself, pretending Luna got brave and Nyx stopped fighting how much he was into her. Who was I kidding? Luna wouldn't even let love break the rules. If Nyx was going to love Luna, he was going to have to do it between classes, before curfew, and most likely in private so no one had to feel bad about themselves.

I found my bookmark wedged between the old pages, and I let the diary fall open to where I had left off. I was hoping Henry Jon would make more sense than Bolton did.

> *Henry Jon*
>
> *I was standing face to face with the Devil's child, and my faith was stronger than ever. I laid in wait, watching my Rosalia get dragged deeper into the lust of the evil. I made no advances on the demon, I had nothing but my faith in my arsenal. I needed answers, and that took time.*
>
> *I prayed every night that God watched over my Rosalia, not letting her slip out of my grip.*
>
> *Every dusk, I went out to the forest to search for clues on how to defeat the devil among us. I found the tusk of the monster deeper into the woods and tucked it into my pocket, hoping this would be the first step to our victory.*
>
> *Pastor Cotton buried himself in his scripture and books, trying to find the beast but we found nothing. The Devil himself was getting creative with his demons, becoming more unknown and made of nightmares.*

There was a knock at the door, and it made me jump as I scanned Henry Jon's cursive ink on the pages. Luna wouldn't ever forget her keys, so whoever it was wasn't my roommate.

I made my way to the door and stood a few inches away asking, "Who is it?"

I waited for their response–none ever came. I mustered up an eye roll before looking through the peephole.

When I leaned in, hands on either side of the small hole, I tried to focus on the shadow. The lock rolled over, unlocking itself. I backed up quickly, not sure who it was or what they wanted but clearly they had some tricks, unexplainable ones.

The door opened to Caellum leaning against the door frame, looking bored to be in front of me, yet here he was.

I didn't believe Bolton for a second that my hands were anything but static zapping against him, but in this moment, in the fear of their enemy, I was willing myself to give into all this.

I held out my hands like a deranged person, hoping they'd protect me. He mocked my idiocy: "They give you a wand with those too?"

I dropped my hands, feeling more stupid than I ever had in my life. I clamped my eyes shut, only for a second, wishing I never actually did that.

"Can I help you? Aren't you supposed to be going back to your school?"

He completely ignored my questions when he invited himself in and took inventory of our room, starting with Luna's side. "How much did they tell you?"

I played dumbed, hoping it was more useful than static-less hands. "Tell me what? How much of a douche bag you are? Kind of learned that on my own."

He saw Henry Jon's diary on my bed, making me a liar and psycho now. He picked it up, scanning the words, before a smile plastered to his face. "Oh, Henry Jon. Such a good Christian. Guess faith can't save everyone."

I wanted to ask him what he meant, what he knew, what he wanted with me this late but he left no time between his thoughts. "Be careful who you trust. Not everyone is on your side."

"But you are? I don't even know you."

He leaned down over me, merely inches from my face, with his hands behind his back, leaning down. "No. I'm on whoever's side wins in the end. Normally, sacrifices don't win."

Sacrifice? Me? Bolton said you can't hurt the circle but maybe I'm not one of them.

I folded my arms against my chest and regained composure, even with his close proximity. "Normally traitors don't either."

I didn't know what actually happened between everyone that made Caellum land on the side of Bolton that was permanently pissed off but he didn't know that.

He stood up, with his eyebrows dipping and assessing how much my face gave away that I knew.

Don't give anything away. Don't give anything away when you know nothing.

Chanting in my head must have helped because he leaned against another wall, giving me room to finally breathe. "You have no idea, do you?" He laughed to himself, pleased as punch, while I kept looking like an idiot.

He sat down on Luna's desk chair, swinging one leg over and his arms pressing into the back of it. "Don't you think you should know my side before you condemn me?"

His sharp jaw, dark eyes, and almost perfect body was distracting me, as the muscles in his arms protruded against his thin shirt. I crossed my arms, sitting on my bed across from him, waiting for him to explain.

"Bolton's always had a hard on for being leader. I don't really care. I appreciate facts and people who don't know what betrayal is. We clashed on everything. He wanted pizza; I wanted ice cream. He wanted to save the sacrifices; I wanted to go home. He didn't have powers; I had too much to handle." He shifted in his seat uncomfortably, like he hadn't thought about any of this until now.

"So you're opposites, cool. That doesn't explain the pure uncut hate."

"It doesn't matter how much we clash. He needs all of us for the ritual to go right. The hate … ? Well, that was born out of you."

"Me? I'm nobody. I didn't even meet any of you until I moved here." I was over deciphering every confusing word, and it was showing. My voice was limp and tired.

"You have the biggest clue sitting on your bed, and yet you're still clueless."

I stood up, annoyed with everything and still a kind of exhausted that stopped begging for sleep; it was now demanding. "Why don't you just tell me instead of the damn riddles?"

He sighed heavily. "You. We always argued about you. He never wanted you to be the sacrifice in the ritual. He wasn't ever sure enough you were one of us … he didn't know if you'd come back. You're always running away, and we are your private army."

Nothing was falling into place, even after the answers I begged for. Caellum was willing to spill every ounce of truth but it didn't matter, because my entire body refused to believe him.

I was just *me*. I wasn't anything but a teenager on the verge of college with a bad attitude and two parents in other places.

Me.

Shooting up off my bed, I started pacing, like often Bolton did. "We don't live in *Twilight*, *True Blood,* or *The Vampire Diaries*. This isn't happening."

Caellum's gritting laugh sounded genuine, unlike his eyes. "Damn straight. We aren't vampires or werewolves. We're gods, crowned in by Zeus himself. Different movie completely."

Everything about him was calm and dormant, like he knew one day he'd have to tell someone, and this wasn't as hard as he thought it'd be.

Good for him.

"None of this is real. You sound crazy. I already have enough problems." My voice was confused, pleading for a sliver of truth in all this. Bolton was a god—a real life mythological god stuck on earth for whatever reason?

"I really thought it would have clicked by now." He should leave the sarcasm to a professional. It was going over like a lead balloon.

"So why can't you go home? Why do you need me?"

He thumbed the pages of Henry Jon's journal, looking for something specific, when he handed me back the book, pointing a few paragraphs down. My eyes found his finger and started to glance over the cursive that was almost unintelligible to read without some history degree.

> *Henry Jon*
>
> We peered through the tall trees watching the Devil's children form a circle around Rosalia, closing her in and suppressing whatever faith she had left.
>
> The Devil's children were always forming circles in the dark, doing their father's bidding.
>
> Rosalia hugged their leader, careful to not use his true name, tightly against her corset, before she laid down on a rock with a smooth top. She trusted him blindly, more than our Christian God.
>
> Pastor Cotton, to my right, clung onto the large cross around his neck, hoping it would save him. I wasn't sure anything would save us, when monsters like these walked around.
>
> I watched the girl moving around Rosalia closely, watching her grind herbs and chant to one of the witches we cast back to hell.
>
> The sky was a heavy shade of black, making the stars seem even brighter than on the clearest night. The others closed in on my prized possession, and it wasn't until their leader spoke that I realized Rosalia wasn't meant to be a vessel or survive but she was to be their sacrifice.
>
> He chanted the words: "The sun, the moon, and the rising.

You will return home to Olympus, and I will never let you out of my sight again."

His words burdened us, while we hid in the bushes, anchoring us in our steps and halting our movements.

Their leader, the sour, lonely child, not much older than Rosalia, disrobed. Every urge for violence and retribution flared up. This was an act of war—one I couldn't ignore. Cotton's hand held me still. There were to be no hasty decisions if we wanted the advantage.

I saw the moonshine hit the silver blade tucked behind his back, while he leaned down over her, and I watched their lips meet.

He was stealing her purity in every form.

His bare chest made him seem so much more innocent, even more childlike but I knew the Devil would tempt my sympathy in any way he could. I fought for Christ, even if that meant slaying the children in the forest.

The dead leaves of the season crunched under my boots, while my adversary pointed to his chest. I didn't want to pull my eyes away from Rosalia, but regrettably, I did, seeing the horns burned into his chest like a badge of honor.

Those weren't the wings of a godsend—an evil I was determined to vanquish. While I was focused on the burn, everything around me sped up in a way I couldn't stop.

Their fearless leader brought his arms up into the air, with the knife firmly between his fists, and as I ran towards Rosalia, the certainty of being too late already corroded my heart. Her body folded up into the knife without fighting the blade lodged into her abdomen. Blood quickly spewed from her mouth in a graceful way that only a pure child could manage. Carefully moving her body from the rock, I held my little girl against my *chest, whispering how much I forgave her, hoping that was enough forgiveness for the Gates of Heaven.*

The boy branded with the horns of the Devil leaned down, pressed his palm into my shoulder, and he told me this would all make sense someday.

It has been seven years since that night in the woods, where I sat on the dirt, rocking Rosalia into her death. As time moved me on, it has also moved my anger with me.

I read the passage and let it all sink in. Bolton had the same mark, only it was a "birthmark" now.

Was Caellum really trying to tell me that they had lived through the 1600's? Complete with religious fanatics and the trials of witches? I was overwhelmed with information that only weighed me down more, making my eyelids heavy to hold up.

"You died that day—luckily for Bolton, not actually. That was just the human form you took while on earth."

"This is too much, okay. I'm not anything but human, and whatever kind of joke this is … ? I'm over it. Tell your pal Bolton getting me naked was punishment enough but I'm not going to bow to him."

Caellum stood up frustrated, and then intrigued by what I had just shared accidentally.

I wasted no time pushing my hands against his solid chest and kicking him out of my room. I felt the same static I did with Bolton only a few hours ago.

"Maybe you should get this pissed at him and let him feel those hands. He wouldn't question … driving that … knife … in you … and sending us back home." The last sentence was full of pauses to exaggerate his point between each word.

"You're a dick. We all get it."

I gave him one hard push, making him step back over the threshold of my room, before closing the door in his face.

Once your body takes on news you can't comprehend, a part of your mind unlocks everything that was every confusing, like friendships that end, why my dad keeps taking jobs that leave me stranded in a stranger's homes, why some people live past thirty and my mom died.

Misery loves company, my ass.

Confusion loves company, and denial loves desolation.

Right now I was firmly in the company of the bad memories still scarring me, before I moved on to the desolation of self-torture—something I knew all too well. Between the tragedy of losing my mother and never having a father figure to count on, I was the poster child for emotional trauma.

I hardly ever let myself cry—at least not over things I could no longer change. However, all the new information was pushing out old memories to make room.

I couldn't even bring myself to read more of Henry Jon's journal before I fell asleep with the tears running down the sides of my face, making stains on my pillow.

Luna didn't come back to the room. She granted me one night of freedom, and I used it to cry.

CHAPTER 23

Arianna

The dreams were getting more active. There wasn't a night my subconscious wasn't trying to scream epiphanies at me.

Last night, I dreamed about the morning my dad broke the news that my mom had died.

It was a cruel joke when your mind makes you relive your worst memories, hoping you'll find what you didn't see before.

In the dream, I was the age I am now, and my dad didn't even wake me up to tell me he went to the hospital. Now he was standing in front of me, breaking news, like I would overlook those small details to mourn. He was wrong. My eyes were becoming brighter, and the violet fused with gold in my irises. My hands were glowing, flecked with gold, and my veins were illuminating my palms, except now it was gold.

Every part of me unexplainably ran gold.

Royal.

Desired.

Myth.

In the dream, I let the lightning spark against my skin, and before I knew it, I was the only thing unharmed when my hands faded back to normal.

Our house was struck down by lightning, burned to a crisp, and barely any beams were still up right, all struck down by *my* wrath.

I could still feel the cold sweat on my back and around my hairline when my alarm went off. I twisted over in my bed, looking behind me to see if Luna was anywhere in sight.

Her bed was perfectly made, meaning she never came back to our room. I was starting to worry, knowing this wasn't a girl who broke any rules.

Last week, she yanked me over to the right side of the sidewalk, because that's apparently the side traveling northbound, and I wasn't leaving room for the southbound students.

Luna was extra everything—innocent, maternal, rule following, and loyal to her friends in a way that made you think of a cult.

I pushed Henry Jon's journal in my bag and decided I was going to skip class today. I needed to tackle all this new information logically. I didn't even bother pretending to glance at my blazer, navy skirt, and maroon knee high socks.

I loathed that uniform. It was meant to make people blend in, and I never did, even in a uniform.

Once I pushed my foot into my Doc Martens, I started to head for the library before anyone was outside, trying not to be seen. I didn't care about getting caught. I was avoiding anyone in this magic circle and their scrutiny.

Stopping for a coffee to warm up my hands wasn't the smartest idea, but after feeling how tight and red my eyes were, I figured they needed some moral support.

Scanning the library for anyone who would rat me out, I decided upstairs where I was last night was probably the most hidden, even from the woman who moved like a ghost.

I dropped my stuff on the same table Bolton had me pinned against and I felt myself suck in my bottom lip as the goosebumps chased the feeling across my skin.

I can't do this with you.

Those words echoed in the back of my mind all night as I cried out my parents lack of attendance in my life, their vacancy, and now, not only was being an outcast not enough, I was also supposed to be some key to *them* going home again.

I slumped down in the seat, already exhausted, and I hadn't done any research at all. I pulled out my laptop and started typing keywords, like "Aries," "gods," and "Olympus," and searching the connections.

> *Aries, "the ram," is the first of the twelve zodiacal constellations, and in Greek myth represents the animal whose fleece was sought by Jason and the Argonauts.*
>
> *Zeus placed the ram's image among the stars in honor of its heroism.*

Everything Caellum and Bolton said had connections back to mythology. The density of the search engine left me wondering which information was more true.

> *Ares, the God of War.*
>
> *Aphrodite's lover and was held in contempt by her husband, Hephaestus.*

Was he a god himself or the ram Zeus honored by literally writing him in the stars?

I was already knee deep when I used a website to calculate my astrological sign and was shocked to see the archer populate in the images on my screen.

I pried my mind open. I broke all the rules but it was hard for me to believe there was something in existence that truly broke all the rules like this.

Sagittarius: Zeus, the God of the Sky, Lightning and Thunder

My mouth hung open too long before my hand clamped over it. I looked down at my shaking hands that shocked not only Bolton but Caellum too. Lightning? My dream threatened another cold sweat, except this time I wouldn't be sleeping.

My twitching fingers moved over the mouse pad and kept reading the information that none of us could really prove beyond the status and the ramblings of an old prophet.

Zeus exposed liars, as he was the keeper of oaths.
Zeus' arrow is equivalent to Sagittarius' archer.

No wonder they were convinced they needed me, they thought I was the most powerful god there was.

I felt like Zeus behind my computer screen, exposing whatever lies I could find and keeping some kind of oath by keeping their secrets.

Guess it was my secret now too?

The deeper I fell down the hole, the more things connected and entwined together like a ball of rubber bands you were trying to pry apart. I had more questions than answers.

If each one of them was a god who represented an astrological sign, then what did that mean for mortals?

Why are they stuck here only now?

Where were they before this?

Why were they together but I was changing schools every year?

It was like all my questions summoned Bolton's existence,

and his quiet steps went unheard, until he leaned down over me, looking at the same screen I was.

"You weren't in class." There was no concern, and his voice didn't go up at the end asking a question. It was just a fact he was stating out loud.

"And? I'm really busy, Bolton."

"Alba isn't a joke. He'll write you up."

He sat on the table next to my computer, and it wasn't lost on me that he was perched up higher than me on a fake throne. Bolton could make anything a throne. From what I had been reading for the last few hours, apparently it was exactly how an Aries should act.

Lust for blood.

Chaotic nature.

Thoughtless aggression.

I focused on the screen, reading though the history I knew Alba wasn't going to teach in class. He just started touching on mythology when I needed something more specific.

Bolton's shoe kicked my leg on purpose as he sat there, staring at me, waiting for me to bow. "Finally finished his journal?"

I shook my head as my words fell out: "Nope. Caellum gave me the CliffsNotes."

I didn't have to be this close to him to realize how tense he had gotten, just at the sound of his name. "Caellum? As in my enemy?"

I twisted in my chair, facing him. "Yes, let me guess ... he's an Aquarius? Power trips, rebellion, and avoids feelings at all costs; that rings a lot of bells. That's why you two really clash—the love of being crowned king."

"Oh, so now you believe it? ... when he tells you?" His mouth fell open, and I watched his jaw freeze, while he mulled over my loyalty for the second time in a few days.

He was the one who told me not to apologize, so I wouldn't.

"I don't know what I believe. This is a lot to swallow. I have too many questions."

He turned to face me, still sitting on the top of the table. "Shoot."

My mind scrambled for a question to ask at the same time my mind searched for a snide comment about gods but my knowledge of unbelievable elements started with *Twilight* and ended with *The Vampire Diaries*. No mention of Greek gods.

"I thought you said you were all children of Zeus? Wouldn't that make you a perv with a fetish for incest?"

His lips stretched into a grin but didn't disrupt his cut jawline that begged to have a tongue swiped over it. He started laughing, while his palm hit his knee at my comment was meant to be an insult. Bolton was hard to insult when he was so comfortable being king. "He's the most powerful god. He rules Olympus. Wait, you actually think you're Zeus? Like *the* Zeus?"

My eyebrows shot up to my hairline, questioning how he put two and two together. That was the only thing I could put together and the only thing that made any sense.

"My hands, you guys need me to go home, the bow and arrow?" My voice was timid and every second more of his rare laughter made me not even believe what I thought I was sure of.

"Zeus was a man, sweetheart."

"Don't be gender bias, dick," I shot back quickly. At least my sarcasm wasn't broken.

"You aren't Zeus. He died a long time ago. You're his daughter."

I shrunk down into my seat. No one liked being wrong but I was pretty sure no one liked being told they were something made of myths either.

Now I didn't just have a dead parent and parent who couldn't stay away; now I had one who I never knew at all.

Just my luck. The constant new girl and the unwanted daughter.

"So why did you all get to stay together?" I looked down at my hands resting on the keyboard of my Mac. I was unwanted in every aspect, unless it was convenient for people.

"It just happens to be you most of the time. You don't like to stay put."

I snatched the coffee sitting against his thigh, just as his fingers held it up with no real grip. "This is crazy, you know that right? I'm not special."

He leaned forward, watching me sip my coffee. "Do you trust me?"

I shook my head no with the cup still to the edge of my lip. I trusted the human parts but this god shit? I wasn't that gullible. He stood up anyways and demanded I come along. To where? I had no idea, I concluded staying in the library all day after skipping was a sure fire way to get caught.

Shoving my Mac back into my bag, I followed Bolton down the stairs, before he stopped, spinning around to face me and towering over me even a step below me. "Just don't tell the circle you know anything."

My eyes hooded, cutting my vision down but not my ability to glare with purpose. I questioned everything, exposed liars for their true nature, and kept important oaths to myself—all the things my research told me I am.

He didn't explain, and I didn't push to know why. I knew enough and that seemed like politics instead of facts.

I followed Bolton into the brisk chill outside when he headed to the edge of campus towards the abandoned building that no one uses, except to blow off steam.

The stairs creaked a loud warning sign that I ignored altogether, before Bolton pushed the heavy door open. It wasn't until I was inside that the part of the brain meant to panic kicked in. We were alone in an abandoned building, after he told me his biggest secret. It was every *Lifetime* movie before the happy ending.

I questioned myself, *Why am I following him down a hallway that smelled like my aunt's attic with a slight hint cologne they must have used to freshen up the scent?*

Once in an abandoned room with all the remnants left behind, glass beakers and posters still up reminding students to be careful in the lab, Bolton slid against a table, watching me awkwardly. "Get mad, Arianna. Your abilities are emotional."

I looked down at my hands feeling nothing but stupid and polished it off with an eye roll.

"I know what happened in Texas now. What about your mom? How did she die?"

He was treading on ground I didn't even like to set foot on. I slanted my eyes, making sure to find his so that he knew there was a special anger saved for him.

That didn't stop him from pushing me and theorizing how my mom might have died as he slipped down, stepping towards me.

"Did what happen in Texas happen before? Do you feel responsible? Did you fight with your mom before she died? Tell me what happened, Arianna." His palms slammed down on the table between us, making demands that I knew I wouldn't meet and answers I forced myself to forget.

I looked down at my hands again, watching my bronzed skin stay perfectly still; there were no veins and no gold, like in my dream this morning. A sweet relief came over me, and I took a deep breath.

Bolton shouted, "Was it your fault?! Did your dad not stick around because he blamed you?! You can't hurt me, Arianna."

It happened in a snap—one quick snap with the right question boring into my soul and crushing all my safeguards I had around my heart. Bolton had actualized my worst fear out loud and made it sound undeniably true. I didn't even feel the tears pour down my cheeks until I opened my eyes again from having them clamped shut.

When I opened them, I expected to see the same damage I did in my dream: a roasted building, with him and I the only things left standing in destruction.

That's what happens when you have a life filled with hardship: you become the anomaly in destruction. Destruction leaves us untouched and toying with how much we can take.

How was destruction not a god?

The damage wasn't the same at all. There were lightning patterns burned into the walls that looked like veins branching off everywhere staining the less than white walls. The tables between us were broken against the lash of my "abilities" that I was unwilling to claim.

Unclaimed lightning from your fingertips. Going once, going twice, anyone?

With my mouth open and chest heaving from the silent tears, I looked down at my shaking hands before I even thought to make sure Bolton was okay. My hands were fading back to normal when I noticed the gold replacing my veins was creeping up my forearms now too.

He unlocked something in me, and now the emotions I kept buried deep were making me vulnerable to not only sarcasm but physically being able to hurt those who hurt me.

Bolton pulled me into his chest. His shirt was full of holes that were burned into the material. There was no blood, and I no longer had a choice but to believe him.

I wasn't different because my mom died, my dad was decorated military, I changed schools multiple times a year, and had an attitude problem. I was different because the blood in my veins was made of gods and myths.

Bolton smoothed down my hair. "It's okay. We're okay. I mean the lab isn't ... " I slapped his arm, willing the tears to dry up with his jokes but I didn't wiggle out of his arms.

Bolton wasn't a god to me. He was my king and only my king.

With my cheek against his chest, I could feel the hard edges of the damage to his shirt. "She died on the way to get me from school. That was the start of being kicked out and suspended constantly." I paused offering him a way out of hearing this if he didn't want to. I knew all too well how nightmares are easily shared.

"What happened?" His voice was less critical than normal, and there was a softness I didn't experience even with his pinning my legs up the night before.

"Fallon Myers was being the extreme bully she was to this girl who would never stand up for herself. She was the easiest target for Fallon. So I pushed her in the hallway, and she hit her head on the lockers. She got three stitches, and I got suspended." I paused again, knowing this was where my memories got less angry and more deep—a depth I felt fill my lungs, slowly drowning me.

"My mom was on her way to pick me up, and someone hit her from the side. The car flipped and caught fire on the way to my school. They said the impact killed her instantly, and she wasn't in any pain when she passed. How can you not be in any pain when you leave everyone behind?"

Bolton's silence spoke volumes I wasn't ready to hear. He was basically a god, and he didn't have any more answers than the mortal I thought I was. No one had the answers I wanted, because nothing would be good enough. Nothing would bring her back.

His hands locked around me, holding me closer. "No one is ever gone, gone. Everyone comes back, just differently."

I don't know why what he said filled the space in my heart that was previously empty but every word fueled the hope I thought

I lost. It propelled my brain into question after question with no real answers.

Was she reborn like they were? Could she have come back as someone else? Would I meet her again? See, hope could answer all of these.

I didn't expect him to fill the silence again but he did: "Guess it's my turn for confessions? The ritual Henry Jon saw is still going to happen. Now we just have to figure out creative ways around it."

"Caellum said you don't trust I'm special enough to *kill me*. That's as sweet as we'll ever get huh?"

I made Bolton laugh, not smirk or grin, but I heard his laugh as he looked down. Aries was the child of Greek gods, with the hard exterior that shattered into a laugh that I wanted to bottle up.

"Sweet? We'll always be hateful, competitive, stubborn, and sparks. Nothing sweet about it. Zeus wrote it into our stars."

I titled my face up toward him, watching his expression for any inconsistencies, even though Bolton was the most consistent person I knew.

Nyx

Three weeks later

I felt like I lived in some PG version of life when all the raw, real, painful parts were left on the editing room floor, and we pretended life was peachy.

Life was only peachy for some of us …

Bolton was smiling on a semi-regular basis when the circle wasn't around. It wasn't hard to pin it on Arianna; all his sudden happiness seemed to dull down the parts of Bolton that rubbed people the wrong way.

He told me everything, and I always made sure to listen, because Bolton didn't do anything without a reason behind it.

In his PG glazed eyes, he told me all about teaching Arianna how to harness her abilities, about our past that she still didn't remember, and keeping it all on the down low. The circle was chomping at the bit to perform the ritual so we could go home.

Being stuck as high school seniors was our own personal hell, one I might have deserved but my penance was over the minute I had to swallow my feelings for Luna all over again every time the fucking distractions failed.

My abilities, strength and speed, were nothing compared to pushing away someone you know you'll fall for if you don't keep yourself in check.

The plain peanut butter and jelly sandwich I made for my lunch seemed plainer when I was staring at her. Nothing else compared when the sunlight poured through the dining hall and lit her hair ablaze. The freckles across the bridge of her nose made her seem even more endearing, even though she didn't need anymore.

She was already painfully aware of others, sympathetic, and overly empathetic.

She was a goddamn sacrificial lamb in a circle of wolves.

I watched her laugh at something Arianna said, just as her fingertips touched her lips trying to conceal it. She was always turned inward, hiding in plain sight inside her shell, not much escaping, unless someone needed it to.

Bolton's heavy boots on the stairs going past me yanked my attention from getting my daily dose of Luna from a safer distance.

"Meeting tonight. No circle. Library. Midnight."

Bolton was always cryptic and somewhat unclear in everything he said. Thankfully one word sentences helped me get on board quicker. Apparently he was calling a meeting without the circle, which meant something was wrong or there was evidence to believe someone in the circle wasn't loyal anymore.

I knew better than to ask why. I felt particularly combative today, seeing as how he ripped my focus from Luna.

I didn't do much talking but when I did it was either filled with cruelty or the lust behind how I felt about this girl. He was the only one who knew how much I could love her if I let myself. That was the problem: letting myself.

I was made up of extremes, too much or too little, no middle ground and no compromising. If I let myself love her, I was going to suffocate her, and if I was hellbent on hating her enough to get by, I would do it with precision.

Right now, I hated her, at least in public. At night, alone in my bedroom, I loved every inch of her that I never had the pleasure of seeing.

The back of Bolton's hand slapped my shoulder. "You hear me?"

I craned my neck, glaring at him behind me. He knew better than to touch me, so I made the playing field even with stupidity.

"I heard you. Why? It's not Wednesday."

"Keep your voice down. I'll explain later."

"I'm not your slave, Bolton. You can't snap, and I'll do whatever you want. You aren't a king here." Everything in me was cruel, cold, harsh.

This was how I had to be when she was around; it was the only way I could be around her with melting into the other extreme.

Bolton retorted, because he couldn't not talk back, "Well, fuck me. Someone piss in your lemonade?"

I got up flinging my bag over my shoulder, even more pissed off than I was when he disrupted my gaze. I wanted to set him on fire. I wanted to hang him up by his ankles and watch him sweat, watch him panic, and only feel satisfied when I could finally smell the sour smell of burned flesh.

Extremes.

Luna had missed curfew last night for the third time in the past couple of months. Every time she broke a rule, I felt it in my fragile, teenager bones.

The first time she skipped curfew I heard about it after the fact from Arianna when she asked if we finally hooked up.

Arianna asked me like she had known me my whole life and was counting down the days until I broke for Luna. She had known me my whole life but we weren't ever friendly like we are now.

Bolton was the only one with memories. Mine were fragments, shards, too vague to tell me anything except I was created out of evil and Arianna was my mortal enemy in Olympus.

One memory kept playing on a loop at night when I couldn't sleep and couldn't be bothered to do anything else.

> Arianna handed me a lightning bolt necklace in a field of flowers. A single tear rolled down her face, "Are you happy now?"
>
> I stood there silently, not sure what to do or say. Arianna was handing me the piece of her father and asking me if I was happy about it.
>
> "You're two halves of what drives people mad: death and sexuality."
>
> I touched her hand enough to close her palm around the delicate lightning bolt. "His lightning isn't lost. It's with you now. You transform, evolve, while I stay stuck between death and sexuality."

The half memory fades there, just enough to make me want more but enough to be satisfying. I started getting these pieces back when Arianna stepped foot here.

I kept them to myself, not even bothering to share them with Bolton. He already had too much power after claiming himself king while we were mortal.

In Olympus, we were all made up of the same shit that made our gods, all ruled by Zeus, all with powerful parents. We all had vengeances or moral dilemmas to right of our own. Bolton was one of us, just more willing to steer the motivation.

Study hall didn't count as a class, and you wouldn't ever find me there. It was a waste of my time. I texted, hoping my guy would hook me up with some bud, nothing much but enough to take off the edge. I was wound up so tightly I felt like a knot.

Nothing else was an option with extremes making up my own personality. I either wanted to fuck or kill. With Luna off-limits, I was down to killing, and that would put a dent in our plan to go home.

The gods would smite us by making it an unbearable loophole: kill someone for fun, and be stuck like this forever.

No thanks.

I preferred using my strengths, not hiding who I was just because the mortals may panic, and not being limited by this mortal body. All it did was hold me back and shit the bed when I needed it most.

I was a fucking god back home—the son of Hades and Persephone, created from jealousy and revenge, forever balancing death and sexuality.

Our abilities weren't meant to be bottled up by flesh and bones.

Luna texted me: *Are you okay? You didn't finish lunch.*

She always knew when someone was fighting their way through emotions, and nothing pissed me off more than her caring when I couldn't.

I snapped when I texted her back: *I'm not hungry, Luna. You've missed curfew a few times now. You don't see me asking about it.*

I could see her small, innocent, freckled features morph into worry even more, while reading my message. I didn't expect her to text back when my phone light up with the please be patient bubbles.

> Luna: *Don't pretend you don't watch me, Nyx. You always know where I am.*

Pushing the earbuds into my ears, I already pressed play on the heavy rock coming through. I was silencing the world with the press of a button, and soon enough, I would silence my feelings the same way.

> **Me:** *I'm not pretending, Luna. There is an open invitation to come sit on this dick. You're too selfless to make yourself feel good.*
>
> **Luna:** *Selfless? More like dangerous. You're a natural disaster. You'll rock things loose that I can't part with yet.*

I didn't bother texting her back. She was right about me. I was a hurricane to Luna, destroying her as she knew it and leaving her to rebuild into something new. Something she didn't ask to be ... or want to be.

There goes that sexuality or death mentality.

Blowing off my steam with some "medicinal" exhales left me feeling like putty on my bed. I didn't realize I fell asleep, until Bolton was kicking the frame of my bed, hoping I'd wake up. "We're in season, you know not to smoke that shit. We can get tested at any time."

I followed his eyes on the makeshift ashtray from an old book I gutted with what was left of my joint, just the ass, the roach. I didn't let any go to waste.

"Sure, Bolton. I'll be okay not being associated with losing the way we are this year." I sat up, wondering what time it was and looking for my phone in my sheets as he scolded me silently. "Library in 20, Nyx. Don't make me come find you."

Bolton was demanding, full of himself, and honestly, the biggest pain in my ass. He told me back home we were friends too but that it was hard to believe I'd put up with him for an entire immortal life.

The only redeeming thing about these meetings was everyone wanting to hear themselves so much that me being silent went unnoticed. This was a smaller meeting, so I didn't know what to expect. If Bolton was having doubts, he didn't share them with me.

I was in the hallway against the railing before Bolton was out of his room. "I'm gonna assume she's learning quick?"

He shrugged. "Not quick enough. She still has no memories. Just nightmares."

"What do you expect when dating you?" My voice cracked into a laugh before it could go up at the end.

The library was the only place on campus our keycard worked 24/7. My wheels turned, wondering where Luna went. I watched her closely but I never followed. I wasn't ready to die that kind of death by stalking my prey.

Luna was already standing on the steps, shivering and waiting by Arianna's side. I shrugged off my jacket without thinking twice. Walking past Luna, so she couldn't refuse to my face, I lightly placed it over her shoulders before I followed behind Bolton to the keypad.

I already knew we were headed upstairs. Bolton hated the obvious, and pushing Kate into complaining more was a past time we all participated in.

"What is this even about? We couldn't do this downstairs?" Kate's complaining always came with a bit of whining and some hopeless huffing. We were all used to it.

Bolton barked out behind him, "I'm not doing this in the open."

Now I was intrigued. Something was wrong, and it demanded privacy.

Bolton thumbed the spines of the old books that were off limits, when all of a sudden we heard gears.

Everything sounded louder in the dark.

The bookcase against the wall shifted, creating an opening I had never seen before and didn't know existed. I wasn't frequently in the library often enough to even know the second level was this big. I preferred firsthand experiences, not reading about them in books.

Luna went to sacrifice herself by stepping into the opening first, my fingers wrapped around her wrist, drawing her back from volunteering. Bolton wouldn't intentionally hurt anyone but I also wasn't taking that chance with Luna.

After everyone slipped through the opening, I took a closer look, "Stop throwing yourself on the damn cross and making me save you."

Reaching out my hand, I waited for her to take mine, while I stood in the catacombs of our school with only our phone's glow bouncing off the walls.

When she was safely through the gap, she pushed my hand away, "That's the difference between you and me. I'll die for someone else but you'll kill."

I didn't let our differences stop my arm from landing across her shoulders and protecting her as Bolton lead us down a long hall, which led to a large room, that had smaller hallways breaking off like veins, like lightning.

Once we all gathered up in the room, I heard footsteps coming towards us. I shifted myself in front of Luna, protecting her, tensing.

Caellum smirked at the room, like he knew no one could really cut him out of their lives for too long.

"Miss me, fuckers?"

"What the fuck is he doing here, Bolton?"

He didn't even let us adjust to the new surroundings when he dove right in, "Stand down, killer. We need all the allies we can get. Alba was hiding Arianna's real file."

Alba? Our mentor? Our friend? The keeper of the balance and virtue? He can't mean the one man I trust in this mortal world, in this prison.

Kate was a walking eye roll and sarcastic tone, "And? I need more theories than accusations, Bolton."

The clash between these two titans made me want to exit stage left and watch the show from a safe spot.

Arianna's questioning voice, still confused and new to this

asked, "Which sign is he again?"

Her dumbass question triggered a response I knew would set Bolton off when I looked at her truly spent. "Have you even been studying? Bolton is trying to give you as much time as possible before the ritual to remember–you're wasting it. On what? Making out? We're all riding on you catching up faster."

Bolton was standing up straighter, and I knew this would end in blows if we argued. Considering he had no abilities; winning was rarely fair.

Luna frowned in my direction as she pushed her arms inside my jacket. I hoped it smelled like her when she was done. "He's a Virgo. Give her a break. It's a lot to take in."

"It's her history, origin. It shouldn't be this hard to keep up, unless you aren't Sag. We haven't witnessed her do anything."

Only in my fragmented memories.

Arianna was the most quiet I had ever seen her, silent, chewing her lips off. I sauntered towards her, only stopping in front of her to leave a few inches, "I don't have to trust you. I've killed enough people that adding you to the body count won't affect me at all. It might break Bolton's little black heart, though … "

I was pushing her into admitting she wasn't who we were looking for or at least proving she was trying to care, learn, be part of the circle for once, instead of always being the one lost.

It had been a few times that the sign we needed to complete the circle wasn't hers. Rare but that dumbass Leo got sacrificed once and cried the whole time. He was dramatic, and thankfully the gods spared us that nightmare again.

I watched her lip biting become more aggressive, and her lips became a cherry color inside of the flesh tone pink they normally were.

Bolton shouted enough from his fake throne, sitting on some table, always perched above us, just to make sure there was no confusion.

I kept pushing her to show her true self or opt out of dying for no good reason, "Just admit it, Arianna: You aren't one of us. You're just a kid whose parents got sick of you making trouble, and instead of being comfortable being an outcast, you clung onto this absurd notion you're the daughter of Zeus, all because your vagina reacts to Bolton."

And just like that she came alive.

"Just stop it, Nyx! I didn't ask to be this different. I didn't ask for parents like this, and I didn't ask to be your damn sacrificial lamb! Fuck!"

I watched her come undone, and a wall of tears glazed her irises in a thick fog. You could still see the flecks of purple matching her hair. I twisted around, bored with being this close to someone about to cry. Luna could tag in when they started to fall, the nurturer.

"Are you happy now?"

I stopped dead in my tracks, and my eyelids went half-mast, trying to discern if I heard her right. I heard the same phrase she barked at me in my memory when her father died.

Slowly turning back around to face her, I examined her face, features, anything that would confirm this was a memory and not some nightmare I created.

"So you do remember. You just didn't tell Bolton."

I don't know when Bolton jumped down from his throne and breezed over to my side, I could see him out of my peripheral vision, looking tense. "Remember what, exactly?" The worry was apparent in his voice but it went ignored.

The room faded out, and the focus was lodged between us, blocking everything else out.

She looked at me through a heavy sheet of tears obstructing her vision as she shook her head in disbelief. "I don't know. Maybe. It's just nightmares so far; I don't know what's real."

I didn't need to see her abilities or hear anymore. I knew we shared a memory and that was enough for me. I had fragments floating in my head at night and none of them were of Luna.

I had no validation for how protective I felt of her but Arianna lived in my head in a way I knew we must have been friends at some point, which was more than I could say for anyone else in the circle.

"I'm the son of Hades. Of course, I'm a nightmare, but it doesn't mean our memories aren't real. Pretty sure the scar on my shoulder is from you."

My cut shirt left openings in the side that showed off the sides of my body easily. I could have been shirtless and showing almost as much. I ran hot, at a boiling, at all times, making my attire justified. I pulled the material towards my neck exposing my shoulder blade to show her my scar patterned after a strike of lightning.

I felt her cold fingertips brush against the embossed skin, no longer flush and taut like the rest of me, with tingling I knew to be the thunder that came before lightning. It made me jump, realizing she was touching me—someone who wasn't Luna, my Luna.

"This is a cute reunion and all ... " Bolton's strained voice was obvious. He didn't like this connection he didn't seem privy to.

I let my shirt settle back over my shoulder, covering up a scar I now knew came from Arianna. I just didn't know how or why yet. We weren't supposed to be able to hurt each other, yet I had a scar branching over the back of my shoulder. I had to regain composure and focus on why we were here: someone's betrayal.

Creating space between Arianna and I, I found a wall to lean against on the other side of the room. "Cut to the chase, Bolton."

Luna's eyes caught mine with not worry or empathy but something I didn't know she felt. It was too selfish of an emotion for her to wear: jealousy. She was jealous I had a tie to Arianna, even though we didn't know what that tie was.

"Alba is working with Cheyanne. I don't know what their plan is. Something is shady. They're both hiding shit from us."

Cheyanne? Probably.

Alba? Doubtable.

Kate yawned loudly on purpose to make her point. "Was that really cutting to the chase, if you didn't know anything?"

"I think they're sabotaging the ritual. Cheyanne knows she has Henry Jon's journal. She freaked out in my room asking me if she has the husk and if we can trust Ari."

I wanted to say, "Maybe we can't," after reevaluating my scar and the tingling in her fingertips that didn't seem to go away—a permanent itch to leave her mark on the world.

Luna's eyes kept pressuring me to hold her stare, to say something, to do something that made her feel better than the jealousy running its course.

She was asking me permission to be selfish. Who was I to deny her? I laced my fingers with hers lazily, not committed or caring, but on the inside, I felt more alive than I ever had.

Luna wanted to be selfish … with me.

Bolton

rying to explain betrayal in a room full of just that had me reeling but the ritual was around the corner. This couldn't wait any longer.

Nyx staring into Arianna like he knew her better than I did wasn't going to blow over any time soon.

Cheyanne was hellbent on using the full moon, which just happened to be the same day as the fucking Harvest Dance.

The Harvest Dance was an old tradition passed down from the early 1400's, that the mortal world took less seriously now by making it a high school dance theme. Settlers who believed if they celebrated the harvest being planted it would bear more fruit.

All the fruit that high schoolers wanted was someone to spike the punch, get laid, and freedom.

At least we agreed on the freedom.

Cheyanne didn't have to convince us; we all knew the significance of the moon and stars. After all, it was what we were made of.

The first time we were set free to bring balance to the mortal world was the 1600's, in Henry Jon's corner of the world, at the same time they were celebrating their own harvest. We knew we needed to influence the town and the people, bring forth new ideas, and propel the mortals forward without their belief in the gods anymore. They had a new God, singular, and none of their new religion involved Zeus or the stars writing their fates. This God was absolute and died for them in an ultimate sacrifice, which we hadn't done, so our gods were cast aside.

I didn't expect the mortal world to capture my attention so much. That was the first time I met Arianna, except her name was Rosalia then. She was the only person in that small town who treated us as equals, instead of as the children of God's enemy—someone named the Devil.

Her kindness seeped into our hearts, and I knew I couldn't leave without her.

I spoke to our gods, always listening and waiting to interrupt your freewill with their own agenda, begging them to give her to me.

Zeus came to me in a dream, explaining that being set free in the mortal world had nothing to do with influence or the people; it had to do with taking Rosalia home to Olympus. Rosalia was his lost daughter who fell out of Olympus and lost her way back home. She took a mortal form, and Zeus patiently waited until she was old enough to trick into coming back home. He sent creatures and signs all meant to enchant her lost memories. When none of that worked, he sent us as a last resort.

Before our gods died, Zeus confessed to being cursed by Hera, his beloved wife, who hated the children he had that she didn't bare. She was always plotting to kill them off, and in her case, she got a mortal death.

I knew Henry Jon was onto us; his watchful eye didn't see much else. His daughter was beautiful and the ripe age to marry. I was sure the entire world was his enemy.

The ritual went off without a hitch when Rosalia laid down on the smooth rock. I didn't think I'd have the strength to make myself drive the knife into her chest but I heard Zeus's voice asking me to bring his daughter home.

That was all the strength I needed to kill her mortal body and go home.

Now the same thing was happening, except there was too much doubt. I doubted leaving. I doubted Ari's abilities. I doubted the ritual. I doubted the rule now that our gods were dead. And, I doubted the circle.

Everyone was keeping secrets, and all I wanted was answers.

I looked around the room at the people I trusted: one bored, one trying to not be in love, one insecure, one confused, and one who loathed me still.

We weren't winning any awards.

The gods would smite us for even giving into the hormones and mortal emotions like this. This was the opposite of staying levelheaded. After fourteen years in this prison, we all had given in to whatever got us by.

"Kate, I need you to get information. You're close to Cheyanne."

Her hands flew up in the air. "Ew. No one is close to her. Not it … "

Wide eyes I looked at her, wondering where she heard a question mark; there wasn't one. Luna volunteered without me having to scold anyone. The ritual was happening, and I needed a plan to keep Ari safe—not me or the circle but *her.*

Without Zeus's power living in her, bets were off; we might be stuck here forever, just as a punishment for the gods dying while we were here influencing the 20th century.

No one planned on being in prison for fourteen years.

I was well over it all—hormones, this body, the rules, the feelings …

"Ari, stay out of it and act clueless still."

She nodded in response, and I was surprised she didn't fight me. She was still reeling from her sudden memories with Nyx that no one expected either.

Now that they knew what was happening in the shadows, we could better prepare for the dance in a few weeks.

Caellum's whistle stopped me in my tracks and urged a grimace across my face that felt tight, strained.

"What Caellum? Don't make me regret bringing you in on this."

"Coming to the dark side, huh? All for some girl who looks petrified to know the truth."

I crossed my arms in front of me, standing tall, "She's adjusting. She's getting better at control,"

Caellum walked by me, with his broad shoulder colliding with mine. "That's not what I'm talking about, and you know it."

I wasn't the only one with memories; Caellum had his memories too—not the same ones. None of it mattered, since he was at another school entirely, after using some black magic to release the chains on himself, leaving the circle behind. He didn't stop to think of anyone else. I didn't need his memories competing anyways.

Every time we had a meeting with the circle, his ego drove a wedge between us, creating sides and opposing ideas. With him gone, I became even more the king.

Caellum almost made his voice sing-songy when he shouted, as he walked away, "Tell her everything, Bolton, or I willlllll … ."

I see he didn't let the threatening tone of his voice go but I needed him for this to work. He was strong, and he was also the only person willing to go against me.

Nyx was her confidant back home. Their friendship was secret, because he was the son of Hades, her father's enemy. She would meet him in the fields of truth and complain of her father's rules, her lack of freedom, and probably about me. We weren't destiny or fate; I was the guy her dad chose for her.

Now Nyx was remembering more than I thought he'd ever care to.

Zeus had almost died more times than I could count. He had many enemies but half of those times could have been pinned on Nyx. He would have done anything for Ari, even if she didn't ask. She complained, and Nyx snapped into some hero act, slaying all her monsters.

When Zeus died for the last time, we were stuck as mortals here. I couldn't blame Nyx for his final death. He was stuck here with me. Everyone felt a sharp pain at the same time, and we knew our home wasn't the same anymore.

Ari was *not* going to end up with Nyx—over my dead body.

As soon as I exited the hall to my secret room, I made sure everything was sealed, and I took Arianna's hand in mine, reminding her that she was mine, despite her new memories leaking into her consciousness.

Her small voice asked me, "What now?"

I squeezed your hand so you know you're mine and I'm not letting you get away this time. That's what now, is what my mind thought but the only words that came out of my mouth were: "Act normal."

Really, I meant act an Ari type of normal: loud, obnoxious, impatient, not the Ari that was still silently digesting the news dropped on her.

After classes, we had been going to the abandoned building toward the back of the campus to control her power and give her a rundown of the gods we now shared.

She didn't know Apollo from Diameter. She was catching on quickly but her memories were still out of my grasp. I couldn't ask Cheyanne to do the voodoo she does without putting Arianna at risk.

Cheyanne was asking too many questions that didn't matter, and I noticed.

Alba was hiding her file from everyone.

People were picking sides without telling me, and that was just cause for the wrath I was about to bring down on everyone during the ritual.

The next morning, I woke up as usual, with a body full of aches and pains from football and a kind or tired that coffee couldn't help. This morning was different; Arianna fell asleep in my bed last night. I looked down at her sleeping with a pillow between her arms and her head barely on it anymore.

My alarm went off, and she didn't budge. Leaning over her, I planted innocent kisses along her shoulder, hoping she'd wake up.

She moved her hand trying to slap me away from waking her up when I whispered into her hair, "We have a test. Get up."

She groaned loudly, rolling over onto her back and looking particularly unmotivated.

"Let's skip. We'll get coffee and hide out," her voice sounded hopeful, like I might agree. I was killing her hope by getting dressed and clapping my hands together just to annoy her this early in the morning.

"Come on, Ari. Don't tempt me with a good time … " I held up my hoodie that she had been wearing for the past week, overlooking the burn marks her lightning imprinted.

She popped up, sitting up, with her arms outstretched in her small black tank, creating a search party for her nipples. I found them. They perked up, getting hard, and I smirked in a satisfied sneer. I tossed the hoodie on the bed, wondering how I kept my hands off her last night.

It wasn't easy. It was hard, and so was I, all night. I remember pushing my hard on into her ass cheek, hoping she'd throw me some kind of bone but my rejection was still living in her head.

She still didn't remember who she was to me but the hormones inside me raged to be between her legs again.

The bed sunk down with a creek as I pushed my boots on, which seemed stupid with khaki pants. Ari, the shortened name

I had gotten used to calling her the past few weeks, her name suddenly too laboring to scold her with, crawled up behind me, pushing her chest into my back and wrapping her arms around my neck from behind.

"Okay, so we can't skip, but can we be late at least?"

My rejection had dropped off her radar, and she was testing my ability to keep my hands off her. My hormones were raging and knocking around my organs trying to land at my dick, which was what I was trying to avoid.

If all the tension found my dick, I wasn't going to be responsible for the aftermath.

Barking out my next move, standing up, and feeling her warmth against me fade, I snapped my suspenders closed on my jeans, "I'll be outside."

I left her in my room, alone, yet no alarms went off inside me.

I wanted the football season to be over so I could finally enjoy a clean scent coming from Nyx's room at the end of the hallway as he poured out. His undone boots, his rings acting as built-in brass knuckles, and his long hair unbrushed were just a part of his "don't care" attitude, when he really did care under it all.

We cared, at least enough to keep us here, tied to those emotions.

He walked by me, pushing his hand into my chest and pinning me into the wall. "When were you going to tell me?" He dropped his arm and stood there, letting me have a fighting chance before he gave me another shiner.

I stayed silent. I was an idiot. I knew what he meant. He wanted to know why I didn't tell him how connected he was to Arianna.

Arianna had timing that left a lot to be desired when she yanked my creaking door open, Nyx's anger only grew into his features, which were all made of stone and forged from fire. "What the fuck is she doing in your room?"

I laughed, only making Nyx more likely to punch me in the face ... or worse, if he felt like it. He killed Zeus more than once. I would be a piece of cake, like butter against his hot knife.

Arianna touched his arm, trying to calm him, which fueled my anger. "Nothing happened ... " Her voice was reassuring the guy who had no privilege to know that information.

I could have been fucking her all night, and it wasn't his business.

He shrugged off her hand, giving me a stare I wasn't about to combat into something worse, and growled, "Forget it."

I heard his unlaced boots stomping down the old staircase, while I waited for him to be out of sight before I made any moves.

"He doesn't need to know what does and doesn't happen between us."

She rolled her eyes at me, and I let her. It was how she managed her emotions by acting out. It was keeping the lightning in her veins inside instead of branching off in every direction.

Class wasn't particularly interesting, and Nyx was avoiding me at all costs, like I had killed his cat. He opted to sit on the windowsill instead of one the empty desks in the room, making it clear how much I shouldn't even bother.

Luna leaned over her desk in History, Alba's class, asking me what his problem was. I wanted to be the asshole that he was making me out to be by breaking her heart in the process. He moved swiftly, making sure to beat my words, before I even formed them in my head.

"Starting more drama, friend? Leave Luna out of it ... " His voice didn't sound familiar or loyal like I was used to.

I felt challenging enough to stand up and let this come to blows if it needed to. "She asked me what your problem was ... You afraid I'll tell her?"

He stood up taller, side stepping and cutting my vision off from Luna, with confliction strewn across his face.

He couldn't understand how to classify his need to protect Arianna and being accustomed to loving Luna silently. "Don't fucking throw your power around, just because you're the only one with memories."

I snickered, letting my body dip down to the desk without letting my weight sit on it fully. My fingers covered a smirk, and I looked up at him through my eyelashes. "You play the tough guy, Nyx, and I'll be the leader I always am. Let's stay in our own lanes."

Nyx had a short fuse—one I just used a match to set off. He yanked me up, fisting the material of the button down uniform shirt we were all forced to wear—forced to resemble each other even though we were all so different.

I felt my shoulder blades slam into the wall, regardless of how toned I kept my body. None of it made up for the powers I didn't have.

Nyx's fist wrinkling my button up resembled Arianna's—gold running through his veins. The blood of the gods coursed through him, and I was at the other end powerless.

I didn't bother flinching; there was no point. His fist was going to collide with my face whether I liked it or not, full force, no holding back ... Luckily, he couldn't leave any real damage; we couldn't hurt each other.

I tried to absorb his fist colliding with my cheekbone as best I could, while Alba tried (and failed) to get Nyx off me. The rest of our class was stunned and watching without any real participation to stop it.

Nyx leaned into me so only I could hear, his lips brushing my cheek and my gaze to one side as I twisted my jaw around trying to break up the pressure: "Heavy is the mother fucking crown who wears it, huh, brother?"

He let go of his grip on me, and I had to bite back retaliation as I got my bearings back. If I was the King of Arcadia Prep, then the knight just embarrassed me enough to dethrone me.

I was still trying to stand up tall and swallow the pain reverberating on my cheek, "Did you tell Luna you've been dreaming of Ari?"

Nyx took me down without any real effort, and I felt my skull hit the hardwood floor with a kind of force that left me dizzy. The sound was muted and muffled; the room seemed to blur; and his hands around my neck made me contemplate if he had the balls to kill the one person with all the answers—well, ones he wanted at least.

My voice was choked up: "Do it if you're going to do it, brother..."

His hands didn't loosen, and I felt his fists around my neck tighten, keeping me quiet by putting pressure on my vocal chords.

It took Leo, Austin, and Alba to get Nyx to let up with the gold shining through his veins like a warning sign—one I didn't take.

Now I had to bear through the sting of my lip being split too. I could taste the tartness that made it seem like I was sucking on pennies. I wiped it away with my knuckles before anyone would notice the color wasn't red like theirs but gold.

Nyx fell down next to me on his ass, elbows slung on his bent knees. "You're a real asshole, you know."

I let my arm fall beside me, outstretched, as I heaved in all the air my best friend just stole from my lungs. Luna didn't dare move until she knew Nyx was okay but when honey and lavender wafted by me, I knew she had taken off in a hurry.

Ari stood above me, offering me a hand, looking just as conflicted with dueling emotions as Nyx did earlier. I took her hand only sitting up and taking my deserved punishment, at least the last hit I earned.

Still catching my breath Ari filled the silence: "What kind of dreams?"

"Not here," I snapped in her direction.

Caellum wasn't even here, and he was forcing my hand in ways I didn't want to. I knew I had to tell her, that left room for her to choose differently and I wasn't giving my crown to anyone.

Heavy is the crown that *I* wear.

CHAPTER 26

Arianna

Nyx was on the floor next to a beaten Bolton, and I didn't know who I was more worried for.

Nothing was getting any clearer now that I had the ability to have lightning spring from my hands.

Nyx couldn't have cared any less about me until he tugged down his shirt and showed me a scar I clearly created with no memory of doing so.

Now to hear he was dreaming of me made me question my connection to him. The closest thing I had to memories was the dreams I was having—my subconscious coming alive, trying to make sense of my new truths.

Luna, the only true friend I had here, ran out of the room, just at the thought of Nyx's attention straying from her.

Kate popped her bubble gum and assessed the mess of us three. "Well … way to go, New Girl. Way to respect boundaries."

She wasn't lying. Luna was my friend; nothing but sweetness and innocence emanated from her. I was the one inflicting new sensations by encouraging whatever magnetism I felt for Nyx that was pulling me to him.

Alba's deep voice was full of authority and annoyance when it sounded: "Detention. Starting now. In the library. I want 2,000 words on the history of the Harvest Dance. Move!"

His hand raised and pointed for the door with a sharp gaze that kind of scared me. He had to be well over six feet tall, and his skin was so dark that the sheen on top almost resembled glitter. His piercing blue eyes weren't anything but serious.

It was hard to imagine someone actually liking teenagers, not to mention wanting to become a teacher at Arcadia.

I grabbed my backpack, waiting for Bolton to get up. Nyx's hand grabbed onto Bolton's, helping him up. Boys get over things more quickly than girls.

If this was Kate and Luna fighting in class, it'd be easy to assume Kate would be holding that grudge for centuries.

I guess literally now.

I waited until we were on the second level of the library to repeat myself. "What kind of dreams? I'm having weird dreams too." I dropped my stuff on the table, standing there uncomfortably talking about this in front of the guy whose bed I woke up in.

Nyx sat on top of the table, fiddling with the heavy rings on his fingers. "Just of memories. You're in most of them. Ask your boyfriend; he has all our memories tucked under his crown, which is not very gracious of a king."

Bolton was leaning against the wood bookcase, trying to pretend he didn't hear him, until our focus bore into him. "What are memories going to do for you? They aren't going to suddenly stick and become yours."

"I don't have any memories, Bolton. This all still sounds crazy, and I've had weeks to adjust. I need something, anything, to just make sense." My voice was practically begging him to tell me something, like it'd spark a torrential downpour of memories.

All the things I forgot.

All the things that sounded crazy.

All the whys, hows, and whats.

My eyes welled up, drowning my perfect vision behind a veil of unshed tears. Bolton's exterior changed from giving no fucks to not wanting to see me cry in seconds, and he rushed to my side, pulling me into him.

I didn't know if he was being so nice simply because Nyx just admitted I'm in most of his dreams or if he was finally tolerating me enough to let me touch him in a vulnerable way.

Bolton only liked to be touched when it was either painful or sexual; anything in between was a hard pass.

His strong arms engulfed me, holding me against him, as a tear slid down my cheek just from the gesture—authentic or not. He spoke, even with my ear pressed against his shirt, and I knew he was speaking more to Nyx, not me. "Back home, you two were close. Zeus hated your friendship, and that's when I came into the picture."

His words fell off, flattening like there should be more. I looked up at him, pulling away enough to see him. "And?"

Nyx's foot stomped down on a chair, silently forcing him to continue with his confession. Letting out a heavy sigh into the air above us, Bolton went on: "Zeus picked me … for you. The son of his enemy didn't have a chance. He knew how much you loved him."

I pulled away, feeling betrayed in a way Bolton wouldn't have stood for. He was helping me learn how to control my powers under stress, letting me sleep in his bed, and keeping secrets that changed everything.

"How do you know that information wouldn't have changed anything? I could have remembered or understood this shit you threw me into."

Bolton's hands didn't reach me; him holding me was for Nyx's sake, not mine. He stood there, defeated, with his hands in his hoodie pocket, looking suddenly not as strong as I once saw him.

He was powerless, in more than one way now.

"You're an asshole—a powerless asshole who can't use it against anyone now that we know the truth." I felt the same kind of anger, defense, creeping up my neck and making the peach fuzz stand up at attention. I looked down at my hands that were glowing gold, outlining my veins.

Nyx took two big steps and held my wrists in place, down by my side. He was bent over, looking me at my eye level: "Relax."

I couldn't relax. I couldn't breathe. I couldn't be anything but pissed off and a heat-seeking missile looking for revenge. My eyes felt wild when I finally focused on Nyx before yanking my wrists out of his grasp.

I needed space to let my anger breathe, and if I did it here, the library would get a remodel that no one approved of.

I wasn't headed anywhere in particular when I stormed past the abandoned building and for the woods. Something about the dark, foggy woods made me feel more calm, like it was home at one time.

I found a spot down by the stream that was deep enough to avoid people but still a straight shot back to campus. The stump was damp and seeping through my skirt and tights that the school made us wear. I didn't care. I need to breathe the cool, fresh air and listen to the calming, quiet trickling of the stream long enough to slow down my pulse. I watched my veins go from being a gold illuminating through my skin back to normal in a few minutes.

Breathing through the change, I forced myself to still and focus on the sound of the stream until all my anger seemed to dissipate. Once it did, I dug in my bag for Henry Jon's journal that I now carried with me everywhere.

It had been a few weeks since I last broke the spine; maybe his words would make more sense than my own.

Henry Jon

My precious, innocent, Rosalia was put to rest today. Her faith was shaken, and the unholy spirit had won her soul in a war we thought we won.

No matter how many Bibles you own, how many churches you step foot in, how long you pray before bed, the Devil has all kinds of tricks up his sleeve.

This time, he sent his children to torment our faith.

Rosalia's death would not go unnoticed. In the wake of her death, the one true God came to me in my sleep, giving me purpose to my life when all felt hopeless. He showed me a path not yet taken, to forge an army to fight His white light against the darkness we don't speak of. We would warn those of the monsters stalking our souls and their tricks.

The day I held Rosalia breathless on the dead oak, the great tree held duality in its roots, just as we would hold duality in our hearts.

I was drunk off the new power my Lord gave me, fueling every step of my mission, as we searched for the Devil's child. The dead oak's stump bore so many clues: the golden liquid, the tusk in the tall grass, the dark magic they used to summon their lord—all left behind like breadcrumbs.

I wanted to smite them all for taking my Rosalia. I wanted to damn them to the Hell they crawled up from.

Pastor Cotton and Blacksmith Samuel forged new weapons—both relics and arrogantly painful. The arrows points were shaved down from their own tusk, the gold liquid melted down and boned with metal to create new bullets, and the dead oak chopped up to make javelins and riffles. We spared no part of what the Devil left behind.

They possessed my Rosalia until there was nothing left of my angel. It started small with the sleepwalking doubling and her Bible studies no longer a focus. It wasn't until their leader

*poisoned her mind, like all young men did when searching
for a wife.*

*It wasn't my Rosalia that passed on that day; it was the
demon child shedding her human skin.*

*We searched the woods for any sign of the children for
weeks, even crossing borders to other territories in our search.
We came up empty-handed every sunset, and every dawn a
new hope was born.*

*It wasn't until Ranger Charles received word one day,
two long years later, that a small town in the deep south was
reporting strange activity. They reported strange settlers that
came to town with no purpose or reason. Ranger Charles rode
out before the sun kissed the ground, riding to chase up to the
Devil's spawn.*

*We rode a half day later with our weapons in tow, ready to
catch up to revenge. The one true God teaches us forgiveness but
I made peace with forgiveness being at the end of my musket.*

Henry Jon hunted the circle for what happened, for revenge over the body I apparently took over and left in my wake in the past. I had no memory of anything before this life; I didn't even remember my hands holding such power.

None of this made sense, and now knowing Nyx was more than someone I trusted was making my head spin.

I trusted Nyx, yet Bolton was the first person to steal more than trust from me as soon as I walked on campus.

Luna was my only friend here, and I found a way to let trouble even ruin that before I packed up and left again.

Typing out her name with a new message, I knew hiding out in the woods wasn't going to help ... or was it? I had been virtually hiding for 14 years, and it seemed to serve everyone pretty well. As soon as I came to Arcadia, there had been nothing but trouble.

I stopped, staring down at her name and a blank text I had yet to type, as I contemplated running. The only thing stopping me was my dad, who wasn't really even my dad, who was in some secret location off saving the world.

I deleted the text and typed out "Dad" instead:

   ↗ *I think I'm in over my head. Call me when you can.*

I knew getting to a phone in the middle of a war zone or third world country was more than hard. I tried to stay hopeful. Something in me needed to keep burning.

I retyped "Luna" out, more stable and calm than a minute ago:

   ↗ *Pizza? Girls' night in? I didn't know about Nyx, and I would never indulge it.*

I felt guilty just typing out his name when it wasn't mine to claim, write, say. All of that belonged to Luna, the one madly and quietly, in love with him.

Everyone could see their true feelings glued to their features when they were in the same room, except them.

They weren't giving in enough to just date, and I had no idea why. Now, maybe I did know: dreaming of another girl can put a damper on even the strongest motivations.

I was stubborn enough to stay in the woods until my hands felt numb and stung from the cold coming in. I pushed Henry Jon's journal in my bag and started back towards campus in the same direction.

I started walking, with every dead leaf and broken branch crunching under my boots, when I felt someone else's presence, strong enough to make me stop in my tracks.

I knew it was stupid as soon as I shouted it: "Hello? Anyone there?"

No one answered, just as I expected. No one was stupid enough to follow someone in the woods as dusk was settling in, just to pop out from behind a tree to respond with a casual, "Hey."

Sinister feelings gripped around my vital organs, making it hard to expand my chest enough to get the oxygen I needed. Someone was in the woods with me, and I didn't know who or why.

Crunch, snap, a hollow step on a rock … all were a flashing neon sign for the sinister one behind me. I was making it easy for him. I kept walking in quick steps, until I saw campus in the wood's opening, and I sighed heavily, hopefully.

Fuck you, sinister fucking woods. Joke's on you.

Just as my head craned back to look at campus and my foot stepped over the threshold onto the perfectly manicured grass, I felt the hand clamp over my mouth, and a strong arm encircled my waist, dragging me back into the woods.

What little movements I could make felt draining as I forced them to become big and threatening. My hands gripped the forearm of the strong person, who wasn't even moving his hand from my mouth, for good reason—they knew I'd scream. My whole body felt a focused sense of anxiety, and I noticed my hands began glowing with the gold I still wasn't even used to.

Suddenly I felt a small pinch in my side, sharp enough to steal my breath and replace it with a jagged one that added to my anxiety.

My tense, small movements became limp as my eyes fell half-mast, too heavy to hold up anymore.

I realized the person was dragging me, and my heels were creating small trails in the soft dirt, like fucked-up breadcrumbs.

CHAPTER 27

Arianna

I woke up with every muscle feeling sore, every bone rattling under my skin, and my heart beating so slow I felt drowsy. I didn't recognize my surroundings as I looked all around me.

I was on the floor, on top of an antique rug, and the only light was a small lamp in the corner with a yellow glow barely illuminating anything at all.

It looked like an old study or speakeasy, with dark accents, comfy furniture that begged you to stay, old paintings hung, and the red walls gleamed like a threat.

Where am I?

I didn't realize I said it out loud until a husky voice responded, "Welcome to my place. Oh, and you're welcome for saving your life."

The shadow in the doorway appeared with his blonde hair pushed to one side. His arms were crossed in front of him, and his necklaces danced on his forearms.

I tried to stand up but my body wasn't ready, so I sat up straight with my arms matching his disgruntled demeanor. "Caellum, how lovely to see you again. I thought we couldn't hurt each other? Felt pretty painful to me."

"Maybe your tolerance for pain is just weak…" He handed me a water and smirked, knowing I was still stuck to the floor, despite my trying to get up. I snatched the water bottle, feeling the inside of my cheeks get tight without any real moisture.

I was a sack of skin, twisted in knots, and so tense it could've produced bruises from Caellum's stunt.

"Maybe you're just an asshole."

He chuckled, pushing his fingers through his hair, looking attractive in all his malevolent ways.

I scolded myself for even thinking that, when he made it clear he was all about himself, only himself, and I wasn't joining that fan club any time soon.

My legs felt less like Jell-O, and I used the chair to get up from the carpet. "What am I doing here exactly? You have my number; that's less work you know."

Stalking over to the desk, I looked at the map he had of the woods rolled out and held down by paperweights made out of ordinary objects: a cup of pens, as football trophy, an ashtray devoid of any ashes.

"Omari was in the woods following you. It was the only way to keep you quiet and out of trouble." He took a marker and drew a black x over the map in a specific location next to the stream, and I wondered what he was looking for.

Me? The journal? The husk?

"And? He's circle."

"Not everyone in the circle can be trusted. Were you not at that exclusive meeting I was forced to attend?" His voice was as sarcastic as mine, every sentence ended in a lashing, reminding me he did it better so I shouldn't bother to try.

"Still didn't have to stick me with … whatever that was … " I was arguing with someone out of my league, and the failure of last time was making me feel small.

"Did you die?" His eyes still shifted down to his map, not seeing me cross my arms and roll my eyes.

"No."

"It's adamantine sickle bore from Gaia. In small doses, it isn't lethal for us."

"So you poisoned me? Wow, can't trust anyone around here."

"Relax, it's not strong enough to damage the immortal flesh melted down." He was casual about almost killing me—so casual that I felt anxiety I never had before bloom inside my chest. I was sitting across from someone who was not afraid to betray those around him—his own kind.

He moved around the room, like I wasn't there, eyed my bag, and dumped it over.

"Hey! That's my stuff. What do you think you're doing?"

He seemed unaffected by my glare or yelling altogether.

His eyes met mine as he poked through my belongings flooding the table. He snatched the journal up and started flipping through, like he knew what he was looking for, like it was his.

I slumped down in a chair on the other side of the desk relinquishing any effect I had on Caellum. He was going to do what he wanted, when he wanted, and I was just an annoyance in his way.

"What are you looking for?"

"Something Henry Jon left behind: a Plan B." He didn't look up and continued thumbing the fragile pages.

I tried to stay neutral, even though my mind snapped to the husk in my bedroom under my bed in a Doc Marten shoe box. It was all that was left of Henry Jon: a journal, a tusk, and some part of his daughter I probably took with me when she died for me to live.

"What for?" I shrugged disinterested, when that's all I was: interested.

He slammed the book shut, slammed his palms on the table, and hung his head between his shoulders, defeated. No, probably just annoyed I existed.

"It's the God-Killer. It's a legend that Henry Jon found a tusk from your beast and used it to make weapons that kill gods." His voice was harsh and curt, like I should know these things but my memories were still missing.

So that's what that little tusk did. Well, what was left. No wonder it was hidden.

"Wait, *my* beast?"

He handed the journal back, and I shoved all my belongings back into the confinement of my bag. "Yes, your pet. Ophiotaurus. Half snake, half bull." The one from the journal that Henry Jon sees Rosalia/me pet in the tall grass.

"Let's just add that to the pile of 'don't know's' and 'now I do's'. It's a mountain now. Did you know about Nyx?"

I watched him drag his fingers through his hair, pushing it back from falling onto his face, still hunched over the desk, slaving over this map, hoping it would take pity on him and give him answers. "I have my memories. Just like Bolton."

I sat up even taller, not hiding how interested I was now. "I thought Bolton was the only one with memories."

"Bolton does a lot to make shit seem one way. Let me guess he was forced to tell you about your connection to Nyx? He probably left out some parts."

Intrigued, also cautious, I leaned forward with my elbows on the desk and looked up at him. I knew he and Bolton didn't have a winning friendship, and that alone made me question every word.

"Bolton wasn't chosen by Zeus for you," he said. "He was chosen only after I decided I didn't want you."

He was aiming to insult me at the same time he spilled some truth. All he really did was add to the pile of confusion sitting next to me, as tall as I was and not going away any time soon.

"You? No offense ... " The shock had my tongue too loose.

Bolton, the loyal ... Bolton, the king ... was also Bolton, the liar.

He was holding all his memories hostage and using them to keep his throne secure.

My hands felt tingly, and the anger inside was only growing with each pause. Bolton weighed everyone's value on how loyal they could be to him when he was just another false god glorifying secret agendas to get his way.

"Royalty marries royalty. We didn't have a choice."

"Who are your parents? Are Bolton's royal too?"

You couldn't not hear the snickering against his closed fist pressing to his lips. "Prometheus, the Titan, and Athena. Inner circle type shit. Bolton's parent is royal; just one, not two."

I sat back, still dumbfounded at all the information.

I was from Olympus.

My dad was Zeus.

When he died, the lightning he conquered transferred to me.

Nyx was someone I trusted.

Caellum was someone I was promised to.

Bolton was second runner up.

He made our connection seem so important, desperate to make me remember when none of my memories would work in his favor. He was ruining any chance with me after I'd remember the truth, yet he still wanted me to have a choice in who I chose without Zeus alive.

"Do you trust Bolton?"

He stopped fidgeting with the maps and his search, placing his hands on his hips. "He's a lot of things—conniving, manipulative, selfish ... but he does the right thing in the end."

Caellum could have him. I was done being betrayed by the people I loved.

Just like my ex-boyfriend who felt me up, let his mom press charges, and not care I was forced into Arcadia Prep. Long distance almost never worked but that asshole didn't even try.

I contemplated everything up until right now—the mess my life had become. "Why is he so worried about the ritual? No one else has lightning coming from their fingers."

Caellum sat down finally, still annoyed and grilling his metallic eyes into mine, like it would make me back down. "He likes sure things. Nothing about you is sure, and with the gods dead, Lady Luck and Fate aren't smiling down on us."

"Wait, those are real people?"

He shook his head in disgust at my inability to tell metaphor and analogy from swirling possibilities. I was never into *Twilight* or *The Vampire Diaries* but knowing who I was made every impossible thought I ever had seem plausible now.

What else was real that I deemed childish?

"Am I free to go now? Am I your hostage?" Folding my arms against my chest, I sulked like a child, which seemed fitting for the tantrum raging inside my head.

"Leave the journal." He was making demands while I was weak enough to overlook them.

He was underestimating me.

Mistake number one.

"No, the journal doesn't leave my sight. Why would I trust you? You're the enemy and looking for the 'God Killer'."

Grabbing the journal off the desk, the spine cracked to its limits and the folds flopped open haphazardly. He was already abusing a key piece of my evidence.

"If I was looking to kill anyone, I would have left you in the woods to die at the hands of Omari. I have no issue with having blood on my hands."

I looked down at his hands, instinctively expecting to see blood. *Damn metaphors.*

"Have you ... has Bolton ... ?"

"We don't get stuck as teenagers for 14 years for good behavior, Arianna. We went to whatever length we had to ... to go home. Sometimes that meant seeing the stars in someone who was only a dark sky."

I looked around the room for my phone, the room was like one of those iSpy books with too much to look at—too many distractions for the object you desired to find.

The anxiety blooming in my chest was fully grown and ripping its way through my vital organs.

Bolton had killed innocent people, and he didn't wear the guilt of his actions.

I was in way over my head, and all I wanted was to sacrifice my love of adventures and mischief for the mundane life I should have been living. I made sure all my things were shoved back into my bag, along with Henry Jon's journal that I wasn't done reading, before I backed my way out of the room. Slowly, I hoped he'd let me go.

I bumped into something hard, and when I peered around, I saw Bolton standing in the doorway, looking downright malicious.

His eyes looked black, so much depth to swim in I almost fell in just taking stock of his presence. His fists were balled up on either side of his hips, and his shoulders were so squared off that it seemed threatening to even me.

Caellum wasn't afraid of him, and he made it clear: "Are you gonna sulk or come in?"

He stepped forward, expertly around me, like I wasn't there at all, when Nyx appeared and grabbed Bolton's arm, holding him back. It was like watching Bolton become glued to the ground out of nowhere. Nyx's strength seemed unreal; then again, all of this did.

Unreal.

Awful.

Insane.

A curse I didn't ask for.

"Fuck you, Caellum. Always have to dip into your bag of tricks, huh? You can't ever just bow to me like you should."

Caellum didn't seem the least bit affected when he moved around the table and perched on its edge, putting his feet in the chair in front of him. "I don't bow to fake kings. Zeus never crowned you, and Arianna never married you. You don't matter any more than the dirt under my boot, demigod."

Bolton ripped his arm away but I saw Nyx loosen his fingers, like Caellum's insult finally crossed a line.

Bolton stormed towards him, wiping the smirk off his face with one unseen motion. I could only see Bolton's hand on Caellum's shoulder. I stood still enough to not make a sound, shocked, when I realized what had actually happened, and where Bolton's other hand was: connected to a dagger that was full-blade deep in Caellum.

He had stabbed Caellum in the stomach with one easy motion.

He stabbed Caellum to feed his own aggression.

He stabbed Caellum, knowing he might be wrong about the rules and that he may not be okay.

Caellum coughed before letting his head fall back, and I saw a trail of gold liquid run down the side of his mouth down his sharp jawline.

"Bolton!"

He didn't turn towards me once; he was soaking the pleasure of draining the life from Caellum, and his upturned mouth proved it.

I saw a ruthless side of Bolton I hadn't seen yet, and for whatever reason … the dangerous parts of me swooned. I could feel every part of me swirl with desire at his brute force protecting me.

I was stuck in a state of confusion that I would feel this way and infatuation for this side of him, even while my morals begged me to check Caellum for a pulse.

Nyx leaned against the wall, looking at his phone more interested than Bolton committing murder in front of us. "Do you feel better now? Can we go now? I have plans."

Bolton stood there, watching Caellum's lifeless body fall back, and his head hung off the other end of the desk. Bolton removed the knife, pushing Caellum's shoulder back. He couldn't take his eyes off him. Nothing screamed remorse or guilt; he was pleased with himself.

Accomplished even.

Standing over a traitor's body, like the king he was and always would be, because we built him up, all the way to the throne, and now he wasn't giving it up—even if he was powerless and every bit as malicious as he seemed.

CHAPTER 28

Bolton

Caellum did enough damage while I turned a blind eye. He chose to make Arcadia Prep our battle ground, and the fight was never about going home but about who would wear the crown that was only made to fit my head.

Demigod.

He dug his own grave when he decided we were hitting below the belt. I may have a human parent, unlike the rest of the circle. I only needed one to be considered royalty in Olympus.

I pushed my way past Arianna, who was shedding a displaced tear for Caellum. I was already a type of pissed off that gets people beheaded, and now she was pushing me even further into the arms of disobedience.

"Whisk those fucking crocodile tears away. He isn't dead, Arianna. It'll just slow him down."

She pushed her face up to look at me. The tears were running down her face, and now her eyebrows pinched together in the middle. "You're a monster."

She was calling me a monster but I could tell by her hard nipples and the extra violet in her eyes twinkling back at me that she was turned on. Arianna was turned on by the monster that had been lying and hiding instead of showing its face.

I shifted behind her, leaning down enough to whisper right into her ear, "I'm pretty sure it's 'Betrothed' to you but 'King' is fine for now."

Nyx was grinning ear to ear, seemingly no longer worried about their history we still couldn't grasp … or he was just trying not to end up on the other end of my blade, like Caellum.

"Nice going, New Girl. Piss off the demon inside him; that'll save us all." He spoke while following Bolton out of the room, with his eyes still glued to his phone screen.

I listened to every word of their exchange, somewhat ready for some safe word to drag all the memories back.

She caught up to his side and asked, "Can I borrow your phone? I have to text Luna."

Nyx twisted out of reach, as her hand lunged for his phone. "What makes you think I'm texting Luna?"

"You always have that stupid grin on your face when you're texting Luna. I know, because she gets the same one."

They both are so in love that their bodies can't help it. Someone wanna fill him in so he can stop being angry about losing Arianna?

"Better than the other faces I make, alone, in my room while undressing her in my mind."

I was sure his confession had her blushing all the way to her core, which was still aching for me.

I had more bad qualities than good right now, yet her clit was throbbing harder than ever for me.

"Use mine," I told her. "We have a game tonight anyways. I'll meet you there. Stay with Luna and Kate."

"We have a game? Since when?"

"Since … any team who forfeits can request a game at any time."

I glared at Nyx, already utilizing his full power and soaked in dream-like memories of Arianna—my Arianna.

"We were supposed to have a girls' night. How long was I even gone?"

I stopped walking away from her, and all the anger she was kicking up abruptly. "Five hours. You stormed off like a child five hours ago. And for five hours of my day I looked all over for your ass. And who came to save you Arianna? Me. So next time you wanna tell me I don't wear a goddamn crown, you better rip it off my head first."

I watched her eyes drown in an ocean of unshed tears, and her face tried to iron out how much it was folding under my harsh words.

Almost—that's how close she made me to feeling bad. She looked broken, stressed, and cursed, just like the rest of us. I had broken her resistance and attitude in a few sentences.

She shoved me out of her way. "You're such as asshole, Bolton. No wonder I ran away when it came time to marry you!"

I let her shove past me, out of my sight, with my phone, because she just remembered something. Her remembering was the best feeling I've had in fourteen years, and I wasn't letting it be ruined by her spite. Knowing Arianna, she'd force herself to forget just to have nothing to say to me.

Nyx loomed, unamused and ready to let the aggression out on the field. "She just keeps running away. Well, well, our king was always without a queen."

He walked past me, the same way she did with a shifted shoulder and palm against my chest, like they'd blow me over in the process.

"I remembered something too. That wasn't your first kill. We've done that before … " he shouted, as the distance grew between us and my patience was thinning.

No shit.

I, Zeus's play-thing, was constantly doing what no one else would, like killing, and finding Arianna every time she disappeared and wiggled her way out from under his thumb.

At least someone other than fucking Caellum was remembering.

The field was already lit up, and the stands were filling in like this was planned. The energy was ringing in the air as I walked out of vision, finding the door to the locker room, before pulling it open with so much force I almost hoped I injured myself.

I had better things to do tonight than tame Nyx and Austin from taking everything out on the other team.

Opening my locker felt routine. I was on autopilot, moving without trying, when I started to get ready. I didn't even see Nyx out of the corner of my eye when he barked behind me. "How many times, Bolton? How many times did we do that? How many times did I take the heat for your actions?"

He was remembering more.

Moments were triggering both of their memories to coming back tenfold.

"I didn't need anyone to take any heat for me, so relax. I had Zeus's blessing in everything I did for the gods!"

The locker room was full, and everyone could hear us but neither of us cared. We wanted to fight it out until gold poured from countless wounds.

He was my best friend, here and in Olympus, and nothing was going to change that—not how much blood was on my hands or Arianna's love. Until he remembered that part, we were perpetually stuck in this hatred.

"Did you ever think the gods were … oh, I don't know … wrong? Maybe this is hell, and we're being punished for all the shit we did!"

His fist plowed through the locked lockers and the puncture of it cracked over my eardrums painfully. I forced myself not to flinch. I had no relay powers, no way to protect myself. I only had my flagrant disregard for their abilities.

That always threw powerful people off—nonbelievers.

"Speaking ill of the dead, now? Is that how much you want your memories to be wrong? No one forced you to balance sex and death; it's who you are."

The locker room seemed quiet as we argued; there wasn't even the sound of anyone moving around or gear being picked through. It made both of us halt our words, letting them push against our teeth to keep them inside.

We both looked around at everyone moving around, getting ready, only we couldn't hear anything, and apparently they couldn't hear us. We were yelling and arguing and damn near blows. No one was cheering us on or videoing it for whatever fucking social media app they preferred.

"What's going on … ?" It wasn't a question; it was an accusation meant for whoever was behind this trick.

I was in the clear. Demigods didn't have power … not like this.

"Jasper! Knock it off!" Nyx shouted at nothing.

Jasper swiveled around a row of lockers, with his beanie covering most of his ink-colored hair, only a few strays stuck out at the edges. His brown eyes were mostly yellow; the gold accents were taking over dominance and the brown became the background. He looked unassuming, uninterested, and cocky at all times.

"You're welcome, *your majesty*." Everything to come out of his mouth was sarcasm.

How did Arianna's own sarcasm not seek him out first? Together they could kill the entire population with a smile and sarcastic remark.

"You can't just use, Jasper … " I pushed past Nyx and his moral dilemma. I had problems that only a gold ring and crown could fix.

Crime and punishment.

He moved a hand gracefully through the air, like he needed to direct the abilities he had. "You could say thank you next time I save your asses."

We weren't Hogwarts students, vampires, or witches; we were gods. No wand needed.

I shoved a flat palm into his shoulder, making it clear there were rules to using now that Arianna was acting as a catalyst, I said, "Does it look I need saving, Jasper? Stay out of this."

Her being at Arcadia Prep alone shifted the air and gave everyone a boost in their abilities—ones we forgot existed, because she'd been missing so long this last time.

"You aren't the only one who can help, Bolton. Zeus made you king but I don't have to bow."

He pushed off the lockers, pushing his back towards me, and the sounds around us swelled up all at once, like the sound was up all the way and you forgot when you pushed play.

Jasper was pushing my last nerve; everyone was, by suddenly questioning my authority.

Nyx whisper-shouted to himself a simple, "What the fuck?"

My ears were still adjusting to the white noise that went missing, and it was surprising I even heard him. He didn't need an answer, and I didn't have one anyways.

Austin tried to lighten the mood by bringing up the Harvest Dance, while we geared up. "I'm gonna ask Kate after the game, so let's try not to lose this one. I don't want a pity yes."

"She's your fucking girlfriend; she's not going to say no, bro."

Kate was deemed a queen, not my queen, by the student body for being full of demands and for her bubbly voice that acted as a double-edged sword. She wore pink and her voice bubbled with friendliness but nothing about Kate was friendly.

Everyone assumed we were together, king and queen; it made sense. Austin worked very hard to make sure people knew they were together, with his public displays, like the one he was describing happening after the game.

It was tradition to ask someone to the Harvest Dance in some over-the-top way.

I never took part in it; no one was worth me going to some ridiculous lengths. Arianna was worth it, I was pretty sure she wasn't talking to me now.

I snapped back into the conversation instead of thinking of my betrothed, who didn't want anything to do with me now.

"I think I'm gonna ask Luna. She deserves it…" Nyx's voice was still unsure.

Peace offering? Trying to avoid feelings for Arianna? Pity on Luna's big heart being destroyed by the truth?

Coach's larger-than-life voice rang through the room: "Let's go! What do I got, a bunch of girls on the team? Hurry up!"

I grabbed my helmet and headed for the door. I wanted this game to be over with, this day, this nightmare… this *curse*.

The lights were on high, illuminating the field, every blade of grass and imperfection in high definition detail. I was c0-captain by definition but leader none the less. I had to lead this team with some kind of motivation, or I might as well throw myself on the bench and let this end in a quick loss. I waved the team over to huddle up, throwing my helmet on the ground and crushing it under my foot.

What was I supposed to tell the faces looking back at me? What kind of king doesn't have the perfect words before heading into battle?

Arianna's words kept repeating in my head: *Powerless. Powerless. Powerless.*

I had never felt like more of a fraud than at her hand, her words. Her absence didn't break me as much as her hate-fueled words.

Without realizing it, I went from looking up at the grey sky to my eyeline falling to the sidelines, looking for her purple hair.

My queen had ruined me in a way I wasn't shrugging off. One look … that's all I needed. One second of our eyes locking, and I would see Fate at work.

This was all written in the stars—her, the circle, the gods dying, this prison. This was the calm, and she was my storm, lightning and all.

Purple hair … there. I had spotted her climbing the stairs with Kate and Luna.

Turn around, Ari. Turn around.

I was pleading in my head, while my team's eyes were all glued to me for some kind of hype, confidence, to win this game.

She stopped turning around, like she sensed my gawking, standing there on the steps, doused with duteousness. Not one thing was *her*, except her damn hair. We let our eyes stay locked, until Nyx's swift hand slapped me across my cheek, eliciting a sharp pain that crawled over my skin. I glared at him for interrupting my moment with Arianna before I could drag any silent answers from her.

"We gonna play a game, or you gonna stare at her the whole time?"

I leaned in, bullshitting my way through some speech about losing the season and this being redemption.

No one can resist a redemption story.

Once we put our hands in and shouted the traditional, "Make them bleed red and see nothing but gold!" we broke, jogging into our places. Our school colors and that saying were created by some past captain while no doubt drunk or on some rage stimulated by the 'roids in his veins.

The game wasn't going terribly. We had a chance of winning. We were up by three and still had one last quarter to push that number further away from their score.

Every chance I could, I looked to the stands at the purple hair, my queen, watching with boredom alive in her eyes. She was taunting me, trying to break me into an apology I wouldn't be giving anyone. The truth was ugly. Who apologizes for that?

Nyx was on the sidelines, pouring water over his hair, before he put the helmet back on, when he shouted into the stands, "Luna!"

She looked alarmed, bewildered, and sat forward like something could be wrong for him to be talking to her so casually in public.

"Go to the dance with me!"

"You're in the middle of a game, Nyx!" I could see her blushing from, here as everyone stopped to stare at what was happening.

"What's it gonna be, little lamb? Wanna go with a wolf?"

She bit her lip, holding a smile captive, as she nodded her head. He got the lamb to willingly go anywhere with a wolf. Nyx was going to eat every innocent part of her.

Austin pushed off his helmet, "Hey, asshole! Way to steal my thunder!"

Nyx shrugged, jogging back with his helmet still off. He stood in front of me in line as I leaned down, pushing my fingers into the ground, waiting for the whistle.

Looking at Nyx, I nodded my head, and we both knew I was lifting the ban on him using his strength. I was losing the game and Arianna in the same day. I was taking this win, with a clear conscience.

I looked to my right at Austin who had two fingers to his helmet, saluting me as he always did. With a stern look, I saluted him back, like I never did, hoping he understood this win was ours to take.

Jasper's arrogance kept him in the dark. He'd catch on eventually, or end up staying out of the way; that was welcomed too.

With the sound of the whistle, everyone moved, and all you could hear was pads colliding. The maroon of our uniforms blended in to the green of our opponents with every yard we stole. I watched Austin carry the ball to the endzone, and a sense of glory immediately felt like the best medicine for the aches and pain created by my queen.

Nyx's arms squeezed around my pads, trying to suffocate me as the win sunk in, rippling through the team.

We were winning ... for once ... as ourselves. Nothing hidden or watered down.

I was never supposed to rule with an iron fist or even submit to being a teenager. I was so concerned with being a silent king and fighting the hormones that I forgot who I was under it all. I was a demigod, the son of Ares, the God of War—not of fucking peace in the kingdom.

I was supposed to learn to let everyone be themselves just like Arianna was—fearlessly.

I was a hypocrite in a plastic crown.

A powerless god.

Another teenager pretending to be invincible.

Fourteen years, that's how long it took for me to feel complete. One woman, with purple hair and dirty Doc Martens, to bring me to my knees.

I was bowing to *her.*

The scoreboard showed a lead and a clear win for the Titans of Arcadia Prep. The team all celebrated in a pile of cheers, all slamming into each other's pads and dancing around like idiots. The stands were mirroring the energy on the field, making it harder to find Arianna.

Jumping over the steel benches outlining the boundaries of the field, I made my way to her. I didn't care if I was still in uniform or sweating like I showered.

I was a man on a mission. I had another battle to win.

Hands kept patting my pads in congratulatory form. I ignored them; I was after only one type of glory.

She stood there, arms crossed, and her gaze just as cross. Her eyebrows were pinched in the middle, and I knew she wasn't going to forgive me easily.

I stood in front of her, towering over her really, in my pads. With my hands on her waist, I placed her on the riser with no fight out of her. No words were going to make the truth pretty, make the past a lie, and make this any easier.

I let Fate speak for herself when I leaned into her crossed arms and pushed my lips to hers. She melted enough to drop her crossed arms, and I felt her hand against my jaw, making it okay to push my tongue past her lips. Our tongues danced and wrestled—everything we did with our emotions. My hand smoothed up the back of her bare thigh past the hem of her skirt, and my fingers touched the material of her panties.

Pulling away enough to speak, leaving my lips still against hers, I whispered, "Hate me tomorrow. Right now, I'm busy bowing."

Her lips collapsed against mine, tangling with mine more, and then she pulled away enough to look down. She was standing above me as my queen, and she knew this was as much I would bow for anyone.

I heard Kate pout beside us, "Seriously? Is everyone gonna get wooed except me? Where is my boyfriend?"

Arianna's arms wrapped around my neck and her fingers wrapped around her other wrist, chaining me in. "I'll hate you tomorrow."

CHAPTER 29

Arianna

H
e was a *monster* and whatever Caellum's insult, "Demigod" meant.

He wasn't boyfriend material.

He hid my past, my memories, from me.

He was a false god, wearing a crown that really belonged to *me*.

So why did I feel a storm of butterflies threaten to ignite all the anxiety that could destroy me?

I was rejected by Caellum, apparently in love with my best friend, Nyx, in another lifetime I don't remember, and Bolton was meant to be my husband.

There was no right or wrong anymore. Right and wrong boiled down to power plays and Fate, who I didn't believe in—gods I didn't know, men I was told I felt for, when all I felt was an ache between my thighs, begging for Bolton.

His lips felt like static dancing on mine. His hands grasped the back of my thighs and felt as warm as the missing sun from this gloomy state. I pushed my tongue against his adding moisture, adding the element that made my mouth open wider inviting more of him in.

I wanted to swallow him whole. I wanted to let him eat me whole, no matter how mad I was at him. Maybe he could chew up and spit out the hate inside me.

I was even more impatient when I felt his fingers brush against my panties again. I shifted against his fingertips trying to get even more of him to touch me. I didn't care where we were or who was watching. I wanted him more than I hated him.

I pulled away, not wanting to. His mouth messily kissed the edges of my lips, even as I spoke with my eyes still closed. "Can we go back to your room now?"

His arms wrapped around my waist, carefully helping me down from the bleachers and now standing on the same level—bringing me down, making us equal. We were king and queen.

No more bowing.

No crowns and royalty.

No more gods' rules.

No more games.

No more lies.

Equal. Our rules. Our truths.

The crowd was still cheering when he gripped my hand so tightly I thought I'd lose feeling. He dragged me behind him down the metal stairs of the raisers. The smile on my face must have been infectious, because even from behind him I could tell he was smiling too.

He only let go of my hand long enough to fumble with his jersey and rip the shoulder pads off letting them drop on the floor. "Jasper, take my pads to the back."

There was no question mark at the end; he was all hormones and feeling as shiny as their win. His hair was flatter than normal, sticking to the sides of his face, glued down by the sweat. He glistened in it. It wasn't helping the ache between my legs. My legs were pinned together so tightly I was hoping the friction gave me some kind of relief until we were alone.

His under armor shirt outlined every muscle he had under the bright lights, and the way he moved to unburden himself.

I forced my eyes off Bolton, sweeping over the yard lines until I landed on Kate standing on Austin's helmet. Her arms looped around his neck, holding him flush against her with their mouths connecting in an innocent kiss.

The romance was in the air, fogging all of our vision and pushing everyone into a confidence they needed to put their hearts on the line.

I took out Bolton's phone snapping a photo of them, the perfect high school cliché: the oddball who scored Miss Popular. He wore fedoras and backwards caps that clashed with his outfits, loud button downs with cats or palm trees, and his pants always rolled up to his ankles.

Self-proclaimed crazy.

It made my smile expand, taking up more room on my face. Even the underdog could win on the battlefield of love. Unscathed.

I looked back at Bolton as the crowd died down and emptied from the field, leaving just the circle.

Even the team had already retired to the showers. Coach stopped yelling for Bolton, Austin, and Nyx to stop with the theatrics. It was just us.

Austin was beside himself, and a dorky wide grin covered most of his face, as he pushed his hair back and said, "Pizza? All these romantic teen drama vibes are making me hungry."

The girls stayed quiet, blushing and biting their lips from smiling too big, like it would be embarrassing.

This wasn't the kind of adventure I had in mind, letting my heart out of its cage, but adventure it was.

Nyx was the only one who didn't look pleased. He looked con-flicted, like Austin suggested sex or death instead. The scariest part was I saw him leaning towards death even after Luna said yes and after however long he pined after her. "I'm gonna go shower. I'll meet you guys there."

Bolton's eyes followed him until even his shadow had disap-peared down the tunnel's mouth. "I've got shit to attend to," he clasped onto my hand, again walking so fast I was taking twice the steps he was, just trying to keep up.

I didn't speak until we stopped moving. I couldn't juggle both speaking and keeping up with Bolton's long legs. I hovered over the banister, trying to regulate my breathing, when he laughed at me. I pushed my hand messily forward, trying to smack him but his agility was on high alert, still riding the adrenaline of glory. "What's wrong? What do you have to deal with?"

He cupped himself through his football bottoms, eye level with me: "This."

I had just got an exclusive invitation and front row seat to see Bolton's rejections take a turn.

Bolton's reserve was unheard of for boys our age. Maybe it's the demigod in him—half uninterested and the other half ready to wage a war over some pussy.

I had been sleeping in his room for days, and he wasn't breaking. Every morning was just as painful as when he rejected me in the library by asking if I was done, like he was some kind of sex toy.

I didn't want the Bolton that bows and gives me what I want. I wanted the Bolton that hated me so much it created a thin line between destroying me and devouring me.

I stood up, letting the back of my hand touch him cupping himself, barely, purposely… "I'm still mad at you."

"Be mad at me while I'm between your legs. I'm not waiting for you to remember anymore."

There was the truth, squeezed from him. He wanted my memories intact while I moaned his name. I didn't have the same requirements.

I grabbed his forearm, waving his phone in front of the keypad, hoping his card was lodged behind his phone like everyone else. The keypad turned a bright green, allowing access. Before I could even get further than the entryway, Bolton pulled me back, right into his solid chest.

His soft lips attacked mine; they were perfectly preserved, unused, not chapped from kissing anyone else.

His lips were *mine*.

His body was *mine*.

His crown was … *mine*.

Our mouths stopped attacking each other only long enough for me to kick my Doc Martens off and shed the school blazer I was still wearing. He pulled off his under armor that looked stuck to his abs and biceps, letting it litter his already trashed room. I sat on his bed, watching him struggle to remove the rest of his football gear, his cleats, and other layers shoved under his pads.

Loosening the wine-stained tie around my neck and the first few buttons of my white shirt, I teased him with my purple bra underneath. Bolton didn't waste any time. He appeared in front of me in just his boxer briefs and waited to have my undivided attention before he hooked his thumbs in his underwear and pushed them down.

His length, already hard, fell out in front of me. My jaw went slack, and I followed the bulging vein right down past the muscles framing his hips, caging his monster.

I licked my lips to help the salivating to hopefully stop. It didn't satisfy the ache anymore.

He leaned down enough to let his mouth take little nips at my lips. My lip was caught between his teeth, while his hands ripped my shirt open. Buttons popped off in the process and hit the wood floors.

Bolton's hands pushed my shirt down my arms messily, just like us. His hands smoothed up the space left between my bra and where my skirt started. I felt the static mixing with the warmth of his hands, until I felt his thumbs push into my nipples, making them even harder.

My head leaned back all the way, soaking his touch in with small gasps. I felt my hair yank, pushing my head further back, just before his lips crashed against my neck.

"Take my panties off, Bolton." I had to push the words out with my head being yanked back and between moans.

Letting go of his grip around the roots of my hair, I moved my legs, letting my thighs rub together, as he pulled down my panties.

"Already wet for me? I've barely touched you. Just wait for it."

I pushed him down to a sitting position for me to straddle his lap, with my skirt still on but no panties underneath. I felt his length against me, teasing me and making me even more wet. Pushing my mouth onto his, I bit his lip hard enough to draw blood, and I watched him recoil in shock.

"What the fuck are you doing?"

"I'm hate fucking you."

"Is that really how you want our first time to be?"

Unclipping my bra from behind me, fearlessly, I asked, "Is it our *first time*?" My voice was cutting through the bullshit.

All I wanted was to be worn as a crown around his head and his tongue buried in his throne … me.

All I wanted was to sit on my throne until I felt the royal benefits of wearing a crown.

He was never soft but his voice was delicate, "No, this wouldn't even be hundreds of times. You love fucking me."

I watched him recoil into himself, knowing I didn't remember us, him, before Arcadia Prep. I wanted to but I didn't get to choose what memories came back. None of them were complete anyways. I was only getting half-truths and whole lies.

I sat on top of him, swaying my hips back and forth against his length, chasing the mood still. "You didn't care that I was close to Nyx?"

He switched our positions quickly, and I fell onto his bed hard. There was nothing soft about it, just like him. He flipped my skirt up, out of his way, before he pushed himself between my legs.

He crawled up me until he was hovering right above me, "You aren't his; should I care how close you are? He can be your *friend* but he's not having you the way I am."

I kissed the skin I could reach: his neck, his collarbones, his strong jaw, until he forced me back down to the bed with my wrists in his punishing grip. He was jealous, and it was showing.

I felt his tongue against my nipples, and the restraint of his grasp kept me down. "Don't mention another guy again."

"Is that why you didn't tell me my memories? So you could hide everything but yourself?"

I felt his hips pushed up against mine even more and his tip was grazing along with me. He was torturing me for mentioning Nyx's name.

"This could go very differently, Arianna. Watch what you say."

I writhed and wiggled under his mouth sucking on my hard nipple and his length teasing my wetness. He was pushing me to the edge before he was even inside me—embarrassingly so.

I wanted to push him, I didn't know what he liked. I only knew what made him tick, what pushed his buttons, and what made him hate me.

"Is that why you hate me, Bolton? Because I'm more connected to him, or because I don't remember you?"

All at once, I felt him fill me between my legs, reaching every depth of me inside and not caring to be gentle. His hips didn't move urgently like teenage boys racing to the finish line. Bolton moved with spite, anger, revenge, hate—all for me and who I was now, instead of being who he remembered.

Leaning down into my space, his tongue licked up from my jaw to my ear. "I hate you for making me wait to do this with you for so long."

I wrapped my legs around him, regretting not taking off my skirt. I was demanding more of him—more than I could take or could give back.

I wanted all of Bolton even though he was a monster.

My monster.

He wasn't boyfriend material.

Because he was a king.

He hid my past, my memories, from me.

To force everything in the background, except himself.

He was a false god, wearing a crown that really belonged to *me*.

He bowed to me.

Arianna

His phone went off more than once while we chased the high of our two bodies rubbing together. It was so faint against his desk I barely heard it. His grunting fell against my lips, and my moans were anything but quiet.

Pushing back onto his knees, he looked down at me as his hands held my hips against his. We were both too close for games.

He brought me over the edge when his fingers dipped down between our bodies pushing the sensitive bundle of nerves around until I felt like I was flying. My back arched, while his fingers kept rubbing me, even though I was already high off his touch.

Bolton didn't care. He wanted to break me—to break everything I knew and put it back together carefully, exactly how he wanted to.

My eyes fluttered open, widening as much as they would after coming that hard to watch him suffer the same fate. He pulled away, leaving me feeling so empty without him inside, as his fist worked his length.

I was going to break him too.

Maybe not now, today, or even tomorrow but I was going to break him for thinking he could underestimate me and who I am.

Hate fucking.

"Someone's popular. Want to get that?"

"It can wait." He fell down onto his hard bed next to me with a thump. The beds at Arcadia weren't meant for two people, let alone the furious movements Bolton just pulled off.

I turned into his side, and his arm folded under his head. I wanted to prod him in his weakened state. "Will I ever remember again?"

"The longer you're gone, the harder it is to remember."

He seemed so sure, so why wasn't I when it came to believing him?

"Was I really promised to Caellum?"

His gaze shifted from the ceiling to me in a snap. "He said that?"

"That wasn't a denial ... "

I propped myself up on my elbow and yanked one of the blankets up to shield me from the cold of his room. Messy, dark, cold ... it was a warning sign.

"Caellum hates me; he'll say anything he can to get inside your head."

It made me wonder why he didn't think Caellum was untrustworthy then. It made no sense. I needed to remember, not go off everyone else's word. "But you trust him ... "

"I trust that he wouldn't ever want you hurt. That's the only trust I need to have."

I sat up, hearing his phone buzzing again, and a painful hunger pinched my stomach, and I realized I had put my body through hell. Between watching Bolton and Nyx fight in class, being taken hostage by Caellum, all the secrets coming out of the dark, and Bolton breaking my body while handing me a crown ... I was surprised I was still operating. "Tell me what happened between you two."

He groaned, thinking a sound effect would be all it took to throw me off from getting an answer. Crossing my arms, I waited, minutes passed by in silence when I poked his exposed side. The blanket was barely covering him and that vein and his muscles trailing down his body were still on display.

Focus.

Answers.

"Fuck, Ari. It's not like one thing happened, okay? It's more like what didn't happen." He turned to face me, leaning on his elbow and looking at me so sternly I almost gave up knowing.

"You want me to remember but you aren't telling me anything. Maybe I should go ask Caellum."

I was letting myself get emotional, desperate even, when I threw my legs off his bed and snagged my shirt up from the floor, along with my bra.

"I want you to remember for yourself, not how I remember shit. You're remembering things without knowing. It's slowly being triggered. Calling me powerless and running away from marrying me? That's all happened before."

I felt overwhelmed again. My head was feeling fuzzy, and now that pinch in my stomach was feeling like the least of my problems. I did my best to force my eyes open, just before my body started to sway and everything went dark.

Running on no sleep and ugly truths eventually always catches up.

When I came to, my eyes barely wanted to open, and through the slits of my lashes, I saw a familiar ceiling—undeniably Bolton's, the dark poster of some British band was taped to the ceiling, making me feel sure.

There was lost time; this position wasn't the last one I remembered at all. I was getting dressed and about to leave when the world got fuzzy enough to give me an instant headache.

The same headache pounded in the space between my skull and brain, pulsing. I sat up slowly with my fingertips digging into my temples, hoping that would provide some relief.

"You passed out. You've been sleeping a few hours."

Bolton was wearing nothing but a towel hanging low on hips, showing off every single muscle glued to every movement. His fingers pushed through his wet hair, making sure it didn't stick to his forehead.

He might be a demigod but he looked nothing but godly to me.

I sat up, even more trying to muster up any kind of words I could. Nothing was coming to mind that was worth saying out loud. I was distracted by how familiar he looked, not from seeing him in class every day but my post headache was dragging memories out of the dark.

A deep, almost scary, baritone rumbled through my mind, causing the now to fade into the background.

"You can't ignore tradition. You can't out run tradition. You will marry him."

I couldn't see anything; it was still covered in a thick layer of fog still. I just heard the voices of my past, and if I clamped my eyes shut, I could hear them ever louder.

"I won't marry him, and you can't force me, Daddy. I don't love him."

"And who do you love, my little tyrant? The dark prince, son of Hades? The boy who brings nothing but destruction and death wherever he goes?"

"Destruction and death, or your everlasting control ... ?At least I can choose for myself."

"You will never be with him, my princess. You will marry him or sit on this throne alone. Do you understand me?"

The memory faded out. I didn't need to see the rest to know what happened next. I ran away, probably one of the first times, certainly not the last. Otherwise, we wouldn't be here, stuck between what I know and don't.

I snapped back to the present, hearing the sound of his voice: "I have to go to the meeting. Can't start skipping now. You okay to be alone? Am I gonna have to hunt you down again?"

I shook my head side to side, without speaking still. I could tell by the look on his face that my silence was only making him worried.

"What is it?" He came closer, handing me Advil and a water bottle from his polluted desk.

Taking it out of his hand and swallowing three pills with a big gulp of water, I debated telling him. I wanted to tell him but I thought I should keep it to myself until I had more to go on.

If I remembered our past, would we have a future? Would I stop hating him as little as I did now? Would I hate him enough to remember loving Nyx, like my own voice just said?

"Nothing. Headache." I hated lying to him. Something in the pit of my stomach created an ocean of nausea at the thought of lying to Bolton.

I was betraying my past self, and it had a vile kind of aftermath.

He kept staring at me while he got dressed, dissecting me and expecting me to speak. He zipped his pants, and I couldn't take my eyes off him when the present faded into the background once more.

"What if I never stop hating you?"

"Then hate me. Hate me until it blurs into something else."

His warm hands were comfortably on my hips, holding me against him, and I could almost smell the forest mixing with his musk. His scent alone was enough to get me drunk.

"What if the line between love and hate never blurs?"

His lips swept against my exposed neck, dragging against my skin with every word. "That line will always be blurred with us, because you already love to hate me."

The small piece of a much larger memory faded as quickly as it came. Bolton was pulling on his shirt, with the arms cut off and the word "THRILLS" in capital letters across his chest, when he came back into focus.

"You look like you saw a ghost."

I felt like I did. It was the first time I was looking at Bolton and truly seeing him.

Swallowing back the turbulence of these memories coming back, I swung my legs off the edge of the bed and sat up. "I'm part of the circle. I'm coming with you."

He stood in front of me with his hands lazily on his hips. "You aren't going anywhere. You passed out, and the memories are all over your face. You're fucking four shades paler than normal."

Standing up on my shaking legs, I grabbed the hoodie hanging off the bed post and wrapped it around me. That same forest and musk scent mixed together, making me want to drool.

"I'm going, Bolton. I'm the one this has to happen to." I was holding myself up as best as I could, while I tried to look more like myself. Crossing my arms and throwing him an eye roll helped.

"The element of surprise was kind of my plan here."

"Well, tough shit. I've had enough secrets."

I pushed my bare feet into my Doc Martens, still wearing my uniform, just even more disheveled. I wasn't letting anyone tell me

I wasn't going to this meeting for the circle I was queen of. I pushed past Bolton and stood in the hallway, waiting for him to catch up.

"You're a pain in my ass, you know that?"

He draped his arm around my shoulders, and he whistled with his gaze down the hallway. I didn't know who's attention he wanted or who would even think a whistle was meant for them.

"Learn to love to hate me ... " I soaked in being pushed up against him.

Walking further down the hallway with no real light, I tensed up, unsure what to expect. He kicked the door with his boot, and all you could hear was rustling behind the door. The inaudible music muffled by the door left a silence in the air when it was turned off abruptly. The door flung open and illuminated Luna, fixing her clothes and hair to be perfect again, while Nyx was pulling his shirt back on.

Bolton was laughing next to me in an unfamiliar way. He was actually amused by corruption.

Nyx was defiling Luna, and he actually thought it was comical.

"What do you want?"

Bolton leaned into the door frame, "Meeting? You kids wanna stay off each other long enough to come to that?"

Luna's cheeks were sunburnt red and matched her red locks. She was embarrassed, and I couldn't figure out why. They liked each other, and when there's enough like in one room, the tension is only bearable with your clothes off.

I knew from personal experience.

Nyx barreled through Bolton and I in the doorway, like a bowling ball, making a complete strike. I followed Luna's gaze to the guy walking away from her, after God, or apparently gods, knew what happened. Linking my arms into hers, I forced her close to me, letting Bolton lead.

"I can't believe he's letting you go," I whispered in a pointlessly hushed tone. Bolton probably had some form of his ears ringing, except more dramatically, like his soul lights on fire when someone talks about him.

"What are these meetings about anyways?"

"The same thing every week. Who's the one, planning the ritual, all the prep that goes into it ... Normally it's Bolton against the majority vote on everything."

I knew I was the one; otherwise, my hands wouldn't reenact *Harry Potter* scenes without a wand. None of that interested me.

I was going, so the secrets could cease and desist once and for all.

Changing the topic as we walked across the grass to the off limits building that gave me the creeps, I asked Luna what upstairs with Nyx was all about. Her cheeks went up in flames again. "Nothing ... we just got caught up. Thank god you interrupted."

Nyx stopped walking ahead of us and charged nearly into us, "This isn't Olympus. You aren't my queen or best friend anymore, so what I do with Luna isn't your business."

He made it clear that he was putting whatever we had in the past and changing his future.

I couldn't remember what we had in Olympus to motivate a fight, so I let him yell he wasn't my business anymore. He was right after all.

Without realizing it, my hand reached out and touched his folded arms lightly. At first, he let me, before yanking out of my reach. A memory was already unlodging itself from deep in my subconscious and coming to the surface.

> *"Run away with me. You don't have to marry him. He'll love you because Zeus told him it's so. I'd love you for all my days, because I can't help it."*
>
> > *"He always finds me. There's nowhere safe from him."*
> > *"Then I'll kill the king and set you free."*

The words echoed in my head: *free, kill, runaway*. All things I wanted to do—anything to get out of this paper bag sealed at the end, trapped with secrets and lies inside.

"Don't fucking touch me," his voice was completely filled with malice and callous.

I couldn't keep my eyes from rolling back over his dramatics. He was the son of Hades, all destruction and death, but his weakness? Apparently being touched was triggering.

I pushed past him towards the door, waiting on Bolton to force the lock undone. This was the one building I didn't even walk by on purpose. The gargoyles perched up top and the dark stone made it feel evil. The nagging feeling I always got right before an adventure crept into my stomach, fluttering up to my chest in a storm of butterflies.

That feeling normally went away once the high of breaking whatever rules took its place.

That kind of high was unmatched; it took over every aspect of me and blurred out the annoyances.

Not this time.

I walked inside, and the mounting storm in my chest only got stronger. It was trying to tell me to turn back, fuck the secrecy, let them have it.

Bolton handed me a ringing phone, and it didn't even register that it was my iPhone wrapped in a purple case. Across the screen it said "DAD" in capital letters, and I hung a left into a spacious room, not bothering to ask how he got my phone back or when.

Putting the phone to my ear, I didn't realize how much I missed him when I had to bite down my trembling lip, summoning tears. "Hey, honey! Sorry it's so late; it's only 3 here. I got your message. Is everything okay?"

"Daddy…" It was all that surfaced to say. I hadn't called him "Daddy" since I was little.

I felt the same kind of innocence wash over me. All the bullshit toughness I played up on the outside shattered, because he knew deep down I was as scared as everyone else, as alone as everyone else, and had lost things no one should.

"What happened?" His rough around the edges voice always screamed he had seen things that change you.

"It's just hard being here," I lied through my teeth. It was too much to explain with continents between us.

"Making any new friends at least?" Smoothing out his voice for my benefit.

"Yeah, some. When will you be home?" I hadn't even realized the holidays were right around the corner when a hot tear ran down my cheek without permission.

I was all alone, and it didn't hurt being without him, real dad or not. All I wanted was someone forced to love me in this moment, and he was too far away for me to feel that. Every mile between us tested my fragile heart, turning it to stone, watching it curse love in all its forms.

"After Christmas, honey. Aunt D said she can have you for the break on some conditions, like no more trouble."

I couldn't produce any words. He wasn't coming home for the holidays.

"I promise I'm trying to work as fast as I can. You'll have fun with your cousins in Texas until I'm back. Chin up."

Even through the phone, he could hear my overpowering disappointment.

"I love you, my Little Archer."

Normally I complained, stomped my foot, and told him I was too old for such silly nicknames. Not this time. Nothing felt more comforting than being his Little Archer—not the daughter of Zeus, not Bolton's promised wife, or not whatever key I was to this circle.

Bolton's arms wrapped around when the line clicked, and the other line went dead before I could tell him I loved him just as much. I buried my face into Bolton's chest and let the tears I was holding free up. His arms felt strong enough to keep me safe, and that was the only comfort I had right now.

His palm swept down my hair and held my face against him, as he said to Nyx, "Tell Alba shit came up. Text me after."

Bolton

A rianna had finally broken—the past and present sandwiched her against her unshed tears, forcing them to fall.

I didn't think seeing her broken would affect me so much.

My shirt was stained with her tears, and her fists were balling up my shirt to the point my nipple was exposed to the cold. An innate need buried in my chest came alive after fourteen years of not protecting her.

One single trail of tears, and it all came flooding back—just like the memories I knew she was deciphering. Her concentration would drop to the floor, and I could see the confusion stirring up her eyebrows and slack jaw.

Right now, all she could focus on was burying her face into my chest and hiding the vulnerable parts she wasn't comfortable with.

Arianna had always been strong, outspoken, rebellious. Fights with her dad in Olympus ended in thunder and lightning that cracked the sky open.

Picking up her legs, I carried her back to my room, hoping she'd sleep this off, just like her headache from earlier. We were already on the side of the clock where trouble lived: past midnight. Balancing her weight, all stuck in her heavy boots, to one side of me to get my door open was still easier than becoming, any sense of the word, comforting.

I was made of stone, even letting her hold onto me. I wasn't the guy who knew what to say or do; I made sure that I always got out before this part came. I was more comfortable killing for her, chasing her, being the guy she hated enough to never let me seep into her soul too deeply.

I fell down to my bed, taking her into my lap, and that feeling came alive in my chest and felt like certain death.

Humanity.

Hormones.

The parts of me Zeus envied, while I hated them.

Feelings that didn't serve me.

I never believed in love before Arianna, before being told how much of an honor it would be to be chosen to marry Zeus's daughter.

It wasn't shocking; my father, Ares, fell for a human, cursing me to being only half god.

Demigod.

Zeus never gave her permission to enter Olympus where I was raised, forcing my dad to sneak off any chance he could see my mom. I never experienced an easy kind of love, and it was no surprise that my fate was the same kind of hardship.

Arranged.

Hateful.

Real.

It was the hate for each other that bred something else.

It was dormant until she appeared at Arcadia Prep with all the same traits I hated on my beloved, making me hate her just as much. She grew on me the same way, and I knew my heart wouldn't ever betray me. The punishment would be turning it off forever.

No, my heart knew Arianna had to be the girl that always ran away, and I chased after her every time.

My thumb cleared the moisture from her exposed cheek as she whispered into the material she was still holding on to with a death grip. "This is stupid. He's not even my real dad."

"He's all you remember right now. Zeus is gone too. There's enough to be upset about without it being stupid." As soon as I said it, I regretted reminding her that her real father was dead.

"How can gods die? Caellum said he was looking for the 'God Killer'."

She was swallowing stray tears and shaking against me less but her mouth was still upside down—a more consolable version of herself. Smoothing down her hair, I told her, "That's only a myth…"

She looked at me displeased and too tired to beg for information. "Henry Jon started the collective that hunts us down, forges weapons from crumbs we leave behind, hates us for taking his daughter's life. Supposedly he passed down the anger and knowledge. I haven't heard or seen of them… Caellum is convinced they're still out there waiting for us to mess up again."

"But you've killed people hoping they were the Sagittarius…"

"My point exactly. Those lives didn't matter? Legends always die young and live on in rumors."

Her voice was so small and quiet it sounded more like a whimper, "I have the husk. I found it…"

Sitting up quickly, I looked down at her in shock. Her hand pushed off my chest enough to make eye contact. "I found it in the woods in a box. Henry Jon hid it far away from the book to keep it safe."

Sometimes legends are true. The hard part is never knowing unless you test legends against reality and see which one wins.

"Where is it?"

"In my bag." Her casual tone made it easy for me to land on the conclusion she really didn't know what kind of dynamite she was holding.

The one way to kill gods was stashed at the bottom of her dirty backpack.

"Don't tell anyone you have this," I said, trying to be as grave as possible. Every other tone was a motivation to defy someone's wishes.

The next morning, I felt like I was on a stopwatch, waiting for the dance tonight. Every hour, minute, second... all were accounted for. Each one pushed the anxiety over my tight muscles to contemplate worst case scenarios.

Ari was still asleep, holding my pillow tightly against her as soon as I snuck out of bed this morning. I had some pent up humanity poisoning my ability to listen to common sense, so I went for a run in the forest. It was the only place other than campus that we could freely roam.

Having this curse lifted was either going to set my soul on fire or free of all the bullshit.

Nothing was absolute.

With my headphones pushed into my ears, I got into a rhythm of my sneakers pounding into small rocks, dead leaves, and sticks cracking. I almost hit the edge of the woods when I swore I saw a shadow out of the corner of my eye moving swiftly between trees. I slowed down my pace trying to be less obvious that I noticed anything at all.

Sweeping the woods, around the barren tall trees, I saw the same shadow. *Following me? Stalking me like prey? Assassinating the king? Divine intervention?*

I slowed down my pace to a halt once I entered the clearing close to where the ritual would take place tonight when I shouted, "What do you want?"

Jasper came around a tree trunk with a sly grin on his face, "Scoping it out for tonight. Is the King of Arcadia Prep scared?"

He always hated me, even in Olympus. Why would high school be any different? This was the perfect place to let his hate run thick and wide for me, and then chalk it up to hormones.

Fingering my earbuds out of my ears, I pretended to not hear his insult. "That's not weird at all. Stay out of trouble. I'm not saving anyone today."

His mom was Persephone, not royal, more like royally fucked.

Hades, Nyx's dad, kidnapped her and drug her to the underworld to be his wife. Somehow that makes them step-brothers but not ones that gave a shit. They stayed clear of each other most of the time.

Here he was equal and ultimately more powerful than back home. He had felt the surge of more power once Arianna got here, and you could see it on his permanent grin. He wasn't going to relinquish that high any time soon.

Pushing the music back into my ears, I prepared to quicken my pace, glaring at him and wondering why he was really in the woods this early. There wasn't one truthful bone in Jasper's body.

As soon as my sneakers hit the pavement of the sidewalk bordering the edge of the woods like a cage, I still didn't feel like I had left Jasper's dubious behavior behind. His sly smile and dangerous grin were haunting me.

I fished the phone out of my pocket to text Nyx and Caellum in a group message. I couldn't be bothered to text them separately about the same thing.

Jasper was in the woods sneaking around. Need any more proof?

We all had different opinions when it came to making someone the villain. Jasper checked all the boxes: motive, opportunity, enough hate to fuel any bad intentions.

My smaller circle of trust was harder to convince to see it that way. Caellum was watching the twins closely, and Nyx had his sight set on Alba. All of us watching someone different just meant nothing should slip past us.

The feeling coating my stomach knew something bad was coming. I could feel the tension in the air, Ari's memories coming back, the Harvest at our feet, and the ritual that was supposed to take us home already feeling like a failure before we even tried.

I slipped my phone back in my gym shorts and jogged back to my room where I left Arianna sleeping.

She was in the exact position she was in when I left. Not wanting to wake her, I set an alarm for 10 minutes and headed for the showers. We didn't have bathrooms in the rooms in this dorm. We had community-style bathrooms with no shower curtains or privacy. We didn't much care; we were all proud.

As soon as I stepped into the hallway, I pulled the door slowly behind me, hoping it would close without that annoying creek my door possessed.

When I looked up, I saw Luna clutching her white tennis shoes to her chest, doing the same thing I was: carefully closing the door and trying not to be seen.

"Luna?" I whisper-shouted in her direction.

I startled her, and her whole body twisted my direction suddenly. The grip on her shoes tightened, and her cheeks flushed to a bright red, like I had caught her stealing.

Technically, she was. Nyx wasn't aware he truly had a heart, and she was hijacking it without him realizing it.

"You didn't see me. I've gotta get ready for class." Her small, carefully quiet footsteps turned to tip toeing, like she knew the floor in front of my door was home to the creeks.

Had she done this before? She was gracefully professional at sneaking—something you'd never expect from her.

Shaking my head, my eyebrows raised, and smirking, I let her slip by me without interrogation, heading down the hallway to the bathrooms.

The bathroom was dark. A few light bulbs were out here and there but none of us were complaining after Caellum's drunk ass ripped down the curtains when he still went here. They never did get replaced.

Standing under the shower spray, the steam engulfed me, and I let it burn my lungs, pushing a cough up my throat. The temperature of the shower wasn't going to wash away anything like modern poetry claimed. I was going to emerge the same man who stripped down and rinsed off the sweat.

Nyx strutted in casually, unknowing that I just saw Luna sneak out of his room at 7:30 AM. I was drawing conclusions and not caring how accurate they were, especially when the chances of them studying or talking was slim.

"What was Jasper doing out there?" I watched him take the shower stall next to me, shouting over the pounding rain of shower head.

"Being a fucking creep. I think he was following me." I pumped the soap into the palm of my hand before lathering up.

"I saw him in the library last week in the off limit stacks. You think he's looking for the God Killer too?"

Too? Had he been talking to Caellum?

He was the only one I knew who was actively looking for weapons. It was still up for debate why he needed a weapon to kill gods. My boycotting of the ritual was so no one died, no one got hurt, and there were no repercussions for our actions if we didn't act at all.

"What would he need that for? All the gods are dead; it's just us now."

His head peeked over the wall dividing the shower stalls. "Exactly. He hates Olympus and, better yet, hates you."

Letting all the soap run down my abs, I spoke candidly, completely trusting him with every word. "If he sabotages the ritual, has any plan to hurt Ari, I won't hesitate to kill him."

"I can be okay with that."

His loyalty didn't go unnoticed. I grabbed the towel swung over the same divider and wrapped it around my waist when I saw Ari leaning against the sink. "Bolton?"

Startling me, I made sure the towel covered what I needed it to, not that she hadn't seen everything already but no one wanted to be naked and afraid at the same time. "What are you doing in here? It's a guys' bathroom…"

Looking towards Nyx, naked and not the least bit caring, I barked, "Hallway now."

"I remembered something. Well, not their face, but the conversation I overheard."

Waving my hand for her to continue, I waited for more to go on in my towel in the hallway.

"The twins, I overheard them plotting to leave Olympus before I ran away. Do you think they don't wanna leave Arcadia Prep?"

Folding my arms against my bare chest, I contemplated her memory. Cheyanne would never betray me. She always had a small crush on me, and I knew it motivated her loyalty. I couldn't get Jasper's behavior lately out of my head. He was acting out, being weird, and pissing me off enough to make me think he was the problem, and not the twins.

"What else do you remember?"

"Just hearing them talk about how awful it was up there. How much they hated everyone in charge, how little they mattered, how much better life would be on Earth for them. It's like a memory, I don't have the beginning or ending, just the middle, that doesn't make sense without bookends."

"Nothing changes. No suspect behavior. We don't have any evidence, and I don't want to spook anyone."

She looked down at her phone, smiling, "Easy. Kate and Luna are kidnapping me to go into town for dresses."

Harvest had started. It was here enough to lift the barrier on campus. We were no longer trapped, at least for now. Harvest only lasts 28 hours, while the moons shifted and the stars prepared for winter.

"Keep your phone on, Ari. I mean it."

Biting her lip, she tilted her chin up, hoping I'd conquer the distance and plant a kiss on her lips. I wanted to keep it interesting by not ever giving her what she wanted.

Her fingertips settled on my towel, leaning further into me. "You were looking amazing in there ... "

"Compared to when else exactly? It sounds like you're comparing." My hand was on her shoulder, as she stood on her tiptoes and finally reached my lips. Mint lip gloss to match her frosty sarcasm.

Slapping her hand to my bare chest, I forced my shoulders straight, not caving in to the lashing. "You know I don't have a lot of memories yet!"

Pushing my lips down to hers again, I let my tongue explore her mouth. Warm and wet—the exact equation to summon my dick to action.

I pulled away only to kiss her exposed neck. "You better run away if you don't plan on opening those legs."

Arianna

I changed so quickly I was convinced my underwear were on backwards. The tag wasn't itching against my skin like it normally did, which aggravated me more than them actually being backwards.

Change was the enemy. No matter how annoying that tag was, I was used to it.

I was used to a lot of things that felt a lot like lies now instead of the truth I once knew.

The girls were waiting in front, giggling and talking to themselves, when I sauntered over to them. "So now we can talk about it right?"

Kate purposely bumped into me casually. "The powers?" She laughed like it was the most out of this world idea to ever exist. Normally I would agree but my gold veins and tingling in my hands proved me wrong.

Luna took pity on me, with her eyes full of empathy and wisdom all at the same time. "It's not always like what you can do. We

just think about something, wish it true enough, and it happens."
She touched my hands, staring into me, like I was a blackhole of
depth and wonderment.

I couldn't describe the warmth her hands held or how comforting it felt to stare into her eyes. Something inside me knew
everything would be okay. Every unshed tear left behind my eyes,
building up strength to threaten my strength again, felt like they
had dried up. She slowly let go of my hands, I paused, staring in
the same wonderment she did a second ago.

"What just happened?"

Her bright smile took over her face. "Comfort. It's no lightning,
but I can take pain away."

"It's not always so extreme like Miss-Fix-It over here," Kate cut
in with a chip on her shoulder.

I could easily sense how much she hated all of this: the power,
being unique, being a god above men. As much as this school fell
at her feet and moved out of her way when she came down the
hallway, in this moment, she seemed to hate every part of the
royalty coursing through her veins.

"She can be Miss-Fix-It, so what's yours?"

"Today is about normal, mundane things, Arianna. We are on
a mission to find the perfect dresses." Her eyes lit up, like someone
just offered her the one thing she always wanted: normalcy.

I roped my arms through their arms, clutching on and walking us all forward together. "Normal day it is. We'll have plenty of
time to talk magic."

Luna's mouth turned down, like she had sucked all the sad-
ness from Kate and saw it as it really was—ugly discomfort she
wore underneath it all. I hugged their limp arms tighter, when we
got to the end of the long driveway and a black town car pulled
up. I wondered if we had incredible timing or if we had believed
enough that today would be normal that we summoned a car to
fulfill our wishes.

I had been here for months, this purgatory, and I hadn't even ventured off campus. The thrill seeking side of me was disappointed in myself.

Bolton could not be all the adventure I'd ever need. He was a handful, but he wasn't going to trap my wanderous heart.

Kate sat up front, comfortably. Squishing in wasn't her strong suit, and being suffocated wasn't mine. She turned back and asked, "You aren't thinking black, right?"

Her eyes were wide and mouth tight, like it was the worst idea she had ever heard of, even though I hadn't mentioned any illusions to this shopping day.

"No ... ? Wait ... What's wrong with black?" I tried to placate her before I realized I was corning myself into some hideous color I really wouldn't want to wear.

I wasn't a fan of shopping. The multiple stores, the idea that everything is going to look exactly how its advertised, the bags, the trying on each thing, while you painfully stumble through finding the perfect piece of fabric.

Not for me.

I was happy with a coffee cup, my old Doc Martens, and the school-required uniform. Before Arcadia, I pretty much threw my beat up jean jacket over everything and prayed no one noticed I was re-wearing clothes just to avoid the mall.

Aunt D was always hellbent on converting me, begging me to go with her, until I broke. I stayed in the main aisles, never getting lost in the racks.

The streets were covered in dead leaves, and the grass peeked through as we drove past houses that looked almost too perfect. I didn't see anyone outside—no signs of life. It was eerie.

Where was everyone? What kind of town did Arcadia sit at the helm of?

Looking out the window and ignoring the discussion of Nyx and Luna, I searched every street we passed for life—any kind of life. Even a fucking squirrel would make me feel better.

"You okay?" Luna's soft voice wasn't bringing any life to my face, as my chest tightened.

I knew she was going to assume how I felt was directly linked to Nyx. Nothing I could do or say could convince someone that history can be dead instead of repeating itself.

That's what everyone was afraid of: history repeating itself. Down to me running away probably.

Nyx made it clear that his ties to Luna weren't my business, and I was okay with being on the outside of them.

Swallowing something other than moisture, my mouth was bone dry; this must have been the panic I did well in avoiding until Arcadia. "Where are all the people?"

She shrugged, like she had never noticed before and couldn't be bothered to care. The one who could take feelings away wasn't doing that in this moment. I was a ball of panic, and its grip on my muscles weren't loosening.

"No, seriously...it's not normal."

Kate spun around, glaring over the seat with a look meant to melt me into my place. "Nothing is normal in Arcadia, Arianna. That's obvious."

The final tone in her voice elicited a pout I wasn't proud of. I felt scolded, like a child chanting why to every question and the parents drained of clever ways to answer.

I didn't have any answers to anything.

The circle.

Arcadia.

My fake parents.

The royalty in my veins.

Abilities I only ever read about in books.

Memories I couldn't remember.

I was forced to swallow a special pill—one that put a pin in everything, for as long as it took.

The mall seemed too big to be real. It made my features twist in to disgust just looking at it from the parking lot. It was full of all the clothes and stores I already loathed.

Turning the focus, I asked Kate about something she'd want to blabber on about: herself. "How long have you and Austin been together?"

She laughed, with a sly look on her face and a dramatic head tilt, analyzing the motive behind asking. "Long enough to not get jealous anymore ... not long enough for the sex to go vanilla."

"You're both strong, very different, amazing queens." Luna trying to use slang casually had us busting out laughing. Nothing modern fit too well on Luna. She was an old soul in every aspect of the word.

"I really hate malls," I mumbled to myself as we walked in.

I followed Kate and Luna's lead, at least there were people here. I punished myself with an eye roll at my own paranoia.

Kate

Shopping with Arianna was a nightmare. She was in the real world longer than us and she possessed no mundane qualities I was hoping to leech from her.

She didn't care what dress or what color, and she didn't bother to pretend to be excited that our cold king invited her as his date. He never asked anyone anything.

He made demands with no apologies.

Luna was firmly on Team Arianna, pretending to not care Nyx asked her to the dance after pining over him since he transferred in.

I felt like the only normal person. Not even for a good reason ... for caring about a damn dance.

Everyone else was hyper focused on the ritual; the two would overlap, leaving the dance simply a distraction.

The one normal thing was deemed a distraction.

Seriously. No, like seriously.

Forcing myself to pretend I cared about the ritual meant not blowing off the meetings, nodding my head like I was listening, and not volunteering for anything. It had been working pretty well. I was sure everyone thought I cared enough to at least revel in the moment Arianna was going to get stabbed.

All I wanted was to be *normal*—as normal as I could get.

Being the daughter of Aphrodite and Demeter set the bar high when it came to the level of not normal I was born into.

Olympus worked solely on royalty (and some incest if we're being honest). The gods were always fighting, killing, playing their wicked games to climb one more rung on the ladder.

My parents played the most wicked games ... not to climb anything, just to laugh on the other end of someone else's heartbreak.

The world had done them wrong already, and all they lusted for was to wrong everyone else to make the playing field even.

I was the opposite; all I wanted was the normal to out-weigh all the nefarious I inherited from them.

Normal could snuff out all the bad with pure boredom.

I was determined to make the Harvest Dance my bitch. Spike the punch, take the cliché photos with Austin, dance to some slow song neither of us knew, and end the night like any formal dance, alone with my boyfriend.

No one was going to get in between me and my hopes for tonight.

We took over the communal bathroom. I dumped all my products and makeup on the counter, smirking at my reflection owning this moment.

"Have you slept with Bolton?" The shock value part of me was never going away. I couldn't snuff that out no matter what I tried.

I used to snap a rubber band against my wrist every time a rude, malicious, callous comment came out. The slight pinch against my sensitive wrist helped for a while, dwindling the comments down to only when truly needed, which was still less, but more than the normal person. I restrained myself to be less like a nightmare.

Arianna tucked her lips inward and tried to stop her mouth from turning up. I popped an eyebrow. I didn't take Arianna as modest, and it was bowling me over.

She liked our cold king more than anyone knew—herself included.

Arianna wasn't the type to admit any sliver of truth to herself, let alone the ones threatening her bleeding heart. She wanted to believe her heart was small, but for her it was the only organ she thought with.

She leaned forward into the mirror, inspecting her messy purple hair. "You and Bolton really never dated? Why isn't Austin king, if the school crowned you queen?"

"Austin isn't king material: he's warm blooded and sensitive. Bolton is, no offensive, cold and heartless … he's the perfect king." Perfecting the concealer step of my process, I watched her turn inward, calculating how much he could care about her if he was heartless and cold.

Rolling my eyes, I turned to face her, dropping my beauty blender from patting the products into my skin. "Everyone has a weakness … you're his. Trust me, he'd be pissed at Caellum for what he did, but not kill him … for just anyone."

Playfully tugging a strain of her purple hair crowding her features, I gave her a genuine smile—well, as genuine as the callous, dried-up parts of me would allow.

That same obvious smile returned. She was falling for Bolton no matter how much she shouldn't.

The powers inside me were wreaking havoc and setting off alarms I was choosing to ignore.

Having parents so rooted in love and lust only transferred their talents onto me like a modern day Cupid. I sensed love, saw their love stories unfold in my head, and it wasn't always a match made in heaven. Sometimes it was a fiery kind of hell.

Arianna and Bolton weren't a match. Neither were Luna and Nyx. I had seen their stories unfold, and they were all full of ache, insecurities, and flaws.

How do you tell your friends when they don't even know your power? How can I break their hearts when love defies the odds every day?

I wanted to pretend I was powerless, so that's what I did.

After putting my face on, I turned to Luna and manipulated her wild strawberry curls in a tight twist along her hairline, creating a crown.

We were all equally royal and going to look it.

My phone went off on the counter, shaking the products closest to the vibration.

    ♓ Austin: *Jasper is missing. No splitting up.*

I kept my phone close to me, so only my eyes were able to read the message. Last thing we needed was Arianna's dramatics and Luna's worrisome eyebrows to dip.

    ♉ Me: *What do you mean by MIA?*
    ♓ Austin: *Bolton poked the bear.*

My fingers were frozen, hovering above the screen. I didn't know what to type back. Bolton was rocking the boat before it was even in the water. Thankfully, Nyx and Bolton weren't keeping the other girls in the loop like Austin was.

Pretending everything was fine was my special talent that I used every other day; tonight was no different.

We spent hours getting ready, talking, and snacking the whole time. It was straight out of a romantic comedy movie. There was always that one montage of the girlfriends together before they figured out how to be normal. Just like this.

I shimmied into my blush pink velvet wrap dress, making sure any static was banished from my look. I sat on the edge of the bench and pushed my feet into pink Balenciaga sneakers for some edge. I couldn't let Arianna's black number with Doc Martens steal the show.

I was on the dance committee, responsible for ordering people around and birthing the idea of the Winter Wonderland dance, but when I walked in, my own jaw dropped. I was seeing my handy work for the first time.

Austin's arm was around my waist as I took in the magic around us; none of it was abnormal or god-like—just magic.

Nyx and Bolton met us here in true bad boy fashion. They weren't going to conform to gentleman, even to walk across the quad to pick up their dates and walk to another building across the same quad.

Stubborn as they are handsome.

Almost all of me was focused on tonight and the dance, but the other half of me nagged at my senses. Something was wrong. Something in the air was grabbing my attention in a disappointing way, and I was hellbent on figuring out what was standing between me and the normal I lusted for.

"Did you have to push Jasper tonight? Of all nights? Are you begging for something to go wrong?" I barked at Bolton, while he was smirking at Arianna's much more polished look.

Bolton's mouth dropped exactly the way I planned to make these alpha men bow before the only women able to keep them in line.

I didn't think she could pull it off, but even with her white Doc Martens, she still looked like royalty. Her lace black babydoll dress fit her so perfectly you almost didn't notice the small hair piece I pushed against the crown of her purple hair. A tiny silver crown.

"He was pissing me off. I gave him an out, and he didn't take it."

A strong gaze from my half-mast eyes, heavy with mascara and fake lashes, and he knew exactly what I was conveying: an easy disappointment at his sloppy attempt to fix the situation before it happened.

He was throwing his weight into a brick wall, one not moving if they could hide betrayal this easily.

I had been feeling like someone was watching me for weeks now. It was a feeling that pushed my senses into overdrive, as I tried to pin the feeling onto someone looking my way or whispering in the distance. I had been searching all week for the culprit, but came up short. Whoever it was, was talented and hiding in the shadows, which is a place I had no determination to go.

Let them watch me.

Let the mystery person see how normal I strive to be.

Let them try to guess what my abilities are and what I can do.

I hadn't even told Austin about this feeling. Not that he wouldn't protect me or throw his weight around like Bolton; I just didn't need him to. I wasn't Luna or Arianna—someone looking for a shield to promote how strong I am. I was strong, and no man on this planet was going to steal an ounce of it.

I worked hard to be considered strong myself, apart from my sovereign blood and football player boyfriend—both equally deemed majestic in their own worlds. The mortal world prided themselves on image, and having a hot boyfriend that people adored was the same as having powerful parents in Olympus.

It made no sense, yet yielded more respect, even from me.

The dance was going smoothly, but the small hairs on the back of my neck were standing straight up still. I kept sweeping the room for threats; we all were. Tonight was the full moon and the start of the Harvest. There was no doubt it would happen tonight.

"Where's Caellum?" My arms were around Austin's neck, as we slow danced, trying to forget everything around us. Too bad my mind was glued to the drama.

"Probably going to blow us off. I heard Bolton really got to him."

I couldn't help the eye roll that came next. Bolton was single handedly playing the fool. It wasn't like him to not play smarter than the average guy.

This was more than protecting Arianna. This was jealousy, anger, payback, and every other bad emotions lingering inside him for fourteen trapped years.

Men, as much as we condemned them to hide how they feel, we never stopped seeing how their actions were rooted in emotions.

My eyes swept the room as I pushed my chest against Austin's, letting my pink velvet brush against his button down, complete with suspenders with small dogs on them. Austin was a rare bird, just like his father, Poseidon.

"Stop worrying. It creates wrinkles…" His voice was smooth and casual, like how I should be. He could feel how tense I was against his chest, relaxing sailed away when the nagging feeling of someone watching me grew even more heavy.

At least he knew me well enough to know how to get my attention.

"Hey! I don't have premature wrinkles! Something feels wrong…" I didn't mean to say the last part outside my own thoughts.

Austin was my safe place, and I knew he didn't cower easily. How could he among the men running into fire, hate, and death just to make points? He learned to let his sensitive heart come second.

I pushed the feeling down long enough to make it through my checklist before Caellum showed up in his gold bowtie and all white suit with tight dress pants to match. He was a show-off and wanted all the attention—something he conquered every time he walked into the room.

Caellum and I dated briefly when we first got trapped here. Living it down was hard when everyone hated him with so many colorful words attached to the end of his name.

I whisper-shouted into him before people noticed he had arrived: "You're late."

He smirked the way someone does when they've seen you naked, vulnerable, and in all the ways that leaves you defenseless. "Birds of a feather, Miss-Preps-For-Dates-Days-In-Advance. Where's the demigod?"

I turned my body, arms folded against me, and swiped my tongue against the inside of my cheek, stopping any words from coming out, as I looked in Bolton's direction.

He had his arm around Arianna and was whispering into her ear, probably some evil-nothings, which are similar to sweet nothings, but nothing was truly sweet about Bolton.

I grabbed his arm as he walked away, "You provoking him isn't part of the plan."

"Calm down. It's almost midnight. It's time."

I could tell by his features set into his stony face that he meant every word.

I looked down at my phone; a watch didn't go with this dress. It was midnight. Just like he said. The ritual was starting any minute, and I had to go back to straddling two worlds: mortal and something godly.

Alba sought us out individually, making sure we didn't lose track of what tonight was truly about.

It had been one year since Cheyanne lost the love of her life by the hands of an old dagger that Bolton had to drive through his heart. No one was forgetting what tonight was about. It was hoping someone would survive the blade or send us home; everything else was happenchance.

Taking Austin's hand tightly, I followed behind him to the secret hallway—part of the tunnels Bolton was so obsessed with that connected almost every building on campus.

They were dark, damp, and cold, like the wind got trapped along with our responsibility. The velvet black robes hung, each separately, lining the hallway, like some kind of fucked up monument to the ritual none of us even liked participating in. I took the robe down carefully, slowly, hoping something would happen before we actually went through with this again.

Arianna wasn't mortal; that much we knew. The rules beyond that were unknown even to us. No one knew what to expect or what waited in the woods for us.

The gods are dead, and we're the last of our kind. That means all bets are off.

Arianna

Bolton's hand grasped mine with such strength it felt like he wanted me to lose all feeling as he watched the circle leave the gym where the dance took over.

I had never seen my dad cry, not even when the news broke that his wife/my mother died on the way to get me from school after acting out. I blamed my stoic dad for the discomfort I felt watching Bolton's eyes turn a lighter version of brown than his normal muddy waters to a tea complete with milk, sugar, and honey. It wasn't hard to tell he was scared; his features formed a giant question mark.

Bolton was a know-it-all, making it all the more alarming when he watched his circle disappear, like they were never here at all.

Watching Alba give Bolton a stern nod, I felt a tingling sensation, not the lighting, but a new sensation: my own fear growing inside the edges of my stomach.

"You're making me nervous," I whispered into his chest, pretending to hide my face, by making his body sway slowly with mine.

"Just keep your head down and play dumb. Come on; it's time."

I had gotten to enjoy the dance until midnight, and that's when the magic seemed to fade out of the decorations. Everything seemed less glittery and even more fragile, like the paper that the snowflakes were made from.

I was all grit, all rude remarks, and not afraid to stir up trouble, until trouble had a face like Bolton. Now I was just as fragile as the glittering stars losing their magic.

He was still trying to cut the circulation from my hand when he dragged me behind him, out of the gym, and through the quad to the edge of the woods I vowed never to go in. My boots were cemented to the sidewalk that bordered the trees on their side, upholding my vow.

"Arianna ... " The brooding tone of his voice was more than annoyed.

Walking me to my death in the forest, I didn't belong. I didn't belong anywhere, but especially there, not after last time. "I forgot something. I'll meet you there."

I tugged my arm back and bolted for the girls' dorms. I felt like I was on auto pilot, even though this had never happened enough to create muscle memory. I knew my soul remembered, if that's what we were calling whatever part of us goes back home.

Mortal ole' me didn't remember shit, and I wasn't going to a knife fight without a gun. They can have their superhero qualities, but nothing does anger justice without a trigger. My trigger was the God Killer, and Henry Jon left it behind for someone to finally win battles against divine intervention.

It wasn't that I didn't trust Bolton; I did, more than I ever wished to. Although, liking someone so much it seems deadly didn't kill off the less desirable parts—the parts that want to run into danger, fight, and fuck the rules. Those can't be killed by anyone but yourself.

Shoving the tusk down the side of my ripped tights, I put on my brave face as I made my way back to the edge of the woods.

Bolton pushed his hand out to take mine, and everything in me went into shock when I took it.

Maybe this ritual, disguised as a hazing the new girl, wouldn't go even how I planned.

The Harvest brought the cold; small snowflakes were flying around us but never landing. It was still too warm for the snow to stick to anything. My heavy boots snapped the branches under my weight, and the only way I could see was by Bolton's phone illuminating a few feet in front of me.

It felt like we walked longer than I expected when he saw the group before I did. Nyx handed Bolton a velvet robe for him to push himself into to match the others, sending chills down my spine.

We were no longer a circle; this looked and felt like a goddamn cult.

I heard a faint voice in the back of my head that sounded like my dad: *Little Archer, what did you get yourself into now?*

Trouble, not the kind I typically chase. No, this is much worse.

The intensity in the air broke when Cheyanne intertwined her arm into mine, binding me against her. "Anyone who joins our little group goes through the hazing. We've all done it." I watched her eyes swiftly move, everyone waiting for them to agree. "It's harmless."

Everyone nodded their heads, agreeing. Everyone had died on this rock just to be reunited in Olympus. Nothing in me was a team player, a joiner, a follower, enough to be convinced by everyone else doing something. My palm fit comfortably over the God Killer still tucked into the band of my stockings.

Omari slipped my jacket off my shoulders, and the drop in temperature felt unbearable, instantly making my limbs shake. Hugging my arms to my waist, I looked at the group, all of them in a lopsided circle around the flat top rock I knew matched Henry Jon's descriptions.

So this is where I've died before—well, have been scarified before. No, set free? Even though I was still fuzzy on the terminology after combing Henry Jon's book more than once now.

Jasper, his venom-filled eyes were unmistakable, even with the hood concealing most of his face in a heavy shadow, handed Cheyanne a heavy book. It looked old and bound in taut leather, just like mine.

Omari's hands were on my shoulders, guiding me to the flat top rock and pushing down on my shivering muscles until I sat. "You all know this is creepy, right? Very 90's hazing sorority vibes."

No one laughed.

No one even moved.

Omari stood in front of me, like he was meant to keep me from running away if this got even more creepy.

I swallowed what little moisture I had left my mouth, which felt dry and tight. Cheyanne started chanting in another language, maybe Latin? Something dead and old.

I searched the hoods for Bolton's eyes and high cheekbones, but I came up short. I found Kate's boredom, Luna's worry, Nyx's reserve, and Caellum's malice, but no Bolton. In a panic, I searched the faces again; when Omari's place was taken by another, a knife caught the moonlight and almost made it look pretty as it shined.

Pushing the hood off, I saw Bolton; maybe it was just a familiar comfort. He was mouthing something, but I couldn't decipher what in the darkness.

I reached out, grabbing his forearm, looking up at him confused and scared. I was letting him see the other parts of me no one did, and I was hoping none of his weaker qualities turned him off enough to leave me in the dark.

Leaning into me, I felt his warmth, "Relax, Little Archer. I won't let anything happen to you."

Everything in me froze. My muscles tightened, and my bones felt like heavy steel. That wasn't Bolton. It was ... my dad? His gruff voice was unmistakable.

"Daddy?" my weak voice whimpered out, making it obvious how much I needed him.

He ignored me, his head low, letting the hood do the work of blending him in.

He wasn't here. He couldn't be. He was an ocean away protecting people who weren't me.

Was I hallucinating? Nothing even happened. Get it together.

Cheyanne took my palm and cut me with something sharp, but the sting felt like she rubbed glass in it just to be a bitch. I kept still, trying to play along, just how Bolton had told me.

No one mentioned my dad being a part of this plan.

She held her own cut palm to my hand and chanted more. I was lost in her chanting-like a lullaby, when everything went wrong—the kind of wrong that made you wonder if there ever was a right way.

I reached out for my dad, but I clutched onto Cheyanne's forearm instead and she cut another piece of me. This time the sharp object cut across my exposed arm. I watched the blood pulsate from the wound, shimmering in the moonlight as gold as could be. Her eyes widened, clearly shocked at the color or maybe just how much I bled as her movements paused, and her lullaby made me feel even more drowsy.

Everything felt like a dream, not bad, natural, as my eyelids became too heavy to hold up anymore.

Was this part of the plan? Was this the ritual? Were my pain sensors on overload or just spared?

Luna

I broke the circle, pushing the heavy hood off and making my way to Arianna, who looked out of it. This had never been a part of the ritual before, and it was worrying me that this was a barrier we wouldn't overcome.

What was Cheyanne doing?

Her witchy tricks weren't ever laid on this strong before. Arianna was ready to pass out, and none of us knew how that would affect separating her soul from her mortal body.

Smoothing down her hair, I tried to relax her, thinking it would help, even though she was so docile it made me think she needed adrenaline to counteract her current state.

I needed Arianna aware enough to understand who was good and bad, what side to take, who to trust … and this wasn't helping.

She was practically faint in my arms when I noticed the tusk poking out past the hemline of her dress creating a hole in her imperfect tights.

Trying to be something I wasn't, sly, wasn't as hard as I thought when I glanced around the circle keeping everyone in focus while I snuck my hand around the weapon I didn't expect Arianna to have on her, but I was glad she did.

The God Killer, the tusk of her pet, was a weapon in plain sight that she had made friends with.

The only thing forged to kill gods.

The only weapon made to destroy the royalty in our blood with one stab.

I tucked the weapon away for safekeeping. Knowing Arianna, she'd yanked it out and start threatening even Bolton, leaving no safety for the rest of us.

I felt my stomach drop when someone with twice the strength ripped Arianna from my arms, dragging her legs against the sandpaper surface and positioning her upright.

"We aren't doing this. We don't belong in Olympus anymore, and you all know it," Omari's voice was unapologetic and a type of blood-curdling I knew not to test.

No, his threats needed to be met with threats. An eye for an eye.

I don't know what snapped inside of me, broke, with such magnificent glory that I matched his movements only clutching Cheyanne with the same hostility. I closed my arm around Cheyanne's bicep and kept her close enough for me to shove the God Killer against her side. "Let Ari go, Omari."

Everything felt foreign.

I was holding a weapon against someone's sensitive pale skin, wondering if I had what it took to push it down their layers and watch the life drain from them.

Am I even holding this right?

I caught Austin's gaze, swallowing it down with the nerves. We both knew Jasper was guilty, but not guilty of betraying this circle. Jasper was the one playing both sides and living to tell us about it. Meanwhile, I was waiting for Omari to call my bluff.

The panic in his wide eyes made me shiver with the fear of possibly losing someone I felt so connected with.

Push it, down.

I kept swallowing my tongue, praying my actions were threatening enough.

"Luna, I swear to the gods if you hurt my sister … " trailing off, I knew Omari never bluffed when I pushed the tip further into her skin.

"Omari, what are you doing?! We can go back home!" Cheyanne wanted to speak, bargain, so I clamped my hand over her mouth stopping any more words.

Their connection was too strong to trust any communication between them. They were probably speaking with their eyes as I held her against me; no one could know.

"Let Ari go, Omari. She's innocent."

"Not all of us want to go back home, Luna. Not all of us are welcomed back to that crooked kingdom."

Jasper

I clapped my hands together over and over for dramatic effect, "Raise your hand if you thought I'm the bad guy?"

The chuckle in my voice almost ruined my statement as I watched Luna carefully. The last thing I wanted was for her to get hurt.

An innocent soul was worse than the blood on our hands already.

Bolton stood tall, looking at me bemused, trying to piece it all together in his head. I'm sure all the roads led to me, and him being wrong wasn't a strong suit of his.

Clapping my hands together again. "Who thought Miss Innocent would be holding the God Killer?" My theatrics were on reserve for moments like this—distracting and getting the last laugh.

Bolton's hands fisted the velvet material of my robe, pushing me against a tree trunk bordering the clearing. "Stop playing games, snake. I know you've been following me."

Even his strength couldn't break the grin on my face, elated to be smarter than the one who wears a crown. It was intoxicating. Now I knew why he was addicted to his own crown; it felt like this.

The power alone could have persuaded me to betray everyone, when Austin came to me asking if I knew anything. I always knew something … this was more challenging, switching sides continuously.

Coated in venom, I spat back, "I'm not playing games. I had to follow everyone in order to figure out who was the real bad guy."

I could tell by his grip tightening that he wanted to hate the truth. He wanted to sentence me to hell and throw away the key.

"Might wanna turn around … it's the guy threatening your girl." I expected his fist to collide with my unblemished skin, but instead, all his anger aimed at Omari.

Every red flag and sensor went off to protect Luna. Bolton angry often meant someone was in the crossfire, and normally they didn't make it out to hate him for it.

I didn't want to scare Luna in the background of Bolton threatening almost everyone. My only concern was Luna—not this circle, not dying or living, and not Nyx throwing daggers my direction for pressing my palms into her shoulders.

I was ready to replace her hand with mine, when her body jerked forward, and I looked down to confirm my suspicion. Luna had driven the God Killer into Cheyanne's side with a firm hand. As soon as the melted gold had hit her knuckles, she dropped her hand from the weapon, and the remorse bloomed all over her face.

Kate

"Luna! These are Balenciaga!" Looking down at my crispy pink platform sneakers now splattered with gold flecks.

No one else would know it was blood, but everyone else would know that's not how Balenciaga sold these sneakers that went perfectly with my velvet wrap dress.

I didn't put two and two together until I saw her clutch release. Luna backed away, and I watched Cheyanne fall to the ground.

My mouth fell open, and my gaze ran between my best friend and something I knew she'd never do: murder … anything.

Omari let go of Arianna and scrambled the ground to catch his twin sister that didn't have any hope of surviving.

The God Killer was rightfully named. No cures. No magic. No fixes. Once it was used, there was no going back.

Watching Omari hold Cheyanne close to his chest made me want to wilt down to the floor with him. He was the bad guy, and I was sympathizing like I never had before.

Bolton shoved Arianna into Caellum's arms, pacing and strung out on destruction. He was in his element, yet he looked so conflicted.

Cheyanne's death radiated through each of us, all struck by her death that came premature. We weren't friends, had nothing in common, but we could all agree that her twin, the sinister one, should have been the one to be sacrificed.

All of us cowardly sank down to the ground, as Bolton continued to pace in front of us. No one had any sarcasm, comebacks, witty one liners. Arianna was in and out of consciousness; Luna was catatonic; Nyx looked almost as shook as Bolton; Omari was inconsolable; Cheyanne was dead; and Austin was holding me against him, even though I wasn't even on the scale of emotional, unless we counted the blood on my shoes.

We had broken the circle.

I forgot Alba was here, until his hood was down and his disappointed eyes fell on Omari holding his dead sister. "All you had to do was get Arianna alone. How hard is that?"

My dipped head lifted to meet his gaze in pure shock. Alba was three times our age, our mentor, our keeper … our *real* betrayer?

The sun was peeking up low between the trees, creating this glow we didn't deserve.

Bolton's hostility was no longer aimed inward at his inability to see the truth in front of us all. It was pointed at the man who walked right out of the shadows and into his line of vision. "What the fuck did you say?"

Alba didn't seem regal or poised anymore. "It was simple, keep your eye on Arianna and get her alone. That's all I needed to make her forget her past."

Alba stumbled backwards trying to find his footing after Bolton pushed him. Nyx held him back, pulling his arms behind him, "Give me one reason I shouldn't let him kill you." Nyx barely spoke let alone threatened anyone.

I didn't know my lips were moving when I thought, "Damn, I didn't even see that coming."

Having the terror twins, Bolton and Nyx, both glare at you at the same time made the chill I got used to feeling seem new. They were bested by one of our own—two actually—and no one made these two feel stupid without their permission.

Alba stood like a giant over us all, anger growing even taller than he already was, "We hold the power here; we are gods above men here. Don't you see that? What's back home? Dead gods and pillars made of gold that hold no value?"

Spitting on Olympus wasn't something any of us did; it was the equivalent of swearing in church, frowned upon.

Bolton reached out his hand and said with a stern tone, "Luna, give it to me."

Pushing myself further into Austin's arms, I wanted to hide inside him. The balance needed to be restored; this night could not end on Luna acting so out of character. I shielded my eyes, shoved my face into his armpit, and tried not to inhale just in case he had anxiety sweat too.

I knew Luna would purge herself of the God Killer without even a blink. She didn't hold onto anything that wasn't truly a reflection of herself.

"Fuck!" Bolton forced us all to look when Alba was no longer there. I didn't realize any of us took our eyes off him until he was gone.

Alba, our teacher and mentor, was gone. He had no intention of going home. He had every bad intention he could, down to turning us against each other and watching death eliminate us emotionally and physically. Omari was still clutching onto his twin, praying the God Killer was still a myth and that she'd wake up any second.

The myths were real.

The gods were dead.

Home? That was an illusion none of us were ready to accept.

We were homeless, orphans, the children of gods, and powerless to change our circumstances.

Bolton

Alba was gone.

Omari's literal other half, apparently all the innocent parts, was dead in his arms.

Austin and Jasper played Devil's advocate.

Luna went rogue.

Betrayal lusted in the air like a bad post sex tension—unignorable and weighing on your morals.

I was shaking with anger, on the inside, but I was still so mad. I felt irresponsible. I wanted to inflict pain until I forgot about my own. None of that mattered when I realized Ari was still docile on the cold ground in Luna's arms.

Leaning down, I touched her cheek with my hand, hoping she'd suddenly come to life. We had never not completed a ritual, and no one knew anything about Cheyanne's voodoo magic.

What if Arianna was stuck like this? What if this was some kind of instant karma for killing one of our own?

Shifting my weight onto one knee, I looked into her eyes, trying to find a smidge of humanity that she had grown being here so long or the divine qualities she learned she had. There was nothing but black in her eyes—not one spec of purple. Throwing her over my shoulder, I knew staring at her in the cold woods wasn't going to solve anything. I could stare at her anywhere and accomplish getting nowhere.

Everything seemed more quiet. My mind snapped to Jasper, silencing everything around us, or maybe just Arianna.

She had been through enough: dead parents times three, missing her only living parent, Arcadia, finding out she had powers... and I'd be dumb to leave myself off that pile of problems. I wasn't the easy road... or the high road.

I was hard to shock, but when I stepped onto the sidewalk, I looked up and saw the gothic old buildings that made Arcadia gone. Well, not gone, but dilapidated and broken. Nothing like the buildings that were in a well-preserved condition only hours ago.

Losing control wasn't an option as a leader. I had to stay calm and collected.

If for no one but Arianna.

Arcadia was all an illusion, a Pandora's box, trickery at its best. We were all fooled, even by the smallest lies.

The circle, now less complete, stood in the quad, gasping at how much we believed there were people around us and beautiful buildings holding us captive.

Arcadia was a prison made up of our nightmares. What's the rest of the world made up of? I continued forward, with or without them, until I reached the iron gates that burned if you touched them for too long. Kicking them open the iron nearly fell apart, displaying a fictional world—one that none know of us had seen in fourteen years.

The real world was full of life. I felt like the four horsemen of the apocalypse coming to destroy everything good, until only I was left standing with Arianna.

I just learned the hardest lesson of all: blood isn't thicker than anything else. Cheyanne was right all along when she told me, "The blood of the covenant is thicker than the water of the womb."

I may have been stuck with this circle, forced together as children of gods, as royalty, but I was still the fucking king. The only kingdom I was going to see was a grave for each of my enemies.

Playlist

POUYA & CITY MORGUE : "Bulletproof Shower Cap"

HALSEY : "Graveyard"

PVRIS : "Old Wounds"

PVRIS : "Hallucinations"

PVRIS : "Death of Me"

MORE BY ELENA

AVAILABLE NOW

The Amherst Sinners Series
The Best Years (Book One)
The Best Moments (Book Two)
The Best Mistakes (Book Three)

The Celestial Bodies Series
Awful Curse (Book One)

AVAILABLE SOON

The Best Flaws (Caden's Novel)

Want to stay in touch? Sign up for my mailing list to receive monthly updates and exclusives no one else gets!

Amazon

Instagram

Twitter

GoodReads

Facebook

About the Author

Elena Monroe grew up in Florida scribbling down stories from a very young age. These stories were really just wavy lines filling the paper. But she knew each word, each emotion, each character's name, and there was no tricking her into forgetting what each line signified. Just like her unconventional way of writing as a toddler,

Elena is setting her own rules and just telling stories.

Much like her debut novel, *The Best Years*, life certainly imitated art. Transplanting from the South to the East Coast, Elena currently lives in Connecticut with her husband, reformed bad boy.

Tell stories, no rules.

Elena is currently writing all the things. My TBW (To Be Written) is as long as my TBR. I can't keep a secret to save my life when it comes to my projects so stay tuned.

Acknowledgments

GEORGE

For not only being married to me but being married to my books too. You let me sacrifice having a life, ignore me when I have to write, and let me talk you to death about all things related. You support my beautiful addiction to writing. I appreciate you.

AS I

GIRL. I literally never have words to express us, you, for someone who writes as much as I do. You keep blowing me away with these graphics, your talent, your wisdom, your dedication, and most all friendship. If the book world teaches me nothing, I will at least have learned to cherish this bond.

GIVE ME BOOKS PROMOTIONS

Y'all deal with my crazy emails and promote my books anyways. That's gotta get a round of applause. No, seriously, you guys make releasing so smooth and easy. I'm officially a stress free author on release week, because y'all are so amazing at what you do!

BRRRJOY

I'll never run out of ways to thank you and beg you to never leave me. I swear. I can NOT release without you. You spin my crazy, flawed, comma-hating, grammar rebellion into gold. You are a type of magic that doesn't exist anymore.

MARIA AT STEAMY READS

These covers slay. I can't fathom how you do what you do, but it takes a village. You are one of those people in my village that makes these books what they are.

RULE BREAKERS

Y'ALL.

You guys are why I write publicly inside of the notes app on my phone in secrecy. All the messages, the edits, the promoting, the reviews, the photoshoots y'all do for my books—THANK YOU.

You do not go unseen, unheard, or unloved.

You have power. You made this happen. And you inspire me.